CORRUPTING
THE
INNOCENT

BY P. RAYNE

THE MAFIA ACADEMY SERIES

Vow of Revenge

Corrupting the Innocent

The Mafia King's Sister

Craving My Rival

THE MIDNIGHT MANOR SERIES

Moonlit Thorns

Shattered Vows

Midnight Whispers

Twisted Truths

STANDALONES

Beautifully Scarred

CORRUPTING
THE
INNOCENT

THE MAFIA ACADEMY

P. RAYNE

AVON

An Imprint of HarperCollinsPublishers

HarperCollins books may be purchased for educational, business, or sales promotional use. For information, please email the Special Markets Department at SPsales@harpercollins.com.

Originally published as *Corrupting the Innocent* in the United States in 2023 by Piper Rayne Incorporated. Bonus epilogue originally published online in 2023.

FIRST AVON PAPERBACK PUBLISHED 2024.

Interior text design by Diahann Sturge-Campbell

Interior art © Oleksandr/Stock.Adobe.com

Library of Congress Cataloging-in-Publication Data has been applied for.

ISBN 978-0-06-341245-3

24 25 26 27 28 LBC 5 4 3 2 1

*To all the women who refuse to settle for
any man . . . unless she's his #1*

AUTHOR'S NOTE

This book contains references to content that may be upsetting to some readers. Trigger warnings include alcohol, attempted murder, murder, profanity, sexually explicit scenes, stalking, physical violence, and gun violence. Reader discretion is advised.

PLAYLIST

Here's a list of songs that inspired us while we were writing *Corrupting the Innocent.*

Out of Control – She Wants Revenge
Stupid Girl – Garbage
Team – Lorde
Haul – Christian Löffler, Mohan
#1 Crush – Garbage
Bullet with Butterfly Wings – Smashing Pumpkins
The Perfect Drug – Nine Inch Nails
Pretty When You Cry – Vast
This Mess We're In – PJ Harvey, Thom Yorke
Violent – Hole
The Boy Is Mine – Brandy, Monica
favorite crime – Olivia Rodrigo
Luck Be a Lady – Frank Sinatra

SICURO ACADEMY — ITALIAN CRIME FAMILIES

Northeast Territory

Specializes in running weapons
Marcelo Costa
(head of the Costa crime family)

Southeast Territory

Specializes in counterfeit rings and embezzlement schemes
Antonio La Rosa
(next in line to run the La Rosa crime family)

Southwest Territory

Specializes in drug trafficking and money laundering
Dante Accardi
(next in line to run the Accardi crime family)

Northwest Territory

Specializes in securities fraud and cyber-warfare
Gabriele Vitale
(next in line to run the Vitale crime family)

CORRUPTING
THE
INNOCENT

CHAPTER ONE
SOFIA

I've never wanted to strangle anyone, but the last ounce of my will-power is stopping me from launching myself across the limo and wrapping my hands around her pretty little neck. It's bad enough we traveled here together, but watching Aurora Salucci cuddle up to the man I've secretly been in love with my entire life is pure torture.

"How am I ever going to survive this?" my best friend, Mira-bella, mumbles beside me.

We're stuck with a front-row seat directly across from her brother, Antonio, and his new fiancée, Aurora, driving from the airport to the Sicuro Academy after the four of us went home to Miami for the week-long break between semesters.

I turn to her. "At least you'll be in New York with Marcelo," I whisper.

Mira squeezes my hand.

Mira is to marry Marcelo Costa and go live with him in New York because he's the head of the Costa crime family and they control the Northeast section of the country.

I, however, will be stuck in the Southeast, where Mira and Antonio's father is head of the La Rosa crime family and my dad is a capo. Since Antonio is next in line to run the empire, seeing him with Aurora is a permanent part of my future.

Antonio and Aurora were arranged to be married by their fathers—announced to everyone during the Christmas break.

Merry Christmas to me. Why not put coal in my stocking too? It's been less than two months since the official announcement and I'm already sick of her baby talk and public displays of affection.

And it's not only because she has Antonio. It's also because she's a class A bitch. A real mean girl. And I don't say that lightly. I'm pretty easygoing and get along with almost everybody. But growing up, Aurora was always jealous of Mira because her dad was head of the family, so she tormented her relentlessly. Even went so far as to put a picture of a pig in place of Mira's senior photo in the yearbook. Basically, she's not a nice person—at all—and the fact that she's going to marry Antonio is like injecting poison into my already withering heart.

"Do you think I should change into a reception dress or keep it old school and stay in the dress from the ceremony?" Aurora asks Antonio the hundredth question about their wedding since we boarded the plane.

My gaze flicks back to them.

He shrugs and continues to look out the window. "Do whatever you want."

His voice is indifferent, and I inwardly preen. Mira confided in me that Antonio's not thrilled about being arranged to marry Aurora, but he'll honorably do what's best for the family. With Mira's marriage to Marcelo shoring up the relationship with the Northeast, their father thought Antonio should be married to someone who would strengthen the family. Since Aurora's father, Oronato Salucci, is the underboss and well respected, Aurora was the sensible option.

"Make sure you wear black," Mira says. "Want the outside to match the inside."

Aurora narrows her eyes at Mira then turns to Antonio. "You aren't going to let her speak to your fiancée that way, are you?"

Antonio sighs and pushes a hand through the dark curls on top of his head. The darkness under his eyes says he hasn't been sleeping well. "Mira, keep it in check."

Mira simply rolls her eyes while Aurora gives her a shit-eating grin.

Thank God, the limo rolls to a stop a minute later when we reach the gates of the academy. The guards go through the security check with the driver, then we roll down the windows so one guard can see who's in the back of the limo while the second security guard checks the trunk and under the car to be sure we're not bringing in any weapons or explosives.

Once we're moving again, we drive for a bit then make another stop at the security building set closer to the main campus. We file out to hand in our cell phones in exchange for the ones the college issues that only call and text other people within the college network. Then our bags are searched for contraband, and finally, "us" before we're back in the limo and on our way to the dorms.

Security is top-notch at the Sicuro Academy. The private college was created by the four Italian crime families that run the United States. You have the La Rosas in the Southeast, where we're from, the Costas in the Northeast, the Accardis in the Southwest, and the Vitales in the Northwest. Three decades ago, after a series of fights over territory that resulted in a bloodbath, killing a lot of young men on the rise to prominent positions, they built the academy. The word *Sicuro* in Italian means "safe."

They can all send their children to the academy after high school without having to worry that we'll kill each other since there's a zero-violence policy—and no weapons allowed except for weaponry class.

Eventually, the board let in other mob families like the Irish and the Russians, even cartel members, and finally, the politicians' kids because it made financial sense. Everyone's astronomical tuition pads the pockets of the four founding families—as well as giving the Italians knowledge about who's up-and-coming in their ranks.

Finally, we roll up in front of the main entrance. The school exudes a sense of grandeur and elegance, with its meticulously maintained grounds and stately buildings cloaked in ivy. The sprawling green lawns and well-manicured gardens are covered with the lightest dusting of snow. The many fountains, statues, and other ornate features add to the effect of refinement and sophistication, creating a sense of privilege and exclusivity.

As soon as the limo comes to a complete stop, I open the door and step outside into the cool air. Mira joins me seconds later, having had enough of the Aurora show too.

"That was the longest trip of my life," she grumbles before squealing so loudly I cover my ears and draw back from her. She rushes forward and, I should have known, Marcelo is standing with his cousin and best friend, Giovanni, outside the Roma House.

It is obvious how much she missed him while they were apart, even though it was only a week. Her anxiousness to see him is so funny to me because six months ago, when he returned from the dead, excitement was the opposite of what she was feeling. She would've done anything to escape their marriage. But it's fair to say that they've worked out their differences and have overcome a lot to be as happy as they are now.

"Hey, Sofia," Giovanni says to me after I catch up.

"Hey, how was your time at home?" I ask.

He shrugs. "Mostly had to listen to this one complaining"—he thumbs toward Marcelo—"about being apart from that one." He thumbs in Mirabella's direction. "You?"

I chuckle. "Pretty much the same."

I glance at Antonio and Aurora as they get out of the limo. Antonio approaches us and Aurora is quick to grab his hand. Antonio immediately releases hers, though, and shakes Marcelo's and Giovanni's hands.

We're from different crime families, but Marcelo and Mirabella's union has done exactly what their parents hoped it would—solidified an alliance between the Costas and the La Rosas.

"Hey, guys," Antonio says to Marcelo and Giovanni. "Uneventful trip home?" He arches an eyebrow.

Marcelo's dark gaze sweeps over all of us before he sets his gaze only on Antonio. "Not as eventful as first semester was, but not entirely uneventful."

We all learned long ago how to read the subtext—he had to take care of some things when he was home, but whatever it was has been resolved. And we all know enough not to ask for details, though it would be hard to top everything he and Mira went through during first semester.

"Glad to hear it," Antonio says with a nod and pulls out his phone, reading a text. "I gotta head to guidance. See you guys later." He gives a small smile to Aurora before walking to the doors.

"Shouldn't you be running after him like a little lapdog?" Mira snipes at Aurora.

Aurora looks at me with narrowed eyes. "Keep your bestie on a leash. Otherwise, she's liable to be mauled by a bigger dog." She flips her long, dark blond hair off her shoulder and struts away.

Marcelo steps forward, but Mira places her hand on his chest. "Leave it."

"You're engaged to the don of one of the four families. She will speak to you with respect." His jaw clenches, and his hands fist at his sides.

"Yeah, well, she's engaged to my brother, who will be the head of the La Rosa family someday, so we're not that different. Besides, I can handle her on my own. I don't need a man defending me."

"She's no one yet," Marcelo grumbles.

I always gave Mira props for being able to stand up to someone as powerful as Marcelo. She's definitely not the traditional Mafia wife.

"I'm going to head in. Our things should be there by now," I say, eager to get out of the cold.

To most people, this weather wouldn't even register as cold, but I'm from Miami. Anything under seventy is freezing.

"I'm starving. Gio and I are heading to Café Ambrosia. You want to join us?" Marcelo asks Mira.

"Sure, I'm kind of hungry too." She looks at me. "Want me to get you anything?"

"No thanks."

"All right. I'll swing by your room in a bit," she says.

"Sounds good."

Last semester, Mira and I shared a dorm room. After everything went down between her and Marcelo and they worked out their issues, she moved in with him.

"I'll head to the dorm with Sofia," Giovanni says.

Marcelo's forehead wrinkles. "Thought you were hungry?"

Giovanni waves him off. "Nah, I'm good. I'll see you guys later."

Marcelo shrugs and wraps his arm around Mira's shoulder and they head down the path while Giovanni and I go into the Roma House.

Each dorm building on campus houses a different faction of the Mafia. The Italians are in the Roma House, the Irish are in the Dublin House, the Russians in the Moskva House, the cartel members are in Ciudad de México House, and the politicians' kids are in the Washington building. For the most part, those of each ethnicity keep to their own. None of us trust the others enough to want to sleep in the same building. Keeping things separate makes things easier and safer for everyone.

"How was your visit home?" Giovanni asks.

I shove my hands in the pockets of my coat. "It was nice to see my parents. And spend some time with Mira away from Marcelo."

Giovanni snickers next to me, making eye contact. "I know, right? It's weird."

"What is?"

"How obsessed those two are with each other. Never thought I'd see my cousin crazy in love." It's clear from the disgruntled tone that Giovanni finds the transition as difficult as I do.

I'd be lying if I said it hasn't been weird not having my best friend around as much as she used to be, but I'm happy that she found her one and he values the type of woman she is. "It's great that they're in love, but yeah, it's taken some getting used to."

"You're too nice, Sofia."

I chuckle. "I'm happy for my friend, that's all."

Although lately, it's taking more of an effort to be my usual upbeat self.

"If you say so."

We walk toward the elevator bank, chatting about nothing. Nicolo and Andrea, Giovanni's other best friends, are in the lounge area, and he nods in their direction.

"I gotta talk to the guys. I'll see you around?" He arches a dark eyebrow.

"Yeah, of course." I smile and walk to the elevator.

When I push the button, the doors open automatically, and I step inside and press the button for the fifth floor. When I step out, I say a quick hello to some of the girls in the hallway and let myself into the dorm room that's now mine alone.

And it feels exactly that—lonely.

CHAPTER TWO
ANTONIO

I head into the guidance office building. They texted when I was getting out of the limo, informing me they needed to see me. But I don't walk more than thirty steps before someone pulls my arm. I whip around to find Aurora with a creepy smile.

"What's up?" I look at her blandly, not sure why she's tracking me down when we just parted ways.

"You can't just leave me like that," she whines.

"I have things to do." She needs to learn that I don't have to explain myself to her.

She frowns. "We're engaged, Antonio. You need to treat me with respect, and we have to look like a united unit in front of other people."

I step toward her. "It's no secret to anyone that we're not a love connection, Aurora."

Her head rocks back and she blinks a couple of times. I don't know why. I've done nothing to give her the impression that I feel anything for her.

"One day, you'll be the head of the La Rosa family, and I'll be your wife. Your sister should show me the respect that title deserves."

I grit my teeth. She has a point, but she hasn't been a saint toward my sister over the years. "Respect is a two-way street. She'll be the first woman in the Costa family soon and you need to remember that." I arch an eyebrow.

"Mirabella is impossible sometimes. It's true we've had our differences over the years, but I've been nothing but cordial and kind to her since our engagement announcement and she's being stubborn by not pushing those old issues between us to the side."

Blowing out a breath, I push a hand through my hair. It's hard to deny anything she's saying. Mira hasn't been shy about her displeasure that Aurora will be her sister-in-law. She *is* one of the most pigheaded and stubborn people I know.

"I'll talk to her."

Aurora relaxes. "Thank you." She leans forward on her tiptoes and kisses my cheek. "I'm going to go catch up with the girls. I'll see you tomorrow."

"See you," I say and watch her leave. Relief comes over me once she's far enough away.

There are worse things than being engaged to Aurora Salucci, but if I had my choice, she wouldn't be my first. But I don't have a choice. It's my duty to marry whoever my father believes will benefit our family's empire. I've had years to prepare for this. Hell, I witnessed my sister's arrangement with our enemy only a semester ago. She's happy and definitely in love now, which will never be the case with Aurora and me, but I'll see my obligation through as I always do. There's no doubt Aurora will bask in her position as a don's wife when the day arrives. She's already pushing boundaries she has no right to because she's not my wife yet and I'm not the don yet. That's where Mirabella has one up on her because she's engaged to a don. Marcelo won't sit back and allow his soon-to-be wife to be treated with disrespect.

For the time being, I push away all thoughts of Aurora and our future and head back in the direction I was going before my fiancée tugged on my sleeve like an untrained puppy. Five minutes later, I reach the guidance department and approach the receptionist, a woman that I don't recognize in her midforties with auburn hair pulled back in a low ponytail, sitting behind a desk. She must be new.

"Hi, I received a text from one of the counselors that said they needed to see me."

She looks up from her computer and offers a welcoming smile. "Your name?"

I'm not used to ever having to introduce myself. Whether I'm at home or here, everyone knows who I am. It annoys me. "Antonio La Rosa."

Recognition lights up her face. "Ah, yes, Mr. La Rosa." She opens the drawer to her left and pulls out an envelope. "Mr. Lewis had to attend to another matter, but he asked me to give you this."

I accept the manila envelope. "Thanks."

I don't open it right away because my father taught me a long time ago to never open mail in front of untrusted company. Although I doubt this is some life-or-death situation, I'll still wait until I'm alone.

She nods and smiles, her eyes falling back to her screen. I make my way back to the exit toward the Roma House. I'm eager to unpack my shit and settle in before classes tomorrow.

The campus is abuzz as students get dropped off in their limos and filter back onto the school grounds, but I only offer a quick hello to any acquaintance I pass, not wanting to get drawn into a conversation. I'm in a foul mood after my conversation with Aurora about expecting me to deal with my sister, who never makes anything easy when it comes to my fiancée.

Once I've reached the Roma House, I step into the elevator and stab the button for the third floor, and since I'm alone, I rip open the envelope from guidance.

The letter is a gentle reminder that I haven't accrued any of the volunteer hours necessary to graduate next year. It's not that I didn't know I hadn't. I've just kept putting it off. It's stupid that we have to give back to the school. Especially the Italians. This school wouldn't even exist without our four founding families. I'd like to think the hefty tuition that comes with being a student here more than counts for "giving back."

The elevator dings and I decide to head to my best friend Tommaso's room to see how his trip was. Rather than return home on break, he and his family went to Italy for a vacation. Not really. He and his dad were on an errand from my father, but covering the reason with the authorities and bringing his family with him was a smart move on his dad's part.

I knock on Tommaso's door and hear a muffled "come in" from the other side.

"Hey, man." I swing the door open and step inside.

"Hey." Tommaso strides out of the bathroom with a white towel wrapped around his waist and another he's using to dry his hair, rubbing it vigorously on top of his head.

I glance around and see that his roommate's bed is still empty.

"Heard things went well in Italy." I sit in his desk chair.

"They did, no issues at all. We flowed in and out of there like water."

"How was the rest of your trip?"

"No complaints. Good food, good wine, good pussy." He grins then goes to the dresser.

"Wish I were you. I had to listen to Aurora, her mom, and my mom talk all things weddings the whole break. She managed to convince both our parents to have the wedding this summer." I blow out a breath and run a hand through my hair.

Tommaso stills, pulling out his boxer briefs. "What about Mira and Marcelo's wedding? They were engaged first."

"No shit. But somehow, she made a case for me being the oldest and how I should be married before Mira and how there's no reason to wait."

Tommaso chuckles. "Bet Mira loved that."

Tommaso is my best friend, and although I sensed he had a thing for my sister at one point when we were teenagers, he understands how difficult she can be. He's witnessed her wrath many times behind closed doors.

"Exactly. Now I have the distinct pleasure of having to put my sister in line because she and Aurora can't play nice."

Tommaso grabs some athletic pants from his dresser and disappears into the bathroom, but I can still hear him. "I'm sure Marcelo will like that."

He comes out with his pants on and goes back to his dresser.

"I'm hoping to get him on my side. He knows better than anyone what she's like. Regardless if he likes it or not though, I have no choice."

"Let me know if you need help."

Tommaso's father is one of our capos, and we've been inseparable since primary school. He doesn't even have to say it, I know he's got my back whenever I need him. He's proven himself time and time again.

"And then I pick up this bullshit from the guidance office." I hold up the envelope.

"What?" he asks, pulling a sweater over his head.

"A reminder that I don't have any volunteer hours yet."

He chuckles and sits on the couch on the other side of the room. "Told you that you should've picked away at those years ago. Now you're going to have to do it this year and next."

"No shit." I stretch my legs out in front of me and groan, tilting my head back and looking at the ceiling. "I wonder what kind of bullshit they're gonna have me do."

"Make sure you let me know so I can swing by and heckle you."

I grab a pen from the holder on his desk and launch it at him.

He ducks and it pings off the wall behind him. "I heard something that might improve your mood."

"Yeah?" I arch an eyebrow.

"Heard some of Dante's crew are working on getting a party together. Might be good for you to blow off some steam."

I push a hand through my hair. "Yeah, maybe."

It's not that anyone on my mind is of any real consequence. My sister can be dealt with, although she's sure to be a pain in my ass. The volunteer work, as grating as it might be, is something I'll have to complete. Aurora . . . well, that is what it is. I always knew I'd be forced into an arranged marriage, and though she's not who I would have chosen, I could do worse.

Who would I have chosen if I had the chance?

That I can't answer. Most of the women I've messed around with were just for a good time, not a long time.

CHAPTER THREE
SOFIA

I set down my book beside me on the bed and look at the time on my school-issued phone, 9:02 p.m.

I roll onto my back and blow out a breath, staring at the ceiling.

When I left Mira after dinner, she said she was going to check in with Marcelo and that she'd swing by my room a little later, but I should have known she wouldn't show. She's so madly in love. They're probably naked and banging against the walls.

It's not that I'm not happy she found love with Marcelo. Arranged marriages rarely come with love. At the beginning of the school year, when he showed back up from the dead, I wanted her to give him a chance and for him to let her in enough that they would fall in love. It's wonderful to see how far they've come in such a short period of time, but a teeny-tiny part of me selfishly wishes things were like they used to be.

I hope one day for my own love to come. Although I'm not arranged with anyone, someday I'm sure to be if I don't find a love match first. I had wished for Antonio, but I should have realized it was smarter for Mr. La Rosa to pick Aurora. Her dad is higher up than mine. I need to let go of this schoolgirl crush on Antonio and concentrate on anyone else in this school. It's filled with powerful men. I'm bound to find someone to keep my mind clear of him.

Still, I feel so lonely.

It's not like I've lost my best friend. We still go to the same school, share all the same classes, and she's probably literally in the same building as I am.

But gone are the days when we had all the time in the world to gossip, laugh, and be silly. I'm slowly growing used to her being gone, but I miss her terribly.

Figuring I'm tired and probably just need to go to bed, I change into my pajamas—a pale-blue silk cami-and-shorts set with ivory lace trim. I throw my dark hair up into a bun on the top of my head and wash off my makeup. I'm patting my face dry with a towel when there's a knock on the door.

Though it's much later than I expected her, a fuzzy feeling in my stomach stirs that Mira didn't actually forget about me. I walk to the door with a smile and swing it open, ready to dig into her in a halfhearted way about taking so long.

But it's not Mira. It's Antonio.

I blink, shocked to find him here. He'd sometimes come by when Mira was rooming with me, but since she moved into Marcelo's room late last semester, he hasn't been by.

His gaze skims down my body, causing goose bumps to scatter after its path, then he meets my eyes before stepping inside without asking permission. His cologne wafts to my nostrils as he passes, and I inhale deeply. Ever since he started wearing cologne in high school, I've been addicted to the scent, even gotten samples I keep hidden.

"What's going on?" I ask, turning to face him. Remembering that I'm not exactly dressed for company, I cross my arms in an effort to shield my nipples from his vision.

"Looking for my sister." He looks around the room as if she's hiding.

I don't know why, but my chest feels as though it caves in when it's clear his being here has nothing to do with me. I was so stupid to think it did.

I may have been half in love with Antonio for years, but he's never paid me any sort of special attention. To him, I'm just his little sister's best friend. "She was supposed to come by. Told me she was going to meet up with Marcelo then she'd pop by, but she hasn't showed. I thought you were her when you knocked."

He frowns. "Mind if I stick around for a bit to see if she shows up? I already tried her and Marcelo's room and they're not there, or they're not answering." His face distorts in an uncomfortable grossed-out expression at the thought of his sister and Marcelo having sex.

I stiffen for a fraction of a second then force myself to relax. I can't remember the last time I was alone in a room with Antonio for any length of time.

"Is everything okay?" I ask, uncomfortable standing in my silk jammies, even though Antonio doesn't even seem to notice.

"I need to talk to her about the way she's acting toward Aurora."

I manage to keep my frown at bay from the mention of Aurora and his apparent need to protect her. What I want to tell him is that Aurora is more than capable of dealing with Mira's attitude herself. She's a viper and doesn't need her fiancé to come to her aid.

"It's no secret that Mira's not happy about your engagement." I walk to my bed and sit on the edge beside my book while Antonio paces in front of me.

"I know, but Mira must show Aurora the respect she deserves for her place in our family."

"That goes both ways." The words slip out before I can stop them.

Antonio abruptly stops pacing. His back faces me and rises and falls with a deep inhale. He turns to look at me over his shoulder. "I told her the same thing."

My eyes widen in surprise.

"Don't look so surprised. I'm not privy to every way that Aurora made yours and Mira's life hell growing up, Sofia, but Mira's been clear to me she wasn't nice."

I blink a couple of times. "Oh. I . . ."

He faces me with his hands on his hips and sighs. "Just say whatever it is you're thinking."

My lips press together, but I decide to tell him. "All right. You seem fine with the whole arrangement ever since your dad told you, so I assume you're happy with her being your fiancée."

He stares at me for a beat and I have no idea what's going through his head. "I know what Aurora is like, so no, I'm not happy that I'll spend the rest of my life with her. If it were my choice, I would have chosen someone . . . different. But I am happy that the engagement and marriage will fulfill the purpose intended and be looked upon as a good match by the members of our organization. I've known my entire life that the choice of whom to marry would never be mine."

"So it's about duty?" The only heirs that are to become dons are the four who reside at the academy, but from what I've heard, none of them respect the duty as much as Antonio. Maybe it's his relationship with his father that's instilled his honor to always do what he should.

"Everything in my life is about duty, Sofia." His words hold the weight of inevitability, something I've not heard from him before.

"I know," I say softly, looking at my hands fidgeting in my lap.

"What are you reading?"

I snap my head up, surprised and thankful for the change of topic. My cheeks heat when I answer. "A romance novel."

Antonio walks over and picks up the book. I lean down before he straightens at the same time, our eyes locking and our mouths mere inches apart.

I suck in a breath and hold it, unable to move. His chin is so chiseled I wonder what it would be like to cast small kisses along it. His skin is a perfect olive tone that makes it appear he's tan all year through, and his dark hair almost shines like silk. Even up close, I can't find one flaw on his face.

He straightens and inspects the front and back of the book, obviously not noticing the heat flushing up my chest to my neck from how close we are. "Guess that's not surprising. You've always been a bit of an aspirational romantic."

My forehead furrows because he makes that sound like a bad thing. "What's that mean?"

He chuckles. "Remember in the third grade when you crushed on Mikey Regallo? You wore blue almost every day because it was his favorite color. And then when you were a freshman in high school and you liked Leo Willard, you and Mira would bake cookies for you to bring to him, like, every day. You forget how long I've known you." He shakes his head and chuckles.

Another stab to the heart that he might know me, but he's never seen me. I could correct him and tell him it was him I liked most in high school, but of course I don't.

"That doesn't make me a romantic," I grumble.

He holds up his free hand, still holding the book in the other. "There's nothing wrong with it. It's kind of admirable and sweet that you can still feel that way after all the shit relationships you've seen in our families over the years."

His acting like I'm an adorable little puppy irks me. All I've ever wanted Antonio to see is me as a sexy *woman*.

"Whatever." I huff.

Antonio flips through the book, then pauses and blinks twice before his eyes skim the page.

Shit.

He laughs. "Or maybe it's not the romance." He reads a passage of the book aloud in a dramatic fashion. "'His cock plunges into me, eliciting every bit of pleasure imaginable. My clit pulses with need and I—'"

I rip the book from his hands, cheeks on fire, mortified.

"Hey, I was getting to the good part."

I toss the book on my other side and stand, grabbing him by the shoulders and forcing him to turn around. "Time to go."

He doesn't fight me as I escort him toward the door, laughing at my expense the entire time. When we reach the door, he turns around and looks down at me, eyes alight with intrigue and humor.

"Don't worry, your secret is safe with me, cattiva ragazza."

"Go!" I shout, pushing him closer to the door.

He turns, laughs harder, and opens the door to leave. When he's gone, I walk to my bed and flop down face-first.

Now he knows my secret. He's the only one besides Mira. In the grand scheme of things, it's not a big deal, but most people would never guess that virginal good girl Sofia Moretti likes her smut.

CHAPTER FOUR

ANTONIO

I return to my dorm room after leaving Sofia's room and lock the door behind me. The image of her in that silk cami-and-shorts set is playing havoc in my mind. Which is weird.

Sofia's been a constant in my life forever and I've never noticed . . . that. I mean, she's my little sister's best friend and nothing more. I've always thought of her with a sort of brotherly affection, but damn, the way the silk cami clung to her nipples when she first opened the door. The dip in her cleavage was visible between the lace V of her cami.

Which solidifies that I'm a healthy male. Any guy who saw her tonight would have had the same reaction. But still, I definitely didn't feel brotherly when thoughts of slipping her out of those silk bottoms came to mind. Reading her a naughty passage out of the book, only to dip my finger past the lace at the bottom of her shorts that left easy access to coat my finger in her wetness and taste her. Shit, I shake my head. I'm promised to another woman who is not Sofia.

Not to mention, this is Sofia. Who is about as sweet and innocent as they come. She's off-limits and not only because I'm engaged but because she's Mira's best friend. My sister would murder me if she knew the direction of my thoughts. Sofia comes from a respectable family and will marry someone within the family someday, have his children, and be the perfect Italian Mafia wife. Of that, I have no doubt.

I run a cold shower in the hopes of getting Sofia and her image out of my mind. I outright refuse to let my hand wrap around my cock because if I do, I'll only think of *her*. And if I do it once, I'll do it again.

But I desperately need to. My dick has been half-hard since I walked back in my room, and my balls ache. Once I'm in bed with the lights out, sleep refuses to come.

I roll onto my side and close my eyes, willing my mind to relax and stop the slideshow of Sofia dressed in silk. When that doesn't work, I turn onto my back and stare at the ceiling in the dark, wondering how I could go from seeing Sofia as nothing to seeing her as sex on a fucking stick.

When I'm still wide awake, I release a growl of frustration because nothing is going to relax me except rubbing one out.

I refuse to give in to my basic instincts and beat off because Sofia spurred some newfound urge.

But after another half hour of sleeplessness, my hand reaches under the covers. Since I usually sleep naked, there's nothing in the way of me easing the tension that has me strung tight.

As long as I don't think of Sofia, it's okay. How hard can that be? I've masturbated hundreds of times and never once thought of her.

At least, that's what I tell myself as my fist wraps around the base of my rock-hard cock and pumps.

I flip the covers off with my other hand and try to recall my past experiences with women or the porn I've watched. It works at first and I keep pumping my length with my fist.

But an image of Sofia pops into my mind. Her and that damn book. She's lying in her bed, holding the book up with one hand while her other hand dips beneath the waistband of her silk shorts.

I grip my cock harder and squeeze the tip.

I imagine Sofia moaning as she rubs her fingertips over her swollen clit and she writhes on the bed, enthralled in what she's reading. She works herself into a frenzy, knowing exactly what will get her off until she's on the edge of coming.

I jerk my hips up into my fist and groan as ribbons of cum lash against my chest. A hefty breath leaves me as the image of Sofia dissolves into nothing in my mind until all that's left is the certainty that this is not the last time I'll come with her name on my lips.

* * *

THE NEXT EVENING, on the way to the dining hall for dinner, Marcelo, Mira, and Sofia are up ahead on the path. I haven't been able to catch up with my sister yet and I almost don't call out for her because she's with Sofia and I fear she'll see what I did last night in my eyes.

I don't share any classes with Sofia since she's two years younger than me, so this is the first time I'll be seeing her since I came all over myself, courtesy of her and my imagination.

But I remind myself that I'm not some starry-eyed teenage simp and I need to figure out this thing with my sister. "Mirabella!"

The three of them turn in unison and wait for me. A quick glance at Sofia and she diverts her eyes to the trees. She's embarrassed— probably because of the book. Maybe I shouldn't have made her feel that way when it's hot. I'm quick to look away from her the minute her big hazel eyes land on me, and the image of her on her bed with her hand down her shorts is front and center.

"What's up?" Mira asks.

"We need to talk."

Her eyes narrow at my tone. She knows me well enough to know that she's about to get a lecture of some kind, and everyone knows Mira doesn't handle discipline very well.

"About what?" She crosses her arms and cocks out a hip, her attitude already heightening.

Yep. She knows something's coming.

Marcelo protectively puts his arm around her shoulders and stares me dead in the eye. It's not an outright threat, but it's his way of telling me to tread lightly because he will intervene.

Fuck him though. She was my sister first.

"You need to curb your attitude toward Aurora."

At the mention of my fiancée's name, Sofia turns and looks off at the landscape surrounding us.

Mira guffaws. "She's a grade *A* bitch, Antonio."

Marcelo shakes his head. If he agrees with me, he'll never admit it because he'll stick by Mira's side until death.

"That may be so, but she's going to be my wife. And I'm going to be the leader of this family someday, and by that right, she deserves a certain level of respect."

"She needs to give it in return because Mira will be my wife and I *am* the leader of my family," Marcelo says.

I nod. "Agreed. And I'll deal with her when she needs to be dealt with on that front."

My sister scowls. "Did she come running to you, feigning hurt? God, she is so full of shit." She looks at Sofia, whose lips are pursed and gaze is floating around, her focus everywhere but this conversation.

"Rest assured, I know exactly who and what Aurora is. But let whatever the fuck happened in high school go. We're all adults now."

Mira's arms uncross and her hands fist at her sides. Her lips flatten into a thin line and she looks as though she's about to scream at me, but instead, she mumbles, "Fine."

I nod, knowing that's as good as I'll get from her. "And if Aurora steps out of line, be sure to tell me."

"Oh, I can handle myself, thanks." There's venom in my sister's voice and I'm sure she's hoping Aurora will say or do something stupid almost immediately so she or Marcelo can handle her.

"Got a second?" Marcelo asks. "There's something I wanted to talk to you about."

Mira's gaze flicks to Marcelo, and I get the sense that she's not in the loop about whatever he wants to talk to me about. He'll be dealing with her wrath later.

"Yeah," I say.

"I'll meet you at the dining hall." He bends and places a chaste kiss on Mira's lips.

She doesn't fully reciprocate until Marcelo doesn't release her. She giggles afterward and Marcelo's smiling as though it's a game to them. God, they're disgusting. He taps her ass as she turns.

"I'm sitting with Sofia today, don't forget." Mira loops her arm through Sofia's and looks at her. "I'm sorry I bailed on you last night."

Sofia glances at me quickly. "It's not a big deal."

"I went by your room last night to have this conversation and you guys weren't around?" I say.

My sister looks at her fiancé with hearts in her eyes. "We were out."

From the looks on their faces, they were at their special spot—the gazebo out by the large pond on school property. I don't know why, but it seems to be their thing.

"It's too cold out for that." Sofia's body shakes as if she's shivering, clearly reading between the lines like me.

Marcelo lets out a rare laugh. "Body heat." He winks and my sister giggles again, making me want to gag.

"Marcelo kept me warm," my sister says, and I swear I taste vomit in the back of my throat.

"All right, you two go ahead. We'll catch up," Marcelo says with a grin, tapping Mira's ass again.

Mira turns with Sofia since their arms are still hooked and they continue on down the path. Once they're far enough ahead, we walk at a little slower pace.

"What's up?" I ask once I've glanced behind us to make sure no one is around to eavesdrop.

"Wanted to give you a heads-up on something. Might be nothing, but I figured it was worth mentioning."

I push my hands in the pockets of my jacket. I'm in agreement with Sofia. It's probably not cold by most people's standards, but when you've spent your life outside South Beach, anything below room temperature feels like a chill in the air. "Okay."

"Earlier this year, we had an issue with the Russians running interference on some of our weapons shipments in and out of the port. We located the source that was passing the info on our side and took care of it."

I nod. "We had the same issue with some of the shipments you were sending us."

Each of the four families has a specialty— my family specializes in counterfeit rings and embezzlement schemes, whereas the Costas primarily dabble in running weapons. Just one of the reasons my dad wanted Mira to marry him.

"Right before break, I got word about a shipment from one of our guys on the docks. He heard that there was something coming in and it was all kept pretty hush-hush. My guys managed to intercept the shipment before it left the docks and it was a bunch of guns."

I stop in the middle of the path, and he does the same. "What does that have to do with us?"

"Those guns were the same ones we sent down to you a few months before."

All the pieces slide into place in my brain. Someone on our end could be selling our guns back to someone else. And without even asking, I know it's not something my father has sanctioned, though I make a note to double-check that fact.

"Someone is fucking with us." My face heats in anger and the veins in my neck pulsate.

"Looks that way. I can't say for sure, but I wanted you to know. I haven't told anyone else." He glances around us.

"Let's keep this between the two of us for now. I'm going to look into it. If someone is running our weapons outside the family and taking the profits for themselves, they'll be dealt with."

He nods. I don't need to say any more for him to know exactly how I'll deal with the snake. We walk again toward the dining hall. Mira and Sofia are long gone from our sights.

"Who do you think the weapons were meant for?" I ask.

"Who knows? Could be the Russians. The Irish. Or the cartel." He shrugs.

"Let me know if any more of our shit ends up on your docks."

He nods.

"So this is why you had to return to New York instead of coming to Miami with Mira?"

"Yeah, and she was not pleased. Especially when I wouldn't tell her what was going on. If Mira asks what I wanted to talk to you about, tell her I was putting you in your place for talking to her about Aurora."

I chuckle. "Please, she'll never believe that. I'll bet you've already told her the same."

He shakes his head as the dining hall comes into sight. "Yeah, but you know how your sister is. She doesn't much care for orders."

"Tell me something I don't know."

We part ways when we enter the dining hall. Marcelo goes to sit with the Costa crime family while I head right to the food line, needing a minute to process everything Marcelo told me before I head to the table where I'm sure my fiancée and sister will be waiting to torment me. Not to mention Sofia, who now seems to torment me equally, in an entirely different way.

CHAPTER FIVE
SOFIA

Aurora sits down across from Mira and me, and my appetite disappears. I've never liked Aurora. She's the queen of evil as far as I'm concerned, but imagine the woman you hate being engaged to the man you've been in love with most of your life. It's brought my animosity toward her to an entirely higher level. A level where I find it hard to even pretend with her anymore.

"Hello, ladies," she says, setting her tray on the table. She looks at Mira's and my trays with garlic bread and pasta with carbonara sauce, then looks at the garden salad on her own, feigning distress. "I wish I could eat like you two. But it's only salads for me until the wedding. I have to look perfect in my wedding dress."

Mira's grip on her fork tightens until I'm surprised the metal doesn't bend. She's about ready to put Aurora on blast, but after the conversation she had with Antonio, I feel the need to save her from herself.

"I'm sure you'll look wonderful in whatever you choose," I say, barely able to spit out the words.

Aurora smiles indulgently at me. "Thanks, Sofia." Then she turns her attention to Mira, flicking her gaze over her shoulder first. "Have you looked for your dress yet, Mirabella? I guess you have lots of time for that. I, on the other hand, have no time to waste."

Mira's fork clatters onto the table and she leans in over her meal.

"I should be the one getting married this summer, not you. I was engaged first, after all. But you had to go behind my back and convince everyone that you and Antonio should be wed first, didn't you? What's the matter, Aurora? Afraid my brother will come to his senses and put an end to this charade if the wedding doesn't come soon enough?"

A smug smile settles on Aurora's face as Antonio comes around the other side of the table to sit beside her. His dark-brown eyes are alight with anger, and when Mira meets his gaze, she shudders.

"What's going on?" Antonio asks, looking between his fiancée and sister.

When neither of them answers, I pipe up. "Nothing. Just a heated debate on what style of dress Aurora should wear for the wedding."

I hate giving Aurora the out because she was poking the bear with Mira and she damn well deserved the bite Mira gave, but I won't throw my best friend under the bus.

"Is that true?" he asks Mira.

She nods and picks up her fork, twirling her pasta.

"What do you think for flowers for the wedding, Antonio? I was thinking a mix of whites and creams, but my mother pointed out that a little color would be a nice contrast."

Mira and I eat in silence while Aurora pesters Antonio with wedding talk. He doesn't seem into it, only answering with one-syllable words.

"Oh my god! I can't believe I almost forgot." Mira turns to me, jubilation on every one of her features.

"What?" I take a bite of the garlic bread.

"Giovanni is going to ask if he can take you to the party this weekend." She claps her hands and squeals.

My garlic bread drops onto my plate. "What?"

Mira playfully rolls her eyes. "He asked about you. He wanted to know if I thought you'd say yes."

"What did you say?" This is so out of left field I'm not even sure what I'm hoping she told him.

"I told him he should ask you, of course. Are you into him?" Her eyes are wide and hopeful.

"I didn't even know he was into me," I answer honestly.

She waves me off. "Please, how could you not know? He's always chatting you up any chance he gets."

I shrug. "I thought he was just being nice because his cousin is marrying my best friend."

"Well, he's not. He likes you. So will you say yes?"

I contemplate my answer. Giovanni is nice and he's definitely one of the top five hottest guys on campus, but . . . my heart lies elsewhere. Which is stupid. Nothing is ever going to come of that, and the sooner I realize that, the better. Antonio doesn't even know I exist in that way, and more than that, he's engaged to be married to someone else.

"Yeah, sure." I try to act much more excited than I feel.

"*Yay!*" Mira gives me a hug.

"Who asks someone to go to a party?" Antonio asks with a tone to suggest it's lame.

I hadn't even realized he was paying attention. When I look at him, he's scowling at the two of us.

"It's sweet, Antonio. God, you're such a guy." Mira shakes her head at her brother.

His gaze meets mine and I frown, wondering why he's so irritated by the idea.

"Imagine if you and Gio hit it off and fell in love and got married," Mira says, getting way ahead of herself. "We'd be married to cousins and then we could live next door to each other and raise our kids together. It would be so much fun."

I squeeze her hand. "Slow down, Mira. It's just a date. And he hasn't even asked me yet."

Her attention moves past me, her eyes widening. She abruptly lowers her eyes to her meal. "Don't look now, but it's about to happen."

I turn and look in the direction she just did and Giovanni is heading toward our table. My breathing picks up and my stomach quivers. All of a sudden, I'm nervous.

"Hello, ladies," he says when he reaches our table. "Antonio." He nods.

Antonio barks out a hello, turning his attention to his meal, stabbing and twirling the noodles around his fork.

Giovanni has a swagger that most girls around campus go gaga over. His confident air is appealing even though he'll never be a don unless something horrible happens to Marcelo. Even then, I'm not sure where he lands in the family line, but I think he's second-in-command since Marcelo trusts him so much. He's got the matching looks to his inflated self-esteem that causes him to come off like a bad-boy heartthrob.

"Sofia, could I steal you for a minute?" he asks.

Mira squeals under her breath as if we're in high school.

"Of course." I push back from the table and follow him toward the doors that lead outside.

He doesn't go through them though. Instead, he trails off to the side and stands by the wall, laying one arm on the brick wall and leaning toward me. "Have you heard about the party happening this weekend?"

"Yeah. Sounds like it'll be fun."

He leans closer to me. "Do you want to go with me?" He clears his throat. "I'd like to get to know you better."

I don't want to lead Giovanni on, but I can't sit around and pine away for Antonio any longer. Maybe I could develop something with Giovanni.

So I smile. "I'd like that."

He shoots me a cocky grin, his light-brown eyes twinkling. "Good."

Then he leans in and kisses my cheek. And though I wish I felt the same kind of tingles throughout my body I felt last night with Antonio, I remind myself this is just a start.

"What time should I be ready?" I ask.

"I'll swing by your room at, say . . . ten?"

"I'll be ready."

His eyes cast down my body, hovering over my lips for a second before landing on my eyes. "Looking forward to it." He smiles again and walks back the way he came.

I remain against the wall, trying to figure out how I feel about the fact that I have my first official date and it's not with Antonio.

It's not like I've never kissed a boy before—there were stolen kisses in high school here and there—but my father never permitted me to date anyone. So although it's not with the guy I really wish it were with, I'm still excited to have a date this Saturday night.

I head back to the table, and as soon as I take a seat, Mira leans in and asks, "Well . . . what did you say?"

"I said yes."

She squeals and hugs me into her side.

I can't resist looking at Antonio, who's glaring at me as if I've done something wrong.

Why would he care? His fiancée is sitting right next to him.

CHAPTER SIX

ANTONIO

The week drags. I don't know if it's because it's the first week back after break or whether it's because every time I see Aurora, all she wants to discuss is wedding plans. Something that, believe it or not, is not at the top of my list of things to do.

I have a duty to uphold. I know that. But that doesn't mean I have to be a happy participant in the wedding planning. Just let her and our moms plan it and I'll show up.

Unfortunately, there's also my creeping suspicion that maybe my shit mood has more to do with Sofia than the previous two reasons. She hasn't left my mind and the image I created of her on her bed, pleasuring herself, is still vividly clear.

What my shit mood should be about is the information Marcelo passed on to me earlier this week. And it is—partly. But it should be the only thing on my mind.

I've pondered all week, trying to remember if I heard or saw anything from anyone when I was home that was even slightly suspicious. Still, I'll be discussing what Marcelo told me with my father tomorrow during our weekly Sunday phone call.

Students at the Sicuro Academy are permitted one outside phone call a week and mine is always with my father. In the past, it's usually been him keeping me in the loop about what was going on with the business back home. This will be the first time I'm bringing something to him.

Well, that's not entirely true. Last year, when Mira got herself in trouble, I brought a steaming pile of crap to his doorstep, but that's in the past.

Tonight is about having fun. There's a party in the woods on campus and I plan to drink and let off some steam.

The only shitty part is that Aurora insisted I accompany her to the party. She said it wouldn't send the right message if we arrived separately, and while there's some truth to that, I really don't want to spend my night listening to her either goad my sister into an argument or ask my take on table centerpieces.

But looking like a united front to the rest of the school is an important part of solidifying ourselves as the future of the La Rosa crime family, so I have no choice but to escort her.

That, of course, makes me think of Giovanni escorting Sofia tonight. Which isn't any of my business, nor should it garner a reaction from me. Unfortunately, that doesn't mean it doesn't.

I wanted to send my fist through the table when he kissed her cheek after she presumably said yes to a date with him at the dining hall.

This newfound interest in Sofia has me wound up like a fucking mummy. It's one thing to find a woman hot and want to fuck her; it's another to feel jealous because another man is paying her attention. Especially when she's never been yours, nor have you even imagined she ever could be.

The fucked part is that if some guy were paying Aurora that kind of attention, I'm not sure I would care. I doubt it would bother me in the least.

I shake my head and knock on Aurora's dorm room door.

She answers right away, springing the door open. "Hi," she says, giving me the once-over as if she'd remark if she didn't like what I was wearing.

"Hey, ready to go?" I ask.

"How do I look?" She steps back and holds out her hands, so I step forward to hold the door open. She's wearing a pair of black leggings and a cream-colored sweater that hugs her curves and ends above where her hips swell.

I don't give her the compliment she's fishing for. I hate that shit. "Put a jacket on. Otherwise, you'll freeze."

"I'll be fine. A coat would ruin my look." She runs her palms over her stomach to smooth out her sweater.

"Ready?" I arch an eyebrow.

"All set."

We ride the elevator down and walk outside. The parties are always at the same spot—in a clearing in the middle of the forest. There will be music and lasers on the canopy of trees surrounding us and probably a keg or two. The kids at Sicuro Academy are used to bribing and extorting to get what they want.

As soon as we get close enough for people to see us, Aurora hooks her arm through mine. That makes it difficult to navigate the dark forest, but I don't argue. She's right in that it's best we appear as a united front to everyone else. They'd all take great pleasure in trying to exploit any weakness they might see, whether it be now or in the future when we're all done with this place and competing as rivals in the real world.

We push through the trees and into the fray. Groups of people are gathered around the clearing. On the outside is everyone who's standing around talking and drinking from their red Solo cups, and in the middle is everyone dancing to the beat of "Haul" by Christian Löffler.

"Want something to drink?" I ask Aurora.

She shakes her head. "I don't like beer."

That's no surprise.

"I'm going to get a cup."

I lead us to the usual spot where the kegs are set up, and thankfully, I have the excuse of having to pour myself a beer as a reason to drop her arm from around mine. Once I have my beer in hand, I walk off out of the way of the next person and Aurora stands next to me.

We move a bit to the beat and I spot Tommaso chatting up some girl from the Vitale family a few feet inside the crowd. He must feel my gaze on him because he looks up and we each nod.

He says a quick goodbye to whoever the girl is and makes his way to us. "Hey, guys. You just get here?"

"Yeah."

I can tell that he's at least a few beers in from the glassy eyes. I'm envious. I'd like to be to the point where all the noise in my head is off and I'm left with no thoughts at all. Where I don't have to think about making sure I can fill my dad's shoes when the time comes, where I don't worry about disappointing him, or the fact that I have to marry what I suspect is a frigid bitch, or that someone is trying to rip off my family and I have to get to the bottom of it, or the fact that Giovanni will arrive with Sofia on his arm.

I toss back the rest of my beer in a few gulps.

"Wow. Hitting it hard tonight, I see," Tommaso says.

"I'll be back in a minute." I step back to the keg and don't bother going to the end of the three-person line.

The kid who's next looks as if he wants to say something but thinks better of it. Wise choice.

I refill my cup and walk back to Tommaso and Aurora, who are talking about the song that's playing. It's a remix of Lorde's "Team."

"How can you not like Lorde?" he says, seeming in disbelief.

"Because some of us have taste, Tommaso," she snipes.

"Lorde's the shit. I don't care what you say." He shakes his head and sips his drink.

Aurora rolls her eyes then shivers.

"Cold?" I ask with derision.

"Yeah, a little." She rubs her hands up and down her arms.

Before I can respond, Mira, Marcelo, Sofia, and Giovanni join the group. I force my fingers not to crush the plastic cup in my hand when I see Giovanni's hand settled on Sofia's lower back.

What the fuck is wrong with me?

"Having fun yet?" Mira asks in a tone that indicates she suspects we're not, then she looks directly at Aurora.

"Don't start." I'm not in the mood for her shit tonight.

"What? I just asked if you were having fun." She gives me her best innocent look, but we both know she's full of shit.

Marcelo chuckles and looks at her. "I'm going to get a beer. You want one?"

"Yes, please." She moves onto her tiptoes and kisses him.

"Do you want some beer?" Giovanni asks Sofia.

Why does it annoy me so much?

She considers it and, after glancing my way, says, "Yeah, that'd be great, thanks."

"I'm gonna come with," Tommaso says and follows the two of them to the keg.

"How's your date going?" I ask Sofia. I don't know why.

My sister gives me a weird expression as if asking why I care.

"What?" I shrug. "Just wondering if we have another defector who's going from the La Rosa family to the Costas."

That sounded legit, right?

Sofia shifts in place and glances at Aurora. "I don't know. Fine, I guess. I mean, it's only been, like, half an hour."

Aurora shivers and rubs her arms again.

I slip off my jacket with a roll of my eyes. "Here."

She looks up at me with a smile that suggests she got what she wanted. "You're so sweet."

My eyes veer toward Sofia and her smile is now an annoyed frown. An ache lands in my chest. I toss back more of my beer.

"I'm going to go see what's taking the guys so long," Sofia says and, without waiting for Mira, turns to walk to the keg.

My vision zeroes in on how the denim of Sofia's jeans hugs her ass cheeks perfectly.

"I'm outta here," Mira says before disappearing into the crowd.

"Guess it's just you and me now," Aurora says, slipping her arm through my free one.

I toss back more of my drink, hoping the alcohol will do me a solid and make this weird feeling in my chest vanish.

CHAPTER SEVEN
SOFIA

Giovanni, Marcelo, Mira, and I are all out in the middle of the crowd, dancing.

Well, three of us are dancing. Marcelo is sort of standing and bopping his head, which seems to be about as much as he wants to do. Giovanni, on the other hand, is a good dancer and apparently up for anything. He's a lot of fun, and truth be told, if I could get my mind off Antonio, he's probably the kind of guy I could find myself liking.

But all I can think about is Antonio giving his coat to Aurora when she had exaggerated being cold. I don't know why. Maybe it's because I've never seen him be chivalrous to a woman before.

I'm driving myself crazy with all the thoughts about Antonio and Aurora. It's like a constant loop in my head, reminding me that she's going to marry him, sleep with him, bear his children. Even if it's not a love match, that does little to salve my wounds—she'll still be the one beside him, sharing his life.

A tug on my hand makes me blink and come back to reality.

Giovanni pulls me toward him.

Oh god, is he going to try and grind against me? I'm not ready for that. So far, he's kept a respectable distance, which I appreciated.

But once I'm close enough to him, he leans in to my ear. "I'm going to get another beer. You want one?"

I pull back and meet his gaze, shaking my head. "I'm good."

"Be right back."

I nod and watch as he gets swallowed by the crowd.

After a couple of minutes, my mind is back on Antonio again and I feel claustrophobic in the crush of people swaying to the music.

"I'll be right back," I shout to Mira, who's grinding against Marcelo, then whirl around and push through the crowd, not giving Mira any time to quiz me on where I'm going.

I just . . . I need space. I don't know if it's possible to get it from your own thoughts, but being surrounded by so many people and the music and the laser show zipping over the trees is just too much.

I stumble out of the crowd into the darkened woods. The light from the party is enough to light my way until I'm fifteen or twenty feet into the darkness and my breath releases. It's a little chillier out here, beyond the body heat and fire, and I wrap my arms around myself.

"What are you doing?"

I whip my head toward the male voice, my heart thrumming as fast as the high-tempo music blasting from the party. Antonio is a few feet from me. I can tell from his walk that he's had a lot to drink. There's more swagger and less intensity.

"What are you doing here?" I place my hand over my heart, willing it to slow down.

"I followed you." He steps forward.

"Why?" My forehead wrinkles.

He shrugs and closes the distance between us. "'Cause I wanted to."

"Where's Aurora?" I doubt her name will ever come out of my mouth without attitude.

"She headed back to the dorm a while ago. She was too cold."

He appears annoyed. Maybe he's upset she's not with him? Have his feelings for her grown since they've become engaged? My chest tightens from the idea.

"That's too bad."

He throws his head back and laughs in a way I've never seen. When he straightens, he meets my gaze. "Don't have to pretend with me, Sofia. You hate Aurora."

I frown and shrug. It's true, but I try to give her the bare minimum of respect and kindness. I'll have no choice but to be nice when she's married to Antonio. My father will make sure of it.

He takes two more steps toward me, leaving us only inches apart. His body heat radiates now that he's so close to me. His beer breath wafts over my face, but the distinct scent of spearmint is mixed in.

"What is it?" His fingers gently trace my cheek.

My entire body freezes and I suppress a full-body shiver. He's touching me. Antonio La Rosa's fingers are on my cheek. What planet am I on?

"What's different?" he says, more to himself than me.

Then his hands are in my hair on either side of my head and he's drawing closer until his lips press against mine. My whole body relaxes and sags into his. For years, I've wondered how Antonio kisses. Would he be dominant and commanding or soft and loving? It's a mixture of both. Pure perfection.

His tongue skates across the seam of my lips and I open for him. Our tongues touch and a fission of electricity travels through my body. My heart beats with a pulsing need as his hand slips from the back of my head down to squeeze my ass. I yelp but draw closer to him, not wanting this to end.

Antonio trails his mouth to my ear and, in a low, guttural voice, whispers, "Your ass was made for these jeans."

He pulls me into his body so there's no space between us and his hard length presses against me. I moan into the night air.

"Do you feel what you do to me?"

I must be dreaming. I tripped and hit my head on a rock and I'm hallucinating and dreaming this entire scenario.

He pulls back and looks down at me, glassy eyes full of confusion and lust. As if he can't control himself, he smashes his lips to mine again. My hands delve into his dark hair, loving the way the soft curls wrap around my fingers like vines. He kisses me like he wants to possess me—deep and thorough and full of need. And then his lips trail down the column of my neck.

"I hope I remember this in the morning," he murmurs against my skin.

His words are like a bucket of cold water and the reminder I needed that Antonio is not in his right mind. Just because *I've* wanted *him* for ages doesn't mean the feeling is mutual. I'm probably a convenient, easy target for him.

I pull away and take a few steps until my back lands against a tree. I fight the burn of tears in my eyes. "This shouldn't have happened."

"Don't say that." He moves toward me, but I raise my hand to stop him.

"You're engaged," I remind him.

His face screws up as if my words are ridiculous. "That doesn't matter. You know I don't love her. She doesn't love me."

"I'm your sister's best friend. And you don't really like me. You're just drunk."

Anger flashes in his eyes, but I can't stick around to find out the cause.

"This was a mistake." I turn and run deeper into the forest, desperate to escape him.

I don't know what that was or why he did it, but I'm in a tailspin as I thrash through the forest until it ends and I come out the other side. I look around to gain my bearings, then run again, needing to get as far from Antonio as I can.

Getting what I always wanted will end up being far worse than never knowing what it was like to kiss Antonio La Rosa. I'll never forget the feeling of his lips on mine, but I'll likely never experience it again.

CHAPTER EIGHT
ANTONIO

I wake up Sunday morning with a groan, my head pounding as I roll over in bed. I drank way too much last night, which isn't like me. Normally, I pride myself on my self-control and ability to push away any reaction to what's going on around me.

Like the first time my father shot someone in the head in front of me. And the time I was called on to take my first person out. None of that rattled me as much as seeing Sofia in a pair of tight denim pants. I had to have her.

I couldn't stop thinking about her, *obsessing* over her all night. So once Aurora was gone and I saw Sofia slip off into the woods, my body just moved in that direction. I didn't plan on kissing her, but she looked so tempting in all her beauty and innocence, the moonlight shining through the trees.

At the time, I wished that I wouldn't forget the kiss in the morning, but that was an error on my part. Because I'll never forget what she tastes like, what her plump lips felt like under mine, what she smells like up close. What her ass felt like in my hands. And none of those details faded through the night.

My cock twitches at the memory of my hands in her hair, my lips on hers, the way she let me lead and set the pace. I haven't kissed Aurora yet, but it doesn't take a genius to see that Aurora's about as soft and pliable as a slab of granite. The exact opposite of Sofia.

But that's part of the reason my dad chose her for me. I'm going to need someone strong by my side when it's my turn to run the La Rosa family. Aurora knows her place in the family but has the backbone to withstand whatever is thrown our way.

Even as I try to convince myself, the needling feeling in my ribs that I'm lying remains.

Whatever.

I roll out of bed and turn on the shower. My call with my dad is early this afternoon and it's almost lunchtime.

Once I'm showered and dressed and have downed a bottle of water and some ibuprofen, I take the elevator down to the lowest level in the Roma House, where all our phone calls to the outside world happen every Sunday.

Each person gets access to a secure room with a secure line to speak with whomever we choose. For me, it's always my father, no one else.

I'm a little early for my call time, so I pace around in front of the security desk where all the monitors sit, displaying the images from the cameras all over the Roma House.

"We have an empty room if you'd like to make your call now, Mr. La Rosa."

I turn to answer the woman and her hand is gesturing down the hallway of closed doors.

"Great. What room number?" I head toward the hallway.

"Room number seven."

I raise a hand in thanks but don't turn around, continuing until I reach the room in question. Once I'm inside, I close the door and sit in the lone chair, picking up the phone on the table. I dial my father's number and wait for him to answer.

"Antonio," he answers on the first ring. "How are you, son?"

We don't have a lot of time, so small talk is kept to a minimum. He's not an asshole to me like Marcelo's father was to him, but our relationship revolves around the fact that one day I'll be taking over the empire he helped build. So he's not going to ask how my classes are going and whether or not Mirabella and Aurora are causing me any problems. He knows I'll handle it. I respect the man and hope one day to earn the same amount of respect in return.

"I was better before I talked to Marcelo."

"What'd Marcelo have to say?" His voice holds an edge.

"He told me that they got a tip from someone on their payroll down at the docks. They intercepted a shipment of guns—the same guns that were headed down to us months ago."

"Cazzo!"

"If I had to put money on it, I'd say they're the same weapons that went missing courtesy of the Russians. But there's no way to be sure."

My father curses, carrying on in Italian. Once that's out of his system, he takes a deep inhale before he speaks again. "I'll see if we have any other guns that have gone missing other than the ones that were courtesy of the Russians."

"Are you sure that's wise?" I don't normally question my father, but we have to be sure to play this right.

"Are you questioning me?"

"Of course not, it's just—"

"It could be someone on the inside. Either the runners stole our guns and sold them back to someone in New York, or someone here is skimming off the top and running their own operation on the side. Talk to Marcelo and find out if any of their regulars aren't buying as much as they used to and keep your eyes and ears open with the Russians on campus. Tell me if you hear anything."

I nod, though he can't see me. "Will do."

"Now, your mother wanted to talk to you before you go. Let me get out of my office and find her."

By the time my dad puts my mom on the phone, I only have a few minutes left of my call, which I'm thankful for since all my mom wants to talk about are wedding details and questions she wants me to ask Aurora on her behalf.

"You can tell me next week what Aurora says. Don't forget to ask her," she says.

"I won't. Talk to you next week. Ti voglio bene, Mamma." I hang up before she can slip in something else about the wedding.

I blow out a breath and leave the room, pushing a hand through my hair. When I reach the elevators, I press the up button and the doors open immediately. Aurora's eyes widen, then her surprise morphs into a smile.

"Hey, you." She steps out, lifting on her tiptoes to kiss my cheek.

"Hey."

"You just finish your call? I have mine in a few minutes."

I nod. "Yeah, just spoke with my dad."

She frowns. "You okay? You seem stressed or something."

"Yeah, I'm fine. I spoke with my mom too and she has some wedding questions for you."

Her eyes sparkle in delight. "Great. How about I come find you once I'm done with my call?"

"Yeah, sure." I step around her and hit the up button again so the elevator doors reopen.

"Perfect, see you then." She smiles wide as the door closes between us.

I don't know what it is about her smile that always creeps me out. I think it's because it never reaches her eyes.

Rather than hitting the button for my floor, I hit the button for the main level. I don't feel like being alone in my room, poring over thoughts of Sofia when I should be figuring out how to get to the bottom of whatever's happening with those gun shipments.

When I step out into the lounge, I immediately see Tommaso sprawled back in one of the chairs with Sofia standing in front of him. They're chatting and she must say something that he finds fucking hilarious because his head rocks back in laughter.

My jaw tics as I approach them. I don't know why. First, it's not like Tommaso would ever go for Sofia. He's known her as long as I have and never once uttered a word about seeing her as anything more than a friend. Tommaso typically likes his conquests to be a little farther from home.

But wasn't it two days ago that I was just like my best friend? I didn't look at Sofia as anything more than my little sister's best friend. But now . . . now, I don't know what the hell is going on with my head. Maybe it's a stress response to knowing I'm going to have to spend the rest of my life with Aurora. Whatever it is, it needs to fucking stop—now.

The sound of Sofia's melodic voice hits me as I approach and I realize I have to decide now how I'm going to deal with the aftermath of our shared kiss.

Should I address what happened and tell her to keep her mouth shut? I don't think it's necessary to threaten her to keep it between us. She's smart enough to know that no good will come from her telling anyone about our little indiscretion. Besides, I'm sure she wants to keep her squeaky-clean image in good stead.

While it won't be a big deal for me to stray after Aurora and I are married—something that's not uncommon in our world, especially when the marriage isn't a love match—being rumored to be my mistress wouldn't bode well for Sofia's marriage prospects.

It's then I decide to pretend it never happened. After all, it can't happen again anyway.

"Hey, guys." I step around Sofia and take the chair to Tommaso's left. My gaze flicks to Sofia's.

She looks at me for the length of a heartbeat, then her gaze darts to the floor.

"You just finish up your call?" Tommaso asks.

I nod. "Yep."

I've yet to decide whether I'm going to fill him in on what Marcelo told me. I have no reason to suspect Tommaso of being anything other than loyal to me and the family, but I need to make sure my trust isn't misplaced. You can never be too careful in our business. Trusting the wrong person is what gets you killed.

When I don't expand on my phone call with my father, Tommaso takes my hint that I won't be discussing it further and changes the subject. "That party was awesome last night."

I shrug. "It was all right. I drank more than I should've. A lot of the night is a blur for me." My gaze meets Sofia's, and to her credit, she doesn't say anything. I swear a flash of hurt shines in her eyes, but it's there and gone in a millisecond. "Did you have fun, Sofia?" I arch an eyebrow as if I'm daring her to out us.

"It was okay." She looks away and around the room, almost as if she's hoping Superman will come and save her.

"You were there with Giovanni, right? You two a thing now?" Tommaso asks.

I hate the way I shift forward a bit, eager to hear her answer.

Her gaze darts down to the floor. "I don't really know what's going on with us."

"Sofia!"

The three of us turn in the direction of Mira's voice. She's rushing over from the elevators, Marcelo casually trailing behind.

"Hey, where'd you run off to last night? Giovanni was looking for you," Mira says once she reaches us.

Sofia glances at me for a beat before giving her attention back to my sister. "Sorry, my stomach bothered me and it seemed best to just get out of there. I would've been mortified if I threw up in front of Giovanni." A wan smile tilts her lips.

The lie slides easily off her tongue, which surprises me, but I'm grateful that she doesn't out me.

Mira frowns. "You feeling all right now?"

"Yeah, I'm good." She smiles. "I think maybe I had too much to drink. It was a weird night."

Weird is one word for it.

Marcelo raises his hand in a wave before he goes to stand beside my sister, wrapping an arm around her waist. I swear those two can't be in the same room without having to touch. It's annoying as fuck.

Mira grips Sofia's hands. "I have to talk to you about Giovanni. I was talking to him last night after we couldn't find you and he is so smitten. I think he's—"

"Jesus, take this hen party elsewhere, will you?" I scowl at my sister, who scowls back.

"What's your problem? Engagement to Satan finally wearing on you?"

I want to shake off the smug look on Mira's face.

Before I respond, Aurora's voice says, "There you are."

"Speak of the devil and she will appear," Mira mutters.

A quick glance at Sofia tells me she's even more uncomfortable than she was moments ago.

"I went up to your room, and when you weren't there, I thought I might find you here." Aurora slips past Sofia, Mira, and Marcelo without acknowledging their presence and slides onto my lap.

I don't know why she's acting as if we're a couple who cuddle, but I'll play her game to convince Sofia that last night will never happen again. Plus, it pisses off my sister.

So I slide my hand around Aurora's waist and let my arm settle across her abdomen. A sick feeling invades my stomach, but I'm not doing anything wrong. She is my fiancée.

Then why does touching Aurora feel all wrong when touching Sofia feels so right?

CHAPTER NINE
SOFIA

The sound of Aurora's voice behind me is like a cheese grater on my brain. I squeeze my eyes shut, and when I open them, she slides onto Antonio's lap as if she belongs there. Which I guess she does. But that doesn't make it any easier to swallow, especially after last night.

To make things worse, he slides his arm around her waist as though he wants to make sure she remains there. It's the first un-coerced gesture of affection I've seen him show her and it's a punch to the chest, knocking the wind out of me.

It shouldn't hurt this much. It's not as if Antonio and I share a romantic past, but it's the drying up of all my silly dreams. It's the knowledge that he's sending me a direct message, telling me that last night meant nothing.

I've been used and discarded like all the whores men in our world accumulate outside of their marriages.

Maybe I was just a warm body who happened to be there, and he was drunk. I don't know, but he's the one who followed me, not the other way around.

Regardless, my gut tells me this little display is for me.

Antonio doesn't have to worry—message received.

"How was your call?" he asks her. "I'm assuming you were chat-ting with your mom about wedding stuff?"

Her mouth is full of perfectly straight teeth, which are on display as always when she's around Antonio and she basks under his attention. "There's so much to get sorted. It's going to be hard to do when I can't talk to her whenever I want, but not impossible." She looks at Mirabella, another dig about them marrying first.

"My mom had a few questions for you too." His thumb strokes over her shirt where it rests on her stomach and a sour feeling coasts up my throat.

She shifts on his lap to face him more. "That's right. What did she want to know?"

"Can you two do this somewhere else? The rest of us don't want to hear it," Mira says.

Antonio's narrowed gaze whips to her. "Mira . . ." His tone is a warning.

"What?" Mira blinks innocently. "I'm just saying we don't want to know all the details. Leave some surprises for the guests."

Aurora grins at Mira and I know before any words leave her mouth that whatever she's about to say won't be well received. "Guest? What do you mean by guest, Mira? I haven't had an opportunity to extend a formal invitation yet, but as my future sister-in-law, you'll be my bridesmaid."

My mouth falls open and my head whips in Mira's direction. Her face grows paler the longer the words sink in. Marcelo entwines his fingers with hers. She opens her mouth but says nothing. Then the shock must wear off because her eyebrows draw down and that fiery look that's so Mira flames in her eyes.

"Think before you speak, sis," Antonio says.

Marcelo's chin lifts in a silent warning to Antonio.

Why does Aurora always stir up shit?

Mira's jaw clenches and she draws in a big breath. "I'd be honored. Of course."

She sounds like a Southern belle who was raised to never offend people. But I'm surprised she's even able to get those words out.

Aurora claps like she's a baby seal. "Wonderful! We can chat about bridesmaid dress styles in a few weeks once I've worked out some other details. I'd ask you to be my matron of honor, sorry, *maid* of honor, but my older sister will be filling that role."

Mira drops Marcelo's hand and steps forward, but he grips her shoulders, stopping her in her tracks, pulling her back to his chest.

"Why don't we head to Café Ambrosia? You said you needed caffeine, right?"

Mira merely nods and lets her fiancé direct her away from the group toward the doors.

Tommaso's hand covers his mouth as he tries not to burst out laughing.

"I'm going to head to my room," I say to no one in particular. I just want out of here.

"I know how you and Mira are practically joined at the hip, but I can't have you in the wedding, Sofia. I'm sorry. But don't worry. You'll be invited to the big day."

I stop at her words and turn around. My gaze flicks to Antonio, whose eyes are on me.

"Looking forward to it." I shoot them a wan smile and walk to the elevator, forcing myself not to run like I want to.

Tears gather in my eyes before the elevator doors have a chance to close, but I suck them back. I can't cry over a man who was never even mine to begin with. I'm being ridiculous.

When the elevator reaches my floor, I step out and walk steadily toward my door. My steps slow for a beat when I see Giovanni there, knocking.

"Hey," I call.

He turns to face me, gracing me with one of his killer smiles that all the girls love. He really is attractive. I just wish I'd get the same flutters in my belly that I get when Antonio turns his gaze on me.

Giovanni pushes his hands into his pockets, breaking the distance between us. The hallway is empty except for the two of us. "I just wanted to check on you after you disappeared last night."

Flashes of my kiss with Antonio sear my brain and I feel my cheeks heat. "Sorry, I suddenly wasn't feeling well and had to rush out of there."

He gives me the once-over. "Everything okay?"

"I think I just had too much to drink."

He nods. "Been there."

"I should have told you I was going back to my room. Guess I don't make a very good date."

He chuckles softly and there's a warmth in his eyes. "I don't know about that. I had a good time with you last night."

"Same." I bite my lip.

And I did. Giovanni was nothing but kind and respectful. He's good-looking and no doubt will have a solid place at the top of the Costa Mafia. On paper, he's everything a girl like me—a girl destined to marry a made man—could want.

But he's not Antonio.

No. I push that thought from my head. It's useless. I need to do whatever I can to get over my feelings for Antonio. Maybe that means leaning into this thing with Giovanni. Even if things don't stick with us, maybe he could be a distraction to get me over Antonio.

"I'm glad to hear that." He steps closer and takes my hand. "I was hoping maybe we could do something on our own next time rather than with Marcelo and Mira?"

"I think that sounds like a good idea. What were you thinking?"

He squeezes my hand. "There're not a lot of options on campus, unfortunately. If we were in New York, I'd wine and dine you and show you exactly what you deserve, but since we're here"—he motions to our surroundings with his hand—"the best I can do for a meal is either the dining hall or Café Ambrosia. I'm thinking the café so we don't have to share a table with everyone else."

A soft chuckle leaves my lips. "The café is fine."

His thumb rubs the back of my hand. "You deserve so much more than fine, Sofia."

I've heard the rumors about Giovanni. He's a sweet talker until you get him in bed. So I'm unsure if I'm like every other girl he's bedded since he's been here or if I'm something different to him. It's not lost on me that if it were Antonio saying these words to me, my chest would be warm and I'd probably be at a loss for words. But as it is, it's still a nice sentiment, so I smile.

"Thanks, Giovanni. When were you thinking?"

"How about tomorrow night?"

My eyebrows rise into my hairline. "So soon?"

"I'm not an idiot. I don't want to waste any time. Otherwise, someone else might try to take my place."

I laugh. "Tomorrow night it is. I have a meeting after my last class, but I should be finished around five or so."

"Do you want to meet at the café after your meeting? That way, most people will be in the dining hall having dinner and we won't have to worry about an audience."

"As long as you don't mind me still being in my school uniform, that works for me." Not having an audience sounds ideal. Especially if there's any chance that that audience would include Antonio La Rosa.

"You look beautiful in anything you wear, school uniform especially. I'll see you then." He kisses my cheek before dropping my hand and walking past me toward the elevator.

I don't turn to look at him as I make my way to my door and unlock it. Once I'm inside, I lean against the door, blow out a breath, and stare at the ceiling.

I hope I'm doing the right thing.

But I need to do whatever it takes to get over Antonio.

CHAPTER TEN
ANTONIO

Tommaso and I push through the classroom doors once the professor dismisses us.

"You coming to the gym before dinner?" he asks.

"Yeah, I'll be there, but I have to head to guidance first."

He laughs. "I see ice cream scooper at the school's spring fair for your volunteer hours?" He puts up his hands like people do when they say *see your name in lights.*

I push his shoulder, and he rocks to the side. "Fuck off. Not a chance I'm doing that bullshit."

"Did you already pick what you're going to do?" Tommaso spins and walks backward beside me to check out a girl I've seen a few times from the Roma House. "Damn, she's hot."

I shake my head. I'm all for hooking up, but Tommaso takes it to a new level. "If you're not careful, you're going to work your way through the entire Roma House by the end of the year. Then what will you do?"

He turns back around. "Move on to the Moskva House, maybe. Did you see that girl in our hacking class?" He lets loose a low whistle. "Legs that were meant to wrap around my waist."

My head whips in his direction. "Don't even think about it."

The Russians are our enemies. We don't fraternize and we definitely don't fuck them.

He holds up both hands in front of him. "I'm kidding. I'll just wait for a fresh crop of chicks to come to the Roma House next year. But you've got a point. Maybe I should pace myself until the end of the year. Make sure I don't run out of options."

I laugh. "Too bad you don't use those problem-solving skills when it matters."

He clamps me on the shoulder. "I do and that's why I'm your right-hand man."

I still haven't told Tommaso what Marcelo told me. I trust him. I do. But sometimes, I question whether he lets his dick make too many decisions for him. And comments like the one he made about the Russians don't help.

"So what'd you pick?" he asks.

I shrug. "I haven't. I ignored them all last week. The text I got today said they've chosen for me now, but we'll see about that. If it's something fucking stupid, I'm not doing it."

Tommaso lets out a wicked laugh. "Oh man, I hope you get stuck restocking shelves at the library or helping hand out food in the dining hall or some shit."

"Not happening," I grumble. Though I'm anxious to know what type of stupid activity they want me to participate in. "I'll meet you at the gym when I'm done."

We split off when he heads to the opposite end of campus, where all the athletic facilities are, and I carry on toward the administrative offices.

I loosen my tie as I walk, and when I arrive, the same auburn-haired woman who was behind the desk the last time I was here looks up at me expectantly. "Mr. La Rosa, we've been expecting you."

At least she remembers who I am this time. "Let's get this over with."

"Mr. Lewis is in his office, waiting for you. Why don't you head on in? Second door on your left."

I nod and make my way down the spacious hallway. The office

door is open, so I don't hesitate to walk in and take a seat across the desk from a balding man I'd put in his early forties. He startles when my ass hits the seat and quickly closes the screen on his computer.

He swivels his chair to face me and links his hands together on his desk. "Mr. La Rosa. Glad to see you came to the meeting. You've been a hard man to nail down."

"Can we just get to the part where you tell me I need to get my volunteer hours and then give me all the shitty options to pick from?" I give him a bored look.

A small chuckle leaves his lips. "Well, last week, there was a list when the sign-ups were open. Now, due to your lack of response, you've been assigned a volunteer task. There's only one spot left, and it's yours."

"And what exactly will I be doing?"

"You've been assigned as one of four students who will be responsible for running the entertainment at Café Ambrosia every Friday."

My hands tighten on the chair arms. "Run those stupid spoken-word poetry and open-mic talent nights?"

"Those are the ones. Though you can do anything you like. Students just generally default to what's been successful before."

I lean forward. "This is complete bullshit."

"Like I said, had you come to see me when I followed up last week, you would have had a choice."

"I was here. You weren't in your office."

He looks down his nose at me. "Mr. La Rosa, we both know I've been texting you all week."

My jaw clenches until it becomes painful.

"You will be responsible for an activity every other Friday. You've been assigned to work with another student. The other two students will run their activity on the alternating Friday to yours."

I think of all the lame shit I've seen on Friday nights at Café Ambrosia over the past few years and cringe internally. "There has to be something else I can do."

"As I explained, the opportunity for that has passed."

Jesus. I'd argue further, but there's no point. Trying to throw my weight around wouldn't do much here. Though I'm higher on the social pyramid than most since my dad is a don, everyone at Sicuro Academy is someone or the son or daughter of someone. And not showing any favoritism is a trademark of this place.

I lean forward in my chair, resting my forearms on my knees. "How long do I have to do this shit?"

"The rest of the semester."

"Jesus." I push my hand through my hair and tug on the curly strands, pissed off at myself.

"And here's your partner."

His eyes shift to the door, and I follow his vision. I still when it's Sofia standing in the doorway, wide-eyed and staring at me.

"Antonio, I believe you know Ms. Moretti."

Sofia recovers quickly and steps into the room with a smile. "Hey."

She sits next to me and the scent of her perfume wafts to me. I resist the urge to close my eyes and draw it in deeper.

"Sofia, you'll be working with Antonio this semester. I'm here to help if you need any advising, but Antonio . . . I expect you both to play an equal role in this effort."

I turn to look at Mr. Lewis. "Can't I work with one of the other two people?"

Sofia jolts next to me and I feel like an asshole. But I need to do whatever I can to get out of this. There's no way I can work with her so closely and not cross that line again. I have the willpower for everything and everyone but her.

Mr. Lewis frowns. "I highly doubt you'll want to work with someone from the other team."

"And why's that?" I don't care if they're the most annoying person in the entire school.

"They're from the Moskva House."

My shoulders sag. Not a chance I'm working with the Russians and I'm sure they feel the same. Besides, there would be no good way to explain to anyone why I requested the change and I know Sofia will probably run to my sister and tell her it was my doing when she's questioned.

"Fine." My voice is like a whip. "When do we start?"

"Right away, I'd say. Your first event is the Friday after this one." He turns his attention to Sofia, who I haven't looked at since she sat down. "I trust that you don't have any issue working with Mr. La Rosa?" He arches an eyebrow.

I move my gaze to her and she briefly meets it, then shakes her head. "No issue, no."

"Good." He claps his hands together as though it's such a wonderful plan that has all come together. "I'll leave you two to figure out when you're going to get together to do the prep and planning. Good luck."

Luck.

I'm gonna need it.

CHAPTER ELEVEN

SOFIA

Unbelievable. I signed up for my volunteer hours to help keep myself busy, keep my mind off Antonio, and now I'm stuck working with him.

"Thanks for stopping in, Sofia," Mr. Lewis says as I rise from the chair and make my way toward the door.

Antonio follows me. I feel his gaze on me like a brand on the skin.

The way he asked to switch partners as soon as he found out it was me he would be working with felt like a jagged dagger to the chest. What have I ever done to him? I kept my mouth shut about him kissing me like he clearly wanted and now it's as if he can't stand to be around me.

Am I a terrible kisser?

Granted, I don't have a lot of experience, but I never had anyone else tell me that was the case.

I say a quick goodbye to Mrs. Greer at the reception desk, and once we're out of the administrative offices, I just keep on walking. Antonio and I need to talk about a plan of action to put together our first event next week, but I can't deal with the thought of being near him. I'm going to have to spend *months* in Antonio's presence, all while he apparently hates me.

I'm not more than five steps out of the administrative area when

Antonio's fingers wrap around my upper arm. The heat of his fingertips burns through my school uniform.

"Fucking wait. Where are you going?" His voice is low and sounds rougher than normal.

"To the café to meet Giovanni."

His hand drops from my arm as though I threw acid in his face, and he walks around me until he's standing directly in front of me with a glare that would intimidate most. I smell the scent of his cologne—the same one he's worn since high school—and I try not to react.

"Are you two dating now or something?" It sounds as if he's disgusted by the idea, though I can't fathom why. He has a fiancée.

"We're going on *a* date."

"That's the second one if my math is correct." He crosses his arms.

I sigh. "Is there something you need before I go?"

His gaze does a slow perusal of my body before coming up to meet my eyes again. "We need to figure out when we're going to get together to work on a plan of action."

I gesture to him with my hand. "It doesn't matter to me. You tell me when you're available."

"No dates with Giovanni that we need to plan around?" He arches an eyebrow.

My impatience and frustration get the better of me. "No dates with your fiancée that we need to plan around?"

He stares at me without saying a word, but his face softens slightly.

"Listen, I'm going to be late if I don't leave in a minute. Just tell me when you want to meet."

He huffs. "Wednesday night. I'll come to your room sometime between seven and eight. That work for you?"

I nod. "Yeah."

Without waiting for him to say anything further, I walk around him and toward the doors that lead outside. It will mean a longer journey to Café Ambrosia this way, but desperation to flee from him claws at my chest.

It's not until I'm out of his sight that I take a full breath again.

By the time I reach the café, I'm still rattled. I expected to quickly pop into Mr. Lewis's office to meet my volunteer partner and that was it, not realizing I'd be paired with the man I'm doing my best to avoid.

Giovanni is already seated at one of the far tables with a drink in front of him and one on the other side of the table. He spots me as soon as I walk in, and I do my best to put on a real smile. He deserves my full attention tonight.

The café has a small stage on the opposite side of the room from the counter you order at. They have a few options for food, but nothing you'd really consider a meal. There's no alcohol, but they do have my favorite—a caramel latte, and that's what is sitting on the table in front of the empty chair when I approach.

"Hey," I say.

Giovanni looks up from texting someone on his school-issued phone and smiles wide. "Hey." He pushes out his chair and stands, drawing me into a hug. "Thanks for meeting me."

"Thanks for asking." I smile back at him. It's a genuine smile. I may not know what to make of my interaction with Antonio, but Giovanni has made it very clear that he likes me. And he's always so kind and respectful.

"I grabbed you a drink. Hope that's okay." He gestures to the mug with the Café Ambrosia logo on it.

"Of course. I'm surprised you know what I love." I pull out the chair and take a seat.

Giovanni sits back down. "I've been paying attention to you for a while."

My cheeks heat as I hook my bag on the back of the chair and wrap my hands around the mug, letting the heat seep into my fingers.

"I wasn't sure if you wanted something to eat, so I waited for you."

"I'll probably get something in a bit. I'm going to enjoy this first." I lift the mug to my lips and take a small sip, careful not to burn my tongue. "Mmm. That's so yummy. What are you drinking?"

He sort of cringes. "Don't judge me, but I'm drinking peppermint tea."

I chuckle. "Definitely not what I expected."

"I only get it when I'm stopping in here by myself. The guys would razz the shit out of me if I did it in front of them." He shrugs. "It's good. What can I say?"

"Well, you like what you like, right?" As soon as the words leave my lips, an image of Antonio flashes through my brain.

"That's certainly true." He gives me a look that makes me think he might be referring to me.

Guilt whips against my skin because the man I really like isn't him. But that can change, right? I mean, I've had a thing for Antonio for years. That's not just going to go away overnight. But that doesn't mean I can't develop feelings for someone else. And falling for someone like Giovanni would be perfect—he's kind, respectful, has a high ranking in the Mafia, and is a part of the same world as mine, understands its inner workings.

Right. I can do this. I can fall for this man seated across from me. It'll just take some time.

"You mentioned you had a meeting before this. What was that for?" Giovanni asks then takes a sip of his drink.

I blink a couple of times as thoughts of my interaction with Antonio come to the surface. So I proceed to tell him about getting my volunteer hours and how I've been paired with Antonio.

Giovanni chuckles. "What are the chances, right? But better him than one of the Russians or the Irish."

I nod. There's very little mingling between factions and the only time it ever really happens is when a professor pairs you up for a project or in-class work. And even most of them try to never let that happen, but sometimes the numbers just don't work.

"Yeah, I guess he didn't sign up for anything last week, so he got stuck with it. I don't think he was happy about it."

Giovanni nods. "It's a lot of work. I'm surprised you signed up for that one."

I shrug off his comment, not wanting him to know the real reason I signed up for one of the more time-intensive volunteer opportunities.

The rest of our evening passes quickly. Giovanni is easy to talk to and fairly laid-back. He's funny, but not in a way that comes off as trying too hard. Anyone would find him endearing. I just don't know if this is an act or not.

Still, Antonio comes to mind more than a few times throughout the night.

"I'd better get going," I say after I get a text from Mira. "I have some homework I have to get done tonight."

He nods and stands from the table. "I'll walk you back to the Roma House."

"Are you sure it's not out of your way?"

We chuckle since we live in the same building.

Once we reach the path that leads us to the side of campus where our building is, Giovanni takes my hand and links our fingers.

"This okay?" he asks.

I nod. It feels kind of weird because I've never had a serious boyfriend who I walked around holding hands with, but it doesn't feel wrong. The idea that someone would be proud enough to show their interest in me so publicly is appealing.

He squeezes my hand a few times as we walk and chat some more, and when we reach the Roma House, he drops my hand so that he can hold the door open for me.

"Thanks."

The lounge area is fairly empty. Most students are probably still in the dining hall. We walk to the elevator together and get in when the doors open. He only presses the button for my floor, so it's clear he's planning to walk me to my door.

Oh God, is he going to want to come inside? I'm not ready for anything like that.

When the elevator doors swing open on my floor, my stomach swoops down to my toes. I'm unsure of what's about to happen. I'm not experienced in this arena, and being here at school with a room of my own is different than if a guy drops me off at my parents' home after a date.

We reach my door and I turn to face him with a nervous smile. "Thanks again for tonight. I had a good time."

Giovanni smiles and steps into me. "Me too."

Then he wraps his arms around me lightly, letting his hands rest on my lower back. My breathing picks up speed.

"Is it okay if I kiss you, Sofia?" His voice is soft and gentle.

I wonder if I look like a deer in headlights because I'm ready to bolt. I force myself to relax, inhaling a deep breath. I nod.

He slowly brings his face toward mine as if he's giving me time to change my mind, but I don't. This is exactly what I need to move on from Antonio.

His lips press gently against mine before his tongue skirts across the seam of my lips. I open to him, and when our tongues meet, he groans deep in his throat. Giovanni's hands tug me in closer until I'm pressed against him with not an inch of space between us.

"What would Mr. Moretti think if he knew his virginal daughter was playing tonsil hockey with a Costa?"

The male voice from down the hall causes us both to pull back. I step to the side to look around Giovanni at Dante Accardi standing in front of a door down the hall with a shit-eating grin on his face. He's next in line to run the Southwest portion of the country and can be a real jerk when he wants to be.

Giovanni turns around to face him. "Fuck off, Accardi."

Dante laughs and knocks on the door in front of him. It whips open a few seconds later and the girl standing there is wearing just her school-issued white button-down and a pair of lacy pink underwear. I don't really know her, but I've seen her around. She's part of the Accardi Mafia.

My eyes widen. Guess those two are hooking up.

Dante looks back at us before stepping inside. "Don't do anything I wouldn't do, kids."

Then he laughs again and slams the door. The squeal of the girl rings down the hallway shortly after.

Giovanni shakes his head and looks back at me. "He's a fucking asshole."

"Most of the time."

"Thanks again for tonight. Can we hang out again? Maybe later this week?" He arches his dark eyebrow in question.

"That'd be nice."

He merely nods and kisses my cheek. "See you soon then."

I watch as he makes his way back to the elevator and steps inside. Once the doors close, I release a long breath.

There was nothing wrong with our kiss, nothing at all. But my entire body doesn't feel as if it's going to combust the way it did when Antonio's lips were on mine.

Getting over Antonio is going to be harder than I thought.

CHAPTER TWELVE
ANTONIO

I've been in a crap mood since Sofia walked away from me on Monday evening, and I don't know whether it's because I'm going to have to work with her and resist her the entire time or because Wednesday night is taking forever to arrive.

Sure, I've seen her in the dining hall, but she's been sitting farther down the table than she normally does or chooses to sit with Mira at the Costa table, where she sits next to Giovanni while she laughs at his stupid jokes. I can't just pull her aside and chat her up where anyone can witness. The last thing I need to deal with are rumors that I'm messing around with my little sister's best friend. I can't imagine how ballistic Aurora would be.

She wouldn't care in the sense that she's fallen in love with me and would be hurt by it. But it wouldn't reflect well on her and there's nothing that woman hates more than giving someone a reason to think she's anything other than perfect and has everything anyone could ever dream of, in this case—me.

"Do you know what type of wedding band you want?" Aurora asks.

She sits across from me at Café Ambrosia. I only agreed to come here after she insisted several times at dinner that we needed to go somewhere quieter in order to talk wedding details. It doesn't matter how many times I tell her that I don't care what she chooses for our wedding, she wants me to weigh in on every little detail. It's annoying as fuck.

"The kind that slides onto my finger."

She rolls her eyes. "Funny. I mean, do you want gold, platinum, silver? What kind of look do you want? Something traditional or something more modern? Diamonds?"

My head falls back and I stare at the ceiling, willing the torture to end. "Why don't you decide what you think will go best with your rings?"

"Oh! Great idea. Okay, I'll figure it out and let you know."

"Or don't. Either is fine." I straighten my head and stare at her.

She juts out her bottom lip in a pout while I check the time on my phone.

"I gotta go." I stand from my chair and slide my phone back in my pocket.

Aurora's forehead creases. "Where are you going?"

This woman thinks that I report to her, but that's not the case. So even though it shouldn't matter what I'm off to do, I don't tell her. Just to drive the point home that any information I give her about my life and my whereabouts is because I want to—not because I have to.

"A meeting. I'll see you around."

I don't wait for her to respond before I walk away from the table. The oppressive weight of being near her lifts with every step I take.

When I reach the Roma House, I head to my room to change into a pair of black jeans and a gray long-sleeved shirt. Then I climb the stairs up to the fifth floor, where Sofia's room is. I could take the elevator, but I don't want to advertise the fact that I'll be in her room alone.

It's funny . . . the night I showed up here looking for my sister, I didn't think twice about who would see me knocking on Sofia's door. But now that I've got this constant hard-on for Sofia, it's a thought in my head. Must be a guilty conscience.

I knock on the door, and when it swings open, I have to swallow hard to keep my jaw shut. Sofia wears a pair of black leggings and a cropped sweatshirt that hangs off one shoulder. Her stomach isn't showing, but the pale-yellow sweatshirt ends right at the top of her high-waisted leggings, like a tease. Her hair is pulled back in a high ponytail, showing off her neck that I would love to nibble on.

Doesn't she understand how effortlessly sexy she looks?

Unlike Aurora, Sofia's face isn't covered in makeup. There's darkness around her eyes, but that's it. She's the epitome of fresh-faced and innocent, and something about her makes me want to smudge her up, get her dirty behind closed doors so I'm the only one to see it while the rest of the world thinks she's still a virginal creature.

"Are you going to come in?"

Her voice draws me from my thoughts, and she's standing with the door held wide open, waiting for me to come in. She must've said something, and I missed it.

"Yeah." I cross the doorway and get a waft of her fresh scent that I've committed to memory like a fucking psychopath.

I glance at her bed, where textbooks and notebooks are spread out. Good, otherwise that'd be asking for trouble. So instead, I head to the couch and sit.

She stands near the door and looks between the other end of the couch and the bed and then seems to decide being as far from me as possible is the best idea. She sits on the bed, legs crossed.

"Any ideas for what we should do?" I ask.

She reaches for a pad of paper. "I was brainstorming different ideas before you arrived. Here's what I've got so far: trivia night, karaoke, a talent show, spoken word performances, musical performances . . ."

She looks at me with her plump lips pressed together as if she's concerned I'm going to make fun of her choices or something.

I nod slowly. "Those are okay ideas. Any idea what the Russians are doing this Friday?"

She shrugs. "No idea."

"We should make sure we're there to see what they're up to."

A crease forms between her eyebrows. "What's it matter what they do?"

I arch an eyebrow. "We're competing with them."

Her head rocks back. "No, we're not. They're volunteering the same as we are."

I chuckle. "You don't think they're going to want to show us up? Of course they will. Whatever we do has to be bigger, better, and more fun."

She considers my words. "What if they think of something really cool?"

"Then we'll top it. Easy."

A smile slowly forms on her lips. "Okay . . . I do hate the idea of the Russians thinking they got one over on us."

I think of the weapons shipments that have gone missing courtesy of the Russians. They need to be dropped down a peg. "Same."

"Do you think they'll be mad that we're there scoping them out?"

I shake my head and smile. "Sometimes it astonishes me that you grew up in the same life I did."

Her mouth drops open and she looks offended. "What does that mean?"

"Because you're so sweet and innocent. Who cares what they think?"

She rolls her eyes and shimmies to the edge of the bed, then gets up and walks toward me. "Do you want a drink? I have water and strawberry-flavored sports drinks."

Her small fridge is against the wall a couple of feet away from the couch and she bends to see inside, her ass on display in those leggings that leave nothing to the imagination. My hands itch. Sofia's ass is amazing. How have I missed it all these years?

"Oh, I have orange juice too." She glances over her shoulder, waiting for me to answer.

"Nothing for me." My cock stirs in my pants.

Unless she's up for grabs.

She turns back and reaches into the fridge, my eyes zeroing in on her ass in those leggings. All my willpower wanes and I lean forward, snag her around the waist, and pull her back toward me. She yelps as she lands on my lap.

"What are you doing?" she asks, still and rigid as a statue.

"Relax, Sofia." I bring my nose to her ponytail and inhale deeply, my eyes drifting closed.

"Did you just smell me?" she asks, squirming to look behind her.

"You always smell so fucking good. How did I not notice before?" I mumble, more to myself than to her.

"Before what? What are you talking about?"

"Before I became obsessed with you." I run my nose along the nape of her neck.

She startles in my lap, trying to get free, but I can't release her.

"Relax," I whisper.

"I don't think this is a good idea." She says the words, but there's no fight in her voice.

"You say the word, bella, and I'll let go."

I wait a few moments, but she doesn't say anything. The only sound in the room is our heavy breathing. When she doesn't argue, I lift her and turn her around so that she's straddling me.

God, the fucking heat of her pussy through her leggings on my lap causes my cock to harden further, and when she rests even more of her weight on me, her eyes widen.

That's right, Sofia, my dick salutes you.

Jesus, she's so fucking innocent. Has she even seen a cock in real life? Had one in her mouth? Watched one enter her? Every part of me wants the answer to be *hell no* because I'd do about anything to make my cock her first.

She stares at me with her big hazel Bambi eyes. My lips tingle with the need to kiss her, so I place them on hers. Sofia doesn't hesitate to wrap her arms around my neck, and her hands dive into my hair. She tugs on the strands with a moan deep in her throat. Our tongues slide and the sensation is like a live wire directly to my cock. It painfully pushes against the denim of my jeans.

Frustrated that I can't do what I want to do to her from this position, I end the kiss and straighten up, pulling her legs up off my lap.

"Did I do something wrong?" she asks as I stand.

I adjust my dick into a more comfortable position and grin at her, then bend forward and pick her up with one hand under her knees and the other around her back. "Not at all. I just want free rein with you and that requires a bed."

Her eyes widen in fear and her hand presses to my chest. "Antonio, I can't . . . I'm a virgin."

Her admission shouldn't turn me on as much as it does. I'm a sick son of a bitch.

"I'm not gonna try to fuck you." I walk to her bed and set her down to the side of all her papers. With one hand, I swipe the books, notebooks, and pens off the bed.

"Hey, that's my schoolwork."

Next, I lie down beside her and place my hand on the side of her head, kissing her again. My erection presses against her thigh and she gyrates under me, sending fissions of electricity through my shaft.

My right hand drifts up under her sweater. At first, I stroke her bare skin, letting her get used to my touch. I don't want to move too fast and scare her away. But when all self-control wanes, I slowly raise my hand, drifting up and over her bra-covered breast. The fabric is a thin cotton and her tight nipple teases me underneath.

I don't want to remove my lips from hers, but I want to explore her, find the little areas that make her moan and squirm from pleasure. I trail my lips over her jawline and down her neck before I nip at her collarbone.

Her hand grasps my curls harder and a rush of air leaves her lips. I lift her sweater and she doesn't fight me. In fact, she raises her hands to help me pull it off.

Unable to not look at her, I draw back to take her in. She doesn't realize how easy she is to read. Her blushed skin and heavy eyelids. Her heavy breathing and her sprawled legs as an invitation.

The bra she's wearing is a simple one, plain gray cotton. Nothing fancy, certainly nothing meant to seduce me, but her innocence is so fucking hot.

I bend down and my tongue traces the skin along the swell of her breasts while my hands glide up her back to unclasp her bra. I pull the fabric away, allowing the bra to hang off her arms and I unapologetically stare at her perfect tits. Full Cs with tight rosy buds for nipples that beg me to suckle them.

"You are so fucking perfect, Sofia." My eyes meet hers and she bites her lip as if she's worried about my reaction. "So fucking perfect."

I grab her tits and squeeze them tightly. Tighter than I should with a girl who has zero experience, but she must like it because her back arches off the mattress, offering them up to me as a deep moan leaves her. My thumbs run over the turgid peaks until my resistance breaks and I take one into my mouth. Her hand is in my hair in seconds, pressing me into her.

I lap at her nipple, suck it and tease it between my teeth, then I do it all over again on the other side. Sofia's hips gyrate beneath me, and I shift to the side so I'm not directly on top of her. I'm likely to blow my load in my pants if I let her keep rubbing against me like a cat in heat.

Instead, I continue to play with her nipples, drawing them into my mouth, flicking them with my tongue before resting my hand over her mound on top of her leggings. Her hips jolt off the bed, moving on their own accord, pressing into my hand.

"That's it, tesoro. Take what you need from me." I suck hard on her nipple.

She cries out, pressing harder against my hand. In no time at all, she's thrusting against my hand while I suckle her tits. I lick the underside and her breast jiggles when I pull my tongue off it.

"I wanna fuck these tits so badly, Sofia."

She groans and I pull her nipple into my mouth again. Never having enough.

Her hips push against me and I press down on her covered pussy. Her heavy breath washes over my forehead, her fingers holding my head to her tit. I dig the heel of my hand against her clit, giving her what she needs to finish herself off. Within thirty seconds, her back is arched up off the bed as though she's doing a yoga pose and she cries out.

I whip a hand over her mouth so that everyone in the Roma House doesn't hear her. After she bucks against my hand a few more times, she sags against the mattress.

When I lift my hand from her mouth, her eyes meet mine. I swear I see something in them. Something I don't like—guilt. Embarrassment. Shame. Not what a woman should feel after an orgasm.

"Has another man ever made you come before?" I'm dying to be her first.

She slowly shakes her head, appearing worried, as if it's not the greatest fucking gift that she's just given me.

I grin at her and bring my lips to hers in a chaste kiss. "Like I said, sei perfetta."

My rock-hard cock strains my jeans, and I roll more to my side and adjust myself with a cringe. I'm going to have to go back to my room and rub one out.

"Antonio . . . I . . .." Sofia's voice is small and unsure.

I wish I knew what to say. I didn't come here planning to screw around with my little sister's best friend—the opposite actually. But something about this woman is too hard to resist now.

I may not know what to say, but I know what I don't want to do and that's have a conversation about what this all means. Because fuck if I know. So I roll up into a sitting position then stand. "I should get back to my room. Want to meet at Café Ambrosia at eight o'clock on Friday night? Scope out what the Russians are up to?"

I glance at Sofia and regret it immediately. The hurt in her eyes causes a nauseous feeling in my stomach.

"Sure." She brings her arm up to cover her bare breasts as though I didn't already commit them to memory.

With a quick nod, I turn and walk to the door. "See you then."

I race out of that room as if Satan himself is chasing me, knowing the woman lying on the bed half-naked deserves more than what I just gave her. But I can't think about that.

I need to remember my duty to my family and stay as far away from Sofia as possible.

CHAPTER THIRTEEN
SOFIA

Ever since Wednesday night, I've dreaded seeing Antonio. That's probably why my pace as I walk toward Café Ambrosia is slower than usual.

What happened with Antonio in my dorm room was . . . well, for me, it was mind-blowing. It wasn't like we had sex or anything, but I've never fooled around with a guy like that. Never had an orgasm I didn't give myself.

But as soon as the bliss fizzled out of my bloodstream and I looked at Antonio's face, all I saw was his regret. And therefore, I felt the same.

Sure, there was the guilt about Aurora, but I placated my conscience by reminding myself how horrible a person she is and that they're in an arranged marriage. It's not a love match and anyone who spends any time with them can see that.

But then there's Giovanni. We aren't serious, haven't even discussed being exclusive, so technically I can still see whomever I want. But I'm keeping it a secret that I'm into someone else, and that just makes me even more confused.

Antonio must be doing his best to avoid me too, because I haven't seen him in the dining hall. Tonight will be the first time I've seen him since we messed around and I'm not sure how he's going to act.

Will he pretend nothing happened like he did after the kiss? Will he want to discuss it?

Probably the worst part about the whole thing is that even after I saw the regret on Antonio's face and the guilt and shame swamped me, I knew deep down I was thankful for having that experience with him. An experience I've dreamed of for years that, years from now, I'll relive in my mind.

With a deep breath, I walk into the café. It only takes a few seconds to spot Antonio sitting at one of the tables by himself. There aren't a lot of people here—maybe twenty at most when the café probably holds one hundred.

He doesn't notice me until I'm only a few steps away from the table, then his gaze flicks up to me and does a slow perusal of my body. The knowing glint in his eyes makes me shiver because it's clear that he's picturing what's underneath the baggy sweater I'm wearing.

My tummy swoops as if I'm on a roller coaster that just went down the first hill. I say hello and slide into the seat across from him.

"Hey." He lifts his chin at me. "You see this shit?"

He gestures at the table between us and I realize that there's a board game. I'd been so intent on looking at him I hadn't noticed. All the other tables also have a board game on them.

"They're doing a game night?"

He shrugs. "Apparently. Hope you like Snakes and Ladders."

"I haven't played since I was a kid." A small smile lifts my lips.

Before Antonio responds, Katerina taps the microphone on the small stage at the far side of the room. A guy I don't know stands beside her while she explains that tonight we'll play games in hour-long rounds. Once the first hour is up, it's time to move to a new table with a different game.

"Lame," Antonio says.

Katerina's gaze flicks to us and her eyes narrow. She tells us to begin, and I pick up the die and roll my first turn. Without saying a word, Antonio takes the die and rolls for his turn. The same thing happens three more times as we're both completely silent.

I'm so uncomfortable, and I can't go through months like this. As much as I don't want to talk about what happened, I think doing so might actually be *less* uncomfortable than us pretending.

I glance around to make sure no one is within earshot. "About what happened Wednesday . . ."

He looks up from the board at me.

I swallow hard. "You seemed angry afterward."

He pushes his hand through his hair with a sigh and it makes his curls a little wilder. He doesn't want to have this conversation. "I wasn't angry. I was frustrated."

I blink and my head rocks back for a beat. Then I lean in and whisper, "Like sexually?"

His head tips and he laughs. "That too. But no, I was frustrated with myself because I didn't go to your dorm room with the intention that anything would happen. The opposite actually."

I nod because I understand. As attracted to him as I am, I had no plans for anything like that to happen either.

"Why did it happen then?" I still as I wait for his answer. I don't really know why I'm prying. It doesn't matter what he says. It's not like we're ever going to be together. He's been told who he has to marry and it isn't me. But still, after all these years, why now can't he seem to keep his hands to himself around me?

"Sofia."

The way he says my name sends flutters through my belly. And the way his light-blue eyes are so intense on me, it feels as if they're spearing me in place.

"It happened because every time I see you, I want you. I want my hands on you and my cock inside you."

Air rushes from my lungs. I'm filled with both elation and crushing disappointment. He's saying everything I've ever wanted to hear come out of his mouth, but it's too late. He's engaged to someone else and will do what his duty demands of him, so we can never be together. I'm not mistress material. I don't want to be the sidepiece he hides in corners. I want to be someone's wife, someone they're proud to have on their arm.

I swear a brief glimmer of disappointment shines in his eyes before he continues. "All that said, what happened Wednesday can't happen again. I will marry Aurora and you deserve more than to be some sidepiece. Let's keep what happened between us a secret and make sure it never happens again. That's what's best for us."

I nod. He's right of course. If we continue down this path and anyone ever finds out that I'm essentially Antonio's goomah, I'd disappoint my parents and never find a respectable marriage within the family. I'd be tainted goods as far as everyone else is concerned.

I always thought Mira was too much "fuck the patriarchy," but I understand why now.

All I've ever wanted was to be in a happy marriage and stay home and take care of my husband and kids. I'm only attending the Sicuro Academy because Mira begged me because her father wouldn't let her attend unless I also did.

"It was a moment of weakness. It won't happen again." My voice is resolved.

Antonio nods.

"Should we continue? I'm about to beat you." I motion toward the game board.

He chuckles and rolls the die to take his turn.

We continue to play for another half an hour. I win the first game.

Antonio looks as though he might win the second, but before he rolls the die for what might be his last turn, he glances over my shoulder and says, "Did you invite him?"

I turn and look over my shoulder at Giovanni making his way to us. "No."

It's an effort to push down my disappointment because Giovanni's appearance means the end of Antonio's and my alone time. Then I remind myself that's a good thing and to put every effort into trying to establish something good with Giovanni.

"Hey, guys. How's it going?" Giovanni asks when he reaches our table.

Antonio mumbles a hello, but I smile and say a proper greeting.

"Thought I'd pop in and see when you thought you'd be finishing up. I can walk you back to your room."

I don't look at Antonio when I answer him. "That'd be great."

"How much longer do you think you'll be?"

I look at Antonio. "Mind if I leave? Doesn't seem like they have any plans to do anything else tonight and I'm kind of tired anyway."

He shrugs. "Whatever. Go."

When I look back at Giovanni, there's a strange expression on his face and panic races through my bloodstream that perhaps it's written all over our faces that something's happened between us.

I push out of my chair quickly. "Great, let's get going then."

Before I lead Giovanni away from the table, Antonio speaks up. "We need to meet up again to go over what we're going to do next Friday. How about Sunday evening? I'll head to your room."

"Sure, sounds good." I hook my arm through Giovanni's and turn him away from the table. "See you then."

Giovanni walks me back to my room and we make plans to meet up at the gym the following morning. I'm not a huge gym person, but it's something to do with him that he enjoys, so I agree. Then he leaves me with a parting kiss that once again doesn't make me feel an ounce of what I feel when Antonio's lips are on mine.

I enter my room, accosted by visuals of two nights ago. How depressing is my life? I have a perfectly good man who wants to date me, but I'm hung up on a man who's engaged to someone else.

CHAPTER FOURTEEN
ANTONIO

Some of the guys and I played poker in my room last night, and since one of them had somehow sneaked a bottle of whiskey onto campus, there's a dull throbbing in my head when I wake up late Sunday morning.

I've never been a huge drinker, but since this obsession with Sofia started, it seems I'll take any option I can get to force her from my thoughts, including intoxication.

I check the time then roll over with a groan. Just like last Sunday, I need to get going so I can make my call to my father. So I shower and change then make my way down to the basement. Security shows me to room number three this time, and I dial my father's number.

"Antonio," he answers.

"What's wrong?" I can tell immediately from his tone that something's amiss.

He sighs. "Another shipment of weapons that the Costas sent us is missing."

I slam my fist on the metal table. "Fuck, are you serious?"

"You know I wouldn't joke about things like this."

"What happened?" My fingers grip the receiver tighter.

"This shipment was coming by rail. No one's sure what happened between New York and Miami. There were two stops along the way to switch off some loads and add others. Those are the only places something could have happened."

My free hand fists in my lap. "I don't think it was a mistake if our load was accidentally removed."

"Exactly. We're looking into the Russians on our end, but so far, nothing. You?"

I shake my head even though he can't see me. "Nah, we all give each other a pretty wide berth, but I haven't heard anything."

"I figured. I'll keep digging both in-house and out of house. I'm going to bring Salucci in on this, see if he thinks we have a rat in our midst."

I nod. As underboss, Aurora's dad is his most trusted adviser and friend. "Yeah, that's a good idea."

"There's more." His voice is even more grave than it was when he first picked up.

"What is it? Is Ma okay?"

"Your mother is fine. Knee-deep in wedding details. Between you and then your sister next summer, I think you've made her the happiest she's been in years."

I'm glad, even if it is because I'm marrying Aurora. "What's going on then?"

"Leo is missing."

I'm stunned into silence. *Tommaso's father is missing?*

"What do you mean he's missing?"

"No one has seen or heard from him in a few days, including Corinna."

"Shit," I mutter and squeeze the bridge of my nose.

I was with Tommaso last night playing poker, so is he going to find out today when he makes his phone call?

"What about Tommaso?"

"I told Corinna she could talk to him about it when they spoke today."

I blow out a breath. "Any idea what might have happened?"

In this life, you never know. Is he a rat who thinks he's close to being caught and he's lying low? Is he on a bender with strippers and drugs and booze somewhere? Did one of our enemies nab him and is trying to pump him for information? There are so many unknowns until we get more details.

Either way, it's not good when someone is out of communication for days at a time.

"I don't know. He was supposed to meet with some of his soldiers a few days back and didn't show. Before that, the last time anyone saw him was Corinna when he left the house that morning."

I stand and pace near the table, unable to sit still. "I hope he turns up." I don't have to add the alive part to the end of my sentence.

"I'll talk to you next week. In the meantime, keep your eyes and ears on high alert."

"Will do. Ciao."

We hang up and it takes me a minute or two to get my feet moving toward the door. I have no idea how Tommaso's going to handle the news about his father, but I need to find him. After I burst out of the room, I head directly to the security desk.

"Has Tommaso Carlotto been here yet today?" I hover over the desk, trying to peek at her paperwork, waiting for her answer.

She must recognize my intense energy and realize I'm not leaving here without an answer. With a sigh, she types something into her computer then looks at me. "He just went into his call."

I don't say a word, turning and stabbing the elevator button to head off to find Marcelo. I want to give him the heads-up about another missing shipment if he doesn't already know from his call with his grandfather today.

When I reach Marcelo's floor, I say a small prayer that he and my sister aren't in the middle of fucking because that's one visual I don't need in my mind for the rest of my life.

I bang on the closed door and no one answers. Right before I'm about to bang again, a pissed Marcelo whips open the door, clad only in a white towel. A quick glance behind him tells me my sister isn't here, but then I hear the shower running and put two and two together that they were probably about to get in the shower together.

I stifle a full-body shiver.

"What?" Marcelo doesn't bother with chitchat.

A quick glance around tells me I'm alone in the hallway, but I keep my voice down even so. "My father told me another shipment went missing. Know anything about that?"

He sighs and shakes his head, tightening the towel in his hand. "Nah, my call's not for a bit."

"Let me know if you do hear anything."

"Yeah, of course. You sure that's all?"

I'm not about to fill him in about Leo Carlotto missing. I trust Marcelo about as much as I trust anyone who's not family. If Mira catches wind of what's going on at some point, depending on how things pan out, she can tell him if she wants.

"That's all. I'll see you around." I turn and head to the stairwell to make my way to Tommaso's room. If he went there right after his call, he's probably back by now.

When I reach the door, I knock and almost immediately, the door opens. It's clear to me that his mom filled him in. His face is drawn, and his jaw clamped tight.

"I heard." I step inside and hug my best friend. Whether his dad ends up being a traitor or not, he's got to be hurting.

He accepts the hug, smacks my back, and pulls away. I make my way to his couch and sit.

"I can't believe it. When Ma told me, I didn't believe her at first. I thought she was just fucking with me or something."

I lean forward and rest my elbows on my knees. "I'm sorry, man. Maybe you should go home."

He shakes his head immediately. "I asked my ma about that and she told me to stay here. Said it's the safest place for me."

His mom has a point. If someone is after the people in the Carlotto family for whatever reason, he's better off here on this high-security campus.

"Do you have any idea where he might be? What might have happened?"

We both know what I'm not asking out loud—do you think he's still alive?

Tommaso sighs and runs his palm up and down his cheek. "None. He hasn't mentioned any funny business or anyone giving him any trouble. I doubt he's on a bender though. That's not like him."

"Yeah, your dad barely drinks."

"I don't know what to think. I just hope he pops up soon."

"Me too."

We sit in silence and I can tell that my friend is lost in his head. I've debated the past couple weeks about filling him in about the missing shipments, and I think now is the time. His defenses are down and I'll be better able to gauge his reaction.

"There's something else you need to know about."

I tell Tommaso about the missing shipments and how some of those guns showed back up on the New York loading docks. He listens intently and I don't see any signs that would make me believe he already knows all this because he's involved somehow. But that doesn't mean his dad isn't.

"Knowing all that you do . . . you think there's any chance that your dad is on the lam and hiding out because he's involved?"

Tommaso stares at me intently, hands fisted on the arms of the chair he's sitting in, probably pissed that I even asked. At the same time, he knows I have to ask, so he just answers me. "Not a chance. My dad is loyal to the La Rosa crime family, you know that."

I nod. I agree. My gut agrees too. But you can never really know.

Even Tommaso himself isn't in the clear, not fully, at least not with me.

But there's nothing I can do today to figure out any more of this. Today I just need to be there for my friend, at least until I head to Sofia's tonight to work on our event for next week.

I blow out a breath. It's gonna be a long day and I'm probably going to be beating off before I fall asleep tonight.

CHAPTER FIFTEEN
SOFIA

I look in the mirror for probably the tenth time.

This is something I should do when Giovanni is coming over, not Antonio. But after our conversation on Friday night, I want to be sure I don't look as though I'm trying too hard. So I purposefully have no makeup on and have my hair up in a messy bun. I'm wearing a pair of black leggings and an oversized sweatshirt that ends at midthigh, covering my ass that he appears to love so much.

The knock on the door startles me because I'm so on edge, knowing I have to share this small space with him for at least a couple of hours while we work out what we're going to plan for Friday night.

My hand lands on my stomach, and I walk toward the door, not too fast, so it doesn't seem like I'm eager to see him, and I swing open the door.

Antonio's elbows lean on the doorframe, both hands over his head and gripping the top. His head hangs down, but once the door is open, he slowly lifts it to meet my gaze.

Something is wrong.

"Are you all right?" I step back from the door and motion for him to come in.

With a heavy sigh, he lets his hands drop and walks in past me, immediately lying on the couch. He pushes his hand into his hair and stares at the ceiling.

Being that it's Sunday, I figure he must've received some bad news from his dad today. But I also realize it's not my place to know what that bad news is. Still, I can't help wanting to fix whatever it is that's bothering him.

"Do you want to talk about it?" I ask.

"No. Let's just get this done. I want to go to bed and erase this day."

I chew on my bottom lip. "Okay." Then I walk to the bed where my notebook is and sit on the mattress, resting the notebook on my knee.

He turns his head to look at me from the couch. "I think we should do a casino night."

If I'm honest, the fact that Antonio has given any thought to this at all surprises me. I thought I'd be doing most of it on my own.

"What did you have in mind? I don't think the school will let us bet real money."

He sighs. "Yeah, probably not. Maybe they'd let each table play for something else."

I tap the pen on the notebook while I think about it. "Oh! What if we asked if they could be playing for some type of special privilege? Like a pass to skip a class or an extra phone call that Sunday, or setting the menu in the dining hall one night for dinner, stuff like that."

Antonio sits up, facing me. "That's a good idea. Everyone would be hyped."

We spend the next half an hour going over all our ideas and making a list of everything we'll need to have brought in, what the prizes should be, and draft a text to the chancellor for approval. Gone is the awkwardness from the last time we were alone together and I ended up half-naked, and in its place is friendly banter and the ease of being in close proximity to someone I've known most of my life.

Somehow we end up sitting across from each other on my floor in the middle of the room, papers sprawled around us.

"I think this is going to be really good." I look up from what I'm writing and smile at Antonio.

"Definitely better than game night." His deep laugh rumbles and I stare at him.

I can probably count on one hand the number of times I've seen this man laugh with abandon the way he is now. Saying it looks good on him is an understatement.

"What?" His laughter stops when he notices me staring at him.

"Nothing." I shake my head.

"Something. What is it?" He tilts his head.

I guess there's no harm in telling the truth. "I just hardly ever see you smile and laugh the way you just did. You should do more of it."

The slight tilt that was left on his lips drops. "Not much to smile about these days. Seems like you're the only one who brings it out of me."

Our gazes lock for what feels like an eternity.

Finally, I can't take it anymore and I look at my hands. "Whatever it is that's bothering you, I'm sure you'll figure it out."

A sort of sarcastic chuckle leaves his lips. "Partly . . . maybe. Let's hope so." He sighs and I look back up at him. "What do you want for your life, Sofia?"

I blink a few times in rapid succession, surprised by the turn this conversation is taking. "I . . . what do you mean?"

"Where do you hope to see yourself in a decade?"

I pull my legs in from where they're stretched out in front of me and cross them, sitting up straight. "I guess I hope to be happily married with a couple of kids."

"Are you like my sister and want to be involved in the family business?" He arches an eyebrow.

I shake my head. "No, not at all. I respect Mira's ambition and I think she's right in that we should get to choose what we want, but I'm content with being an old-school Mafia wife." I shrug. I feel silly saying it and my cheeks heat.

"Yeah, I thought that might be the case." His voice sounds . . . I don't know . . . wistful maybe? "Do you think you'll be in an arranged marriage, or are you hoping for a love match?"

I don't know why Antonio is asking me these questions, but this one, in particular, is an easy answer. "I want a love match. I'm not like you and Mira. My dad's just a capo. It doesn't matter as much who I marry."

He nods. "That's good. You deserve that. I hope you get it."

Our gazes lock and hold. My body is pulled in his direction by some unseen force that I can't resist.

Antonio slowly leans toward me. "Why are you even here at Sicuro Academy?"

"What do you mean?" My voice is whisper soft.

He's on his hands and knees now, inching toward me. "If all you want is to be a Mafia wife, why be here?"

"You know I came for your sister. So she could attend." I don't remove my gaze from his.

"But she and Marcelo have settled things now. You could leave, go home and look for your future husband."

He's right of course. "Because I'd be lonely," I whisper.

"Are you lonely here?" His face is only six inches from mine now and my breath lodges in my throat.

I nod slowly and something passes through his pale-blue eyes. "More now than I used to be."

He closes the gap between our lips to only an inch. I should back away, tell him this can't happen again. But the truth is, I don't want to. I shamelessly want to take whatever Antonio will give me.

"Me too."

His lips press against mine for a split second and I open for him. When our tongues meet, his low moan vibrates all the way down to the apex of my thighs. One of his hands trails around to the back of my head and he gently leans me back until I'm sprawled on the floor beneath him. He lies on top of me, his weight pressing me onto the floor, and every point of contact between our bodies feels delicious.

My legs spread of their own accord, and Antonio's hips fall between them and his arousal pushes against my mound. He grinds his hips into me, and I grip his hair, pulling harder from the perfect friction he's delivering.

His hand trails under the hem of my sweatshirt and he palms my bra-covered breast, teasing the nipple through the thin fabric. I arch into his hand and his tongue delves deeper into my mouth. I wrap my legs around his waist and his erection presses against my aching clit. When he shifts his hips against me, a small cry leaves my lips.

He pulls back and nips on my bottom lip. "Christ, Sofia, I could get lost in you for days."

I'm about to tell him I feel the same when there's a sharp rap on the door. We both still, looking at one another, then scramble. He pushes up off me, eyes wide, and I stand, smooth out my hair, and make sure my sweatshirt is in place before I walk to the door and open it.

Giovanni is smiling and holding a drink tray with three beverages from Café Ambrosia. "Thought maybe you guys could use a pick-me-up." He walks in and kisses my cheek.

Guilt coats me like a can of paint dumped over my head.

"Oh, wow. Thank you." I step back to let him in and turn to look at Antonio.

He's no longer sitting in the middle of the rug. He's standing and making his way to us, avoiding any eye contact with me. "Thanks, man. I was just leaving though. I'll take mine to go."

"Cool." He pulls one of the drinks out of the tray and holds it out.

Antonio accepts it and says thanks. "See you guys later."

He walks out and I hear the elevator ding a second later. I should be glad he's gone and that Giovanni interrupted, right? His appearance effectively put the brakes on whatever else could have happened and that's a good thing. At least it should be, even if it doesn't feel like it.

"I guess that means you're free?"

Giovanni's voice pulls me from staring at the empty space where Antonio just left.

"I guess so."

"Want to take a walk? I got your favorite." He holds my cup up at my eye level and wiggles it as if to entice me.

"Sure, let me grab a coat."

He chuckles from behind me while I make my way to my closet. "You Miami people crack me up."

I roll my eyes. "It's chilly out. Especially this late at night." I slip my hands through my jacket.

"It's hot to us New Yorkers."

I stick my tongue out playfully while he chuckles again and passes me my drink. "Thanks."

We leave my room and ride the elevator down before heading to one of the lighted walking paths that wind around the campus.

"Seems like you guys were able to get a lot accomplished pretty quickly," Giovanni says.

I sip my drink to buy myself some time to let my guilt dissipate. It doesn't work. "Yeah, we have a great night planned. We're going to do a casino night, and the winner of each table will win different privileges on campus—if the administration agrees."

"That's way better than game night," he says.

"Right?" I turn and smile at him. "That's what we said. Hopefully the chancellor won't push back at all."

"If he does, you should ask Marcelo to talk to him. He seems to have some sway with him after everything that went down last year." He brings his drink to his lips.

"As he should."

"Of course, you'd have to be able to reach Marcelo. He and Mira are like hibernating bunnies who spend most of their time fucking."

I laugh, but it's followed by a pang of sadness at the fact that I don't get to see my best friend as much as I used to.

We walk in silence for a beat, and he takes my hand. It's a small gesture in comparison to what I was just doing with Antonio, and panic wells up in my chest.

"Giovanni, I . . ."

I what? What am I going to say? *I want to like you. More than anything, I want to like you and think about you more than I do Antonio, but I just can't seem to make it happen.* Not likely.

I stand in place, keeping us from walking, and he turns to face me, concern in his eyes.

"I just want to make sure we're both clear on what this is," I say. "I'm not sure I'm looking for anything serious."

He sighs. "Was it too much, me interrupting with drinks tonight?"

I shake my head. "Of course not. It was really sweet and thoughtful. I just want you to know where my head's at, that's all. I don't want to feel like I'm leading you on. I'm sure you're really experienced with physical stuff . . ." I fidget, uncomfortable. "But I've never really done anything, and I don't know what I'm ready for. I don't know. I just want to be up front." I cannot believe I just admitted that to him.

He squeezes my hand. "I won't deny that I want more with you." His gaze lingers on my body and I'm guessing he means physically too. Of course he does. He's experienced. "But I've been on my best behavior because Mira threatened to rip off my nuts if I pressured you into anything. And when Mira is mad, so is Marcelo." He rolls his eyes. "But if I made you feel like I was expecting anything—"

"It's not that. It's really not. I just don't want you to think I'm ready to jump into anything serious, that's all."

This is all my guilt talking, but I don't want to hurt Giovanni. I need to make sure he doesn't think this is more than it is. I hope to want something serious with him at some point, I'm going to give it all the energy I've got, but I don't know if I'll ever get there with him when Antonio is lingering around.

"Message received. I'd still like to spend time with you. See if I can't change your mind." He smiles and squeezes my hand again.

I return his smile. "I'd like that."

He nods then turns to face the path and we continue on our walk. The entire time, I wonder, *Why can't I fall for this man instead of the one I can't have?*

CHAPTER SIXTEEN

ANTONIO

Sofia and I have only communicated via text this week about to-night's event. It seemed best to avoid temptation. Being around her makes me want things I can't have. Why torture myself?

But I'll have to see her in a few minutes during the event, which is precisely why I invited my fiancée to come along. Even if she's not exactly at the top of my list of people I want to spend time around, I guess I might as well get used to it.

And in true Aurora fashion, she's making it known to everyone that she's with me on our way to Café Ambrosia. I don't know why she bothers to give others the impression that we're into each other. It's not the end of the world if outsiders know we're not in love, as long as they know we're committed to each other and would never go against the other. Aurora is protected by her relationship with me regardless if it's love attaching us.

I chuckle internally when I walk in and spot Sofia and Giovanni together. She must've had the same idea I did. Or maybe she really is into the guy. A lot of girls on campus love him. But the thought of Sofia being one of them makes me grind my teeth.

"Hey, sorry we're a little late," I say when we approach them. "Aurora had to finish getting ready."

"You can't rush perfection." She bats her eyes at me and I do my best to pretend it affects me when really she looks ridiculous.

I turn my attention back to Sofia, who looks as if maybe she's trying to stop herself from rolling her eyes at my fiancée, and I keep my expression blank, forcing myself not to look below her chin. While we were walking toward them, I saw that Sofia's wearing a black A-line dress that's fitted around her chest and flutters out from there, showing just a small amount of cleavage. I can't allow myself the pleasure of looking again. Otherwise, I'll steal glances all night.

"What do you need me to do?" I ask.

"Giovanni and I already got all the tables set up." She looks at him and smiles and I fist my free hand. "Here're the little signs I made that say what the prizes are for each table." She holds them out, and I use the opportunity to remove Aurora's arm from around mine to take them. "If you guys could set one on each table, that'd be great. I need to set up the playlist for tonight. I picked songs that remind me of Vegas and the Rat Pack."

"Awesome. We'll take care of it." I look at Aurora. "C'mon."

She sticks out her bottom lip in a pouty way as if she's not thrilled about having to help, even this little bit.

Café Ambrosia fills with students, and when Marcelo and Mira enter, I lead Aurora over to say hello.

"Hey, guys. You ready to lose big tonight, Marcelo?" We do that guy-shake, hello-hug thing and he grins.

"Too bad we're not playing with real money. Then I could really clean you out," he says.

Mira and Aurora stand there sizing each other up, but I guess that's better than their usual bickering.

"Hey, sis."

"Hey." She gives me a hug. When she pulls away, she nods at Aurora. "Aurora."

Seems my sister is on her best behavior tonight. Marcelo must have bribed her with sex or something.

"Where's Sofia?" Mira asks.

I nod toward the stage. "Getting the music set up."

"Let's go say hi." She pulls Marcelo away.

I chuckle. "That could have gone worse, I suppose. At least she moved on before she said something nasty."

Aurora's chin rises. "I'm glad she's finally affording me the respect I'm due."

I could argue that statement all night, but there's no point. We're stuck with each other, and I'll make the best of it. My duty is to marry this woman for the good of the family and I will. Why make it worse than it must be?

"What game are you going to play? Blackjack, craps, or roulette?" I gesture to the different tables set up around the room.

Her eyes cast across the room, considering them all. "I think I'm going to try roulette." She gestures to the table that has one of the guys from Dublin House and a girl from the Vitali family. "What about you?"

We tend to keep separate from each other during social events like this, but on campus, we're forced to interact.

"I'm going to be at one of the blackjack tables. Not sure how much time I'll have to gamble, but I'll play if I can."

She nods. "No Tommaso tonight?"

Everyone knows something's up with Tommaso this week, but not what exactly. There's been no communication from the outside this week and I assume that if Leo turned up—either dead or alive—someone would have reached out through the administration to let him or me know.

Tommaso's been lying low all week, curbing his player tendencies, and I don't expect he'll be making an appearance here tonight.

"Not sure if he's planning to come." I play off her comment. "I'll see you later then."

"Okay." She rises on her tiptoes and kisses my cheek.

I head to the stage where Sofia is. "You need me to do anything?"

She's by herself and stiffens at my appearance until she decides to act as if nothing is amiss between us, lifting her chin and plastering on a smile that doesn't reach her hazel eyes. "I was just going to grab a microphone and tell everyone how it works tonight. Unless you want to do it?"

I shake my head. "No, you should take the credit. You've done most of the work. But I'll stand up there with you for support . . . if you want?"

"Yeah, sure." She steps across the stage in front of the microphone and taps her finger on it.

Some of the people in the café look in her direction, but most of them continue with their conversations.

"Hello, everyone . . ." she says softly into the mic and everyone ignores her.

I lean over her to speak into the microphone. "Hey, everyone, listen up." My voice is loud and commanding.

Everyone immediately stops what they're doing and turns to look at the stage.

"Thanks," Sofia says, cheeks red.

I nod and step back from the microphone.

"I just wanted to take a moment to thank everyone for coming tonight on behalf of Antonio and myself. You'll see what prize you're playing for at each table, and each table will run three one-hour games, so you'll have three chances to win tonight. And yes, you can win multiple times. Feel free to switch tables or games after the first hour if you like. Any problems at all, please let me or Antonio know. And before I leave you to it, I want to thank everyone who volunteered to be a dealer for tonight's event. Good luck, everyone!"

Sofia starts the music and Frank Sinatra's "Luck Be a Lady" plays. Of course she began with good ol' Italian Blue Eyes.

"Great choice," I tell her.

She smiles. "Thanks. I'm going to go wander around and make sure it's going flawlessly."

She walks around me and off the stage, and I curb my irritation at her clearly wanting to get away from me.

Really, I should be thanking her for doing us both a favor.

* * *

THE FIRST TWO rounds go smoothly. I check in with Sofia after the first hour to see if she wants me to do anything, and she tells me to go play at one of the tables, so that's what I do.

I opted out of craps—I fucking hate craps, so I don't know why I even sat down at that table—about twenty minutes into it. Now, with only ten minutes left in the final round, I'm sitting on the stage, staring at the way Giovanni pulls Sofia onto his lap. My jaw aches from clenching it so hard watching her there.

He says something to her and her head tips back in laughter. He uses the opportunity to move his arm around her waist, his hand resting across her stomach.

Is that what she wants? A fucking clown for a boyfriend?

I push my hand through my hair and tug, then her eyes find mine. Has she sensed me staring at her from the moment her perfect ass hit Giovanni's thigh?

She says something to him and gets up off his lap, making her way to me. I loathe myself for the relief I feel as soon as she's away from him.

"Only two minutes left," she says. "You want to announce it over the microphone this time?"

"Nah, you go ahead. You've done a great job being the spokesperson so far." I don't add that I like the fact it will keep her away from Giovanni.

"You sure?"

I gesture to the microphone. "Your time to shine, dolcezza."

The term of endearment slips from my lips easily and without any thought.

Her eyes widen, but she doesn't comment before going to the microphone and announcing that the night is ending. There are some groans throughout the room, presumably from people who aren't going to win. Sofia thanks everyone for coming.

When she makes her way back to me, I ask her what she needs me to do for cleanup.

She waves me off. "Giovanni offered to help me with it."

What a fucking prince.

"You sure? It's my responsibility too."

She glances at the crowd, at Aurora specifically. "I don't think your fiancée will be keen on sticking around to help out." There's a bite to her tone and I have a feeling she used the word fiancée as a reminder to me.

Fair enough.

"All right then. I'll see you later."

Without waiting for a reply, I stalk off in Aurora's direction to escort her back to the Roma House, my footsteps heavy with resentment because I'm walking toward the wrong woman and away from the right one.

CHAPTER SEVENTEEN
SOFIA

I'm lying in bed in the dark, waiting for sleep to come, but my mind is tripping over my thoughts. I hadn't really seen Antonio between the last time he left my room and tonight, and like a silly girl, I was hoping my desire for him would have faded. But when he walked in with Aurora on his arm, my stomach rumbled and not in a good way.

I have to stop this. Antonio is not mine. He will never be mine.

I roll onto my side and close my eyes, just wanting this day to be over. I'm still lying there a few minutes later when there's a soft knock on my door.

What the heck?

Maybe Mirabella and Marcelo had a fight?

I crawl out of bed, unlock the door, and open it a crack, blinking in rapid-fire succession when I see him standing there.

Antonio places his hand on the door and gently pushes it, forcing me back into my room.

"What are you doing here?" I keep my voice down, not wanting anyone on my floor to know he's here.

He steps all the way in and closes the door. He's still wearing what he was earlier this evening. A black suit that does justice to the handsome man he is.

He doesn't say anything, just steps toward me as I step back. He closes the distance between us, and when I have nowhere else to go, his hands dive into my hair and his mouth slams to mine. I melt into the kiss for about five seconds before common sense rings a bell and I turn my head away, using my hands to push against his hard chest.

Antonio scowls.

"You need to go." I point toward the door behind him.

"Don't pretend you don't want me too." He breaks that distance once more and I sidestep him.

"This can't continue to happen. You're engaged and I'm seeing someone." I cross my arms.

"You're not exclusive."

"You are." I arch an eyebrow.

I don't want to admit to him that I told Giovanni I'm not looking for anything serious. He'll use it against me to prove his point and I'm doing the right thing by pushing him away even if my body is begging me to allow him to stay.

He scoffs. "You know we're not a love match. She knows it too." He shrugs. "She knows how things work in our world."

I'm sure everything he says is true. In our culture, Antonio can screw around with whomever he wants and Aurora can't say anything about it. That doesn't mean I want to be his side chick.

"It doesn't matter. This can't happen again. There are too many people who will get hurt—Mira, Giovanni, Aurora." Me, I think, but don't say.

"Sofia—"

"Just go, Antonio. I don't want to do this with you."

His lips press into a thin line before he turns and stomps toward the door. I'm sure he wants to slam it, but he doesn't because that could alert someone to his presence in my room in the middle of the night.

I lock the door and slip back under the covers, proud of myself.

Turning him away felt near impossible, but I did it. And if I can do it tonight, I can surely keep him at bay until my feelings dissipate.

I fall asleep, ready for a fresh start tomorrow. One where I fall out of lust with Antonio and into like with Giovanni.

* * *

THE WEEK PASSES in a blur, and by the time Friday night rolls around, I've only had to see Antonio a handful of times at the dining hall during meals and that's just in passing because I've chosen to sit with Mirabella at the Costa table all week.

We have to speak eventually, given that we have next Friday's event to figure out, but the distance from him has been good for me. Time isn't a miracle worker though. My breath still hitches and my belly flutters every time I see him, but I feel closer to accepting the inevitability that there's going to be nothing between us.

Today is my birthday, and normally I really enjoy celebrating, but I'm not much in the mood this year, so when Mira asked me earlier in the week what I wanted to do, I told her I'd be content hanging out with her on our own.

"So how's it going with you and Giovanni? You've been oddly tight-lipped," Mira says, her eyes lit with anticipation.

She'd love it, and I would too, if I found something more than friendship with Giovanni. Sadly, I'm not even close.

We're walking back from the dining hall after dinner. It's just the two of us, Marcelo and Giovanni and the rest of the guys took off earlier to do . . . whatever it is they do. I'm not sad about it. I covet any time I get with my best friend these days.

"He's really nice."

Mira loops her arm through mine. "So is Mr. Smith, but I don't want to date him."

I laugh. "I don't know. This is all new territory for me. I want to take it slow."

She pulls me to a stop. "He's not pressuring you into anything physical, is he? Because I warned him—" Her face is already morphing into her "I'm going to kick his ass" expression.

I raise my hand. "Not at all, and yes, he told me all about your warning to cut off his balls."

She shrugs and grins, unrepentant. "But do you like him?"

I nod and we walk again. "I do."

It's the truth. I'm just not telling her I don't like him as much as I like her brother.

"Oh my god, can you imagine if you fell in love with him and got married? We'd live close to each other, married to cousins, and raise our children together."

She's repeated that exact phrase to me more than once since this thing with Giovanni started. And I'd love for it to happen, but sadly, it's not the future I envision. A part of me—a big part—wishes for that to come true. But motivation alone won't get me there.

"That would be pretty awesome."

We approach the Roma House doors and Mira motions for me to go ahead of her. As soon as I step through the doors, shouts ring out.

"Surprise!"

My hands fly up to cover my mouth and my eyes widen.

Mira comes up beside me. "You should know that this is all Giovanni's doing."

My gaze slides across the crowd and snags on where Antonio stands beside Aurora before continuing to Giovanni. He's smiling wide, arms outstretched as he walks toward me.

"Are you surprised?" he asks, then places a chaste kiss on my lips.

"Very." I chuckle.

"I know you said you didn't want to do much, but I couldn't let your birthday pass without doing something."

I smile up at him, placing my hand on his cheek. *God, Sofia, love this man.* "Thank you."

He turns his head and kisses my palm. "You're welcome." Then he takes my hand. "Come on, let's make the rounds."

He leads me through the room and I thank everyone for coming, steeling myself with every person that draws me closer to Antonio.

He's standing with Aurora and Tommaso. It's apparent that whatever is going on with Tommaso is still haunting him. His normally affable nature is missing.

"Thanks for coming, guys," I say once we reach them.

Antonio's gaze flicks down to where Giovanni's and my hands are linked.

"Of course, we wouldn't miss it. Though Antonio wanted to, I told him it's important that, as the representative of the family on campus, he needs to be here." Aurora smiles as though she didn't just lob a thinly veiled insult my way.

"Well, I appreciate you coming."

We make awkward chitchat for another minute before Giovanni says, "I think it's time for you to open your present."

"You didn't have to get me anything. This surprise party is more than enough."

He scoffs. "I'd be doing a shit job at trying to woo you if I didn't get you a present."

I laugh.

Antonio groans and plays it off like he's tired by fake yawning and blaming a night of shit sleep.

"Excuse us," Giovanni says before leading me to the center of the room and shouting to get everyone's attention.

Someone turns down the music and all eyes swing in our direction. Suddenly, my body goes on alert. What does Giovanni have planned?

"I just want to take a moment to wish Sofia a very happy birthday." His hand is on my back and he's rubbing it up and down as though we've been a couple for months. Everyone claps and there're a few hoots and hollers. "It's time for the birthday girl to open her present from me."

He picks up a small package wrapped in silver paper off one of the tables by the couches and hands it to me. I hadn't even noticed it there beforehand. Fear settles in me, worried about what's hidden under this wrapping. I know for sure it's going to be something over the top before I even make a rip in the paper.

I'm proven right when I find a Patek Phillipe watch. This is something you buy for a girlfriend, at the very least, not a girl who told you last week that she wants to take things slow.

My mouth hangs open as I stare at the extravagance.

"At a loss for words?" Giovanni takes the watch case from my shaking hands and pulls out the watch before sliding it on my wrist. "A perfect fit."

He grins, and I smile at him, grateful but overwhelmed at the same time. The truth is that I don't wear a watch because I find them uncomfortable. But Giovanni doesn't know that.

"It's beautiful. Thank you so much." Then I rise to my tiptoes and kiss his cheek.

My gaze catches Antonio's over his shoulder and we lock eyes. His gaze is intense, laser-focused, jaw tight, eyebrows drawn down. It's the look of a powerful man who is not happy, and I flinch that it's directed at me. He'll make the perfect don one day.

I pull back and direct my attention to Giovanni. "This is too much."

He places his hand on my cheek. "Hardly."

Mira comes up beside me and wraps her arms around my waist, squeezing. "Do you love it?"

"It's really beautiful," I say honestly.

"Yay!" She squeezes me again before letting go.

When I watch the way she looks between Giovanni and me with such a hopeful expression, my chest tightens as if there's a band around it that someone's pulling taut. Regardless, I force a smile and enjoy the rest of the party. Giovanni stays close by the entire time, and I try to ignore the feel of Antonio's gaze following me throughout the room.

CHAPTER EIGHTEEN
ANTONIO

"You sure you don't want to hit the forest party?" I ask Tommaso.

It's Saturday night and we've been mindlessly playing video games in his room—no online play of course, because then we might be able to communicate with the outside world.

"You keep asking because you want to go?" He doesn't look away from the screen. "Aurora on your ass about not attending?"

"Surprisingly, no." Which is out of character for her. I'm not even sure if she's planning to go. I didn't ask because I don't care what she does with her time. But I am surprised I didn't get a whiny "What will people think if I'm there and you're not?" from her.

"Why do you seem so hell-bent on going then?" he asks.

I can't tell him the truth—that ever since Sofia's surprise party last night, all I can think about is Giovanni's hands and lips all over what's mine. It's driving me fucking crazy and I know they're probably at the forest party. Guess I feel like torturing myself.

"I'm not. Just thought you might want to get blackout drunk rather than hole up in your room like you have since you heard about your dad."

He drops the controller and looks at me, so I hit pause on the game. It takes a lot for Tommaso to get pissed, and I can tell he wants to tell me to go to hell. But he knows better, so he clamps his jaw shut until he gathers himself. It was a shit thing I said. His dad could be at the bottom of the fucking ocean and all I'm concerned about is Sofia.

"I'd love to get blackout drunk, but what if I get an emergency call about my dad? I need to be ready for whatever comes."

I nod. He means he needs to be ready to dole out retribution should the worst happen. "We'll get an update tomorrow on our calls."

He nods and picks the controller back up, unpausing the game.

We play for another couple of hours, and he beats me at almost every game because my mind keeps wandering to Sofia and what she and Giovanni may or may not be doing. Losing pisses me off, even if I wasn't already agitated by the direction of my thoughts.

"Fuck." I toss the controller on the couch when I lose yet another game. "You want something to drink?" I get up from the couch and walk to the small bar fridge set under the window.

"I'll take an orange power drink."

As I bend down to open the fridge door, something catches my eye outside. Marcelo and Mira are walking up the path from the forest. A short way behind them are Sofia and Giovanni, hand in hand. The watch he got her for her birthday catches the light on the pathway and glistens on her wrist.

My fist clenches at my side. It's not like I didn't suspect they were together tonight, but fuck is it infuriating seeing it. It's probably a good thing I wasn't at the forest party. Who knows whether I would have been able to keep myself in check? Lately, it seems like any control I used to have is melting away like the polar ice caps.

I bend and pull Tommaso's drink from the fridge then walk back to the couch. "Here you go." I toss him the bottle. "I think I'm going to get going. I can't take losing any more tonight."

Tommaso laughs. "Thanks for hanging with me. I know there are a lot better things or girls you could be doing."

I laugh off his comment. "What do you mean? I'm an engaged man."

"Yeah . . . okay."

Does he know something about Sofia and me? How could he?

Then his face draws tight. "We'll talk tomorrow after our calls."

I nod. The weight of the unknown hangs between us.

Once I see myself out, I make my way to my room, passing Angelica on the way.

"Hey, Antonio, is Aurora back in her room now?"

I stop walking, forehead creased. "How would I know?"

Her head rears back. "She said you guys were doing something tonight."

I make a mental note to figure out what Aurora's playing at. "We were supposed to, but something came up. I'm not sure what she ended up doing."

She frowns for a beat before recovering. "Okay, well, I'll catch up with her tomorrow, I guess. Thanks!" With a wave, she flits on down the hall toward the elevator.

When I get to my room, I fuck around for a while, listening to music and reading. I shower then finally force myself to sleep. It refuses to come.

Every time I close my eyes, all I see is Sofia shirtless and lying beneath me, her ample tits in my hands, my mouth around her nipples. My raging hard-on is a constant reminder of how much I want her, how much I'm apparently willing to risk to have her.

Finally, I can't take it anymore. I fly out of bed, pull on a pair of pants from the floor, then head out of my room to the stairwell, shirtless with no socks or shoes. I'm like a man possessed as I walk up two floors, taking the stairs two at a time. I'm panting when I arrive at her door and don't stop to question what the hell I'm doing when I knock.

But once I hear the sound of my knuckles rapping on the door in the quiet night, I realize how fucking stupid this is. What if Giovanni's inside with her? What the hell will I say then? I have no excuse.

My pulse throbs in my neck at the thought of what they'd be doing in there in the middle of the night.

Another side of me argues I don't fucking care if he's in there. I'll figure something out. Make up something on the spot and I'll be happy to have interrupted. I knock again, more determined than ever to . . . to what?

I have no idea. All I know is that I need to see her.

The door opens and Sofia's wearing the same silk cami-and-shorts set she wore the night my obsession began. What little self-control I still had flees as I step inside, swinging the door closed with my foot, and pull her into me and claim her mouth.

She's surprised at first, as she always is, but she doesn't push me away like she did the other night. Instead, her hands dive into my hair and her tongue meets mine, vying for control. But we both know I won't give it to her. I ease us into a steady pace that's less demanding. I don't want to scare her off, but God, I want to mark this woman. Just me. No one else. The idea that someone else will coax out her innocent sexuality makes me insane.

I walk us to her bed, and when the backs of her legs hit the mattress, she stumbles and falls back onto it in a sitting position. Her big doe eyes stare up at me, full of lust and . . . trust. That is such a fucking turn-on coming from someone like Sofia, who has no sexual experience. That she would trust me with her body is a privilege and I'm not going to allow her to regret her decision.

"Take your shirt off." My voice comes out raspy.

She hesitates for the briefest moment, then pulls the silky fabric up over her head.

My hands reach out the moment her perfect tits are in view, and I hold the weight of them, squeezing and running my thumbs over her nipples. She shudders with pleasure and sighs. I want my lips on her skin but force myself to straighten up.

"Now the shorts."

Sofia immediately brings her hands to the elastic of her silk shorts and shimmies them down her legs before kicking them to the side.

God, she is fucking perfect. Sexy as hell and yet still so innocent.

"Now lie back."

She does as I ask, her hair spilled across the comforter beneath her. Only then do I fall to my knees in front of her. She sharply inhales when I spread her legs, swinging them over my shoulders, and yank her ass closer to the edge of the bed.

No other man has ever had the view I have now—her perfect pink pussy glistening and begging for my tongue. The thought that in a few seconds, I'll be the only one who knows how this woman tastes makes my cock harden until it's painfully pushing against the cotton of the pajama pants I'm wearing.

I place gentle kisses up her left leg, starting at her ankle and working my way up from there. When I reach her inner thigh, Sofia's breaths become more pronounced and she grips the blanket beneath her.

Eventually, I move my face directly between her legs and inhale deeply while I meet her gaze. Her scent is equal parts sweet and musky, and I can't wait to delve my tongue between her folds. Sofia turns her head.

Oh, no, she's not going to be embarrassed.

"Don't look away from me, dolcezza. Our desire is nothing to be embarrassed about."

"I . . . I've never done this," she says in a whisper-soft voice.

"I know. But trust me, you're going to love it." I spread her open and swipe my tongue all the way from her puckered asshole up to her clit and her back arches off the bed.

Her hand dives into the curls on the top of my head and pulls until there's a bite of pain when I concentrate my efforts on her swollen clit. Sofia's hips buck and I use one hand on her stomach to hold her in place while I feast on her pussy.

The sounds she's making will become my new soundtrack when I beat off.

I bring my face down and fuck her with my tongue, and she raises her head to watch. My eyes take in her heavy eyelids and the way her teeth nail down her bottom lip. My ego grows to infinite proportions because I'm the one who put that look on her face. Me.

"Do you think Giovanni could make you feel this good?" I murmur against her wet flesh before swiping my tongue from bottom to top.

Her gaze moves from watching what I'm doing to meet mine.

"Answer me, tesoro."

She shakes her head, still holding my gaze.

"I want the words." I nip her inner thigh.

She moans. "No," she strangles out.

"Only me."

"Always you," she admits.

I don't know what she means by that, but her words light a fire in my blood.

I double my efforts, letting my finger trace the rim of her entrance while I alternately suck on her clit and flick it with my tongue. A minute later, her thighs squeeze the life out of me, clamping around my head as she comes on my face, crying out.

I lap up every bit of her pleasure as she heaves for breath. I should probably give her time to recover, make sense of what just happened. Instead, I crawl up over her body and kiss the living shit out of her, forcing her to taste herself on my tongue.

Rather than pull away, she groans and wraps her arms and legs around me before pulling away and staring me straight in the eye. "More, Antonio."

My cock twitches and I chuckle into her neck. "Let's walk before we run, piccolo innocente."

"I don't want to be innocent anymore. I want you to be my first."

My head snaps up to meet her gaze. "You can't be serious."

Does she realize what she's saying? Of course she does. She grew up in the same life I did. Sleeping with me would soil her for marriage. She'd no longer be pure for her husband. That is a line I cannot cross.

"You deserve more than to be a goomah, Sofia." I pull away from her and roll to my side.

The hopeful look on her face falls to disappointment. "I'm not asking to be a goomah. I'm just asking you to be my first." She covers her tits by throwing an arm over them.

"Why would you want that? What will your husband think one day?"

Her eyes narrow. "Mira's right about the men in the family." She sits up, and though I want to force her to lie back down beside me, I don't.

"I don't think that, but most of the people in our world do. You know this."

She walks over into her closet, returning a moment later wearing a robe that matches the silk pajamas she wore earlier. She has it tied around her waist with a bow and her nipples poke through the thin silk fabric. "Maybe I don't care what everyone thinks."

I arch an eyebrow. We both know that, unlike my sister, she cares a lot about what other people think.

"Maybe I don't care as much anymore." She shrugs.

"And why is that?" I stand from the bed.

She opens her mouth as though she wants to say something then snaps it shut. "Never mind. It doesn't matter." She walks around me to pick up her pajamas off the floor, and once she has them in her hand, her back still to me, she says casually, "Maybe I'll see if someone else can help me lose this pesky virginity. Perhaps Giovanni will help me out."

Sofia just waved a red cape and I'm the fucking bull.

CHAPTER NINETEEN
SOFIA

I don't see him coming. One moment my comment, meant to piss him off, is flying out of my mouth, and the next, I'm pinned face-down on the mattress with Antonio's chest and hips pressed to my backside.

"Don't you even think of letting that stronzo into your body," he hisses into my ear.

"You're acting like a jealous boyfriend," I spit out, growing wetter, loving the way his arousal is pressed between the cheeks of my ass.

"You think he deserves you because he throws you a party and buys you an expensive watch? A man who doesn't even know that you don't like to wear watches?"

I still underneath him. "How do you know that?"

"I've known you forever, Sofia. I remember the time your dad bought you a watch for your fifteenth birthday and you never wore it because you said it bugged you when you wore things on your wrist."

My heart swells over the fact that he remembers such a mundane detail from so many years ago.

"Tell me what you were going to say a moment ago."

I struggle underneath him, but his weight easily holds me in place.

"Tell me, Sofia. Tell me what it is you don't want me to know."

"It's nothing."

"Liar. Why would you tease me and tell me that you want me to steal your virginity?"

I press my lips together in an effort not to let the truth spill from them. Maybe it wasn't a good idea to push him. I was just so embarrassed and angry after his denial and talk about virtue.

"All right then. Maybe I should go about this a different way."

His weight lifts off me and I suck in a full breath now that he's not pushing me into the mattress. At the same time, I miss the heat of his body close to mine. He rolls me over so my back is on the mattress and he's hovering over me. I've never seen Antonio's pale-blue eyes so intense before, so determined, and I swallow hard.

"Let's try this again." His voice is softer now, smooth as his hand moves to the belt on my robe, but he doesn't release it. I inhale. "Now tell me the truth, Sofia . . ." His finger brushes over the silk until he finds my nipple and he circles it lightly, drawing it into a tight point. "Why did you ask me to take your virginity?"

I suck in a breath when he pinches my nipple between his finger and thumb, not breaking eye contact with me. I shake my head that I'm not going to answer and he grins as if I've given him what he wants. He pulls the edge of the belt and the robe loosens, opening for him, revealing my naked body. He drags his hand from my sternum, between my breasts, and down to my mound. But he doesn't touch me where I'm craving him most and my hips lift in invitation.

He clucks his tongue. "Now, now, cara. You don't get what you need until I get what I want. Tell me the truth, why did you ask me to take your virginity?"

He continues to roam my body with his hand but not offering any relief. I mewl like a kitten and arch my back again, desperate for him to *really* touch me. This is pure torture.

The truth is that I surprised even myself. I hadn't planned to offer my virginity to him. I hadn't planned on doing anything with Antonio ever again, but one touch of his fingers and all the strength I'd built up crashed down into a pile of rubble. Because somehow, it just feels right. I've been half in love with this man for years, and even though I shouldn't, I want him to be my first. It will only be a memory I hold sacred my entire life, regardless of the fact that we can't be together.

"C'mon, you know you want to tell me." Antonio's lips fasten around my nipple and I moan when he sucks hard, adding a sharp sting of pain to the overwhelming pleasure.

The moment his finger brushes my engorged clit, not enough to give me any real relief but enough to stoke my desire even higher, it's useless trying to hold out any longer. This man owns my body's pleasure and I'll take the risk of telling him the truth if I really want him to give me what I so desperately need.

"I want it to be you because . . ."

When I pause, he laps at my nipple and applies even more pressure to my clit while staring up at me through his dark eyelashes.

"Because I've liked you for years." The words leave my lips in a whoosh and I hold my breath, waiting for the consequence.

Antonio's head snaps up and meets my gaze.

Surprise.

"You have?"

I nod, pressing my lips together. "No one else knows. Not even Mira."

His gaze roams my face, then he takes my chin in his hands and presses his lips to mine. He kisses me like a man unmoored, but he doesn't bother whispering declarations of how he feels the same. I wouldn't want him to lie to me anyway. I know it wasn't the same for him. He hasn't pined over me for years the way I have him. It's enough that he's here now and wants me.

I wrap my arms around him, and he deepens the kiss, coming

to lie on top of me. My legs have a mind of their own, spreading so that he can fall between my hips. The hard line of his cock presses against the juncture of my thighs and I can't help but arch my hips up into him. He groans into my mouth and thrusts against me before pulling away.

"Are you sure?"

His kind eyes tell me it's my call. If I change my mind and ask him to leave, he will.

I nod. "I'm sure, Antonio." My hand drifts up to press against his cheek and a pained expression slashes across his face.

"It won't change anything. It's still my duty to marry Aurora."

A piece of me loves that he's worried about my feelings and is being up front and honest with me, but another part of me wants to smack him for daring to say her name in this moment. That woman is like poison even when she's not around, but I refuse to let her infect this moment.

At some point, my emotions about not being able to be with Antonio will come crashing down and I'll be trapped under their rubble, but in the long run, I'll be grateful to have shared this experience with him. Pain of loss is the cost of love and I'm willing to pay the price to have a brief moment of happiness.

"I know."

He nods then pushes up off the mattress and stands. For a second, I panic, but then I realize that he's doing so to get undressed. He's already shirtless and the muscles in his abdomen and arms bunch and move while he tucks his hands under the waistband of his lounge pants.

I'm not prepared for the sight of him entirely naked. It feels surreal almost. It's not like I've never seen a naked man before—I did have free rein of the internet before I arrived on campus—but I've never seen *this* man naked.

This man, who is perfection, reminds me of all the statues

carved out of marble that I saw when I visited Italy last summer with my parents, except for what hangs between his legs. He's got the statues beat tenfold in that department.

His erection stands thick and proud, arching toward his belly button. For the first time tonight, I'm nervous about the idea of it being inside me.

"Are you scared?" he asks, his tone soft and caring.

"A little."

"I promise I'll be gentle, Sofia."

His hand moves between his legs and he moves it up and down his erection and my fear gives way to arousal. I wouldn't have thought it would be such a turn-on to see a man touch himself the way he's doing.

"Lose the robe."

It's an order and I obey immediately, sitting up and slipping it the rest of the way down my arms and tossing it to the side.

"Touch yourself." When I hesitate, his voice becomes firmer. "Do it. You have no idea how many times I've imagined just this."

His words give me confidence and I place my hand between my legs, as I've done so many times before.

Antonio studies me for a long moment, licking his lips, his hand pumping up and down his shaft. He takes one step toward the bed then stills, cringes, and pushes a hand through his hair. "I don't have a condom with me. I have some in my room . . ."

The last thing I want is for him to leave. What if he changes his mind once he leaves my dorm room and doesn't return?

"I'm on the pill for my periods and I haven't been with anyone else . . ."

"I had a physical with our doctor when I was home at Christmas, so I know I don't have any STIs. I've never had sex with anyone without a condom before, but it's up to you. I can run to my room and come right back."

I'm shaking my head before he's even finished speaking. "I trust you."

All the tension leaves his body, and his shoulders relax. The look he's giving me as he steps toward the bed, I'm not sure what to think. It feels like more than just lust.

Rather than coming directly on top of me as I assumed he would, he lies on his side beside me, his erection prodding my hip.

"What are you doing?" I ask.

He leans in and drags his tongue up the column of my neck. "I want to make sure you're prepared. I want to hurt you the least I can."

My eyes flutter closed as he nips my ear. His hand drags over my breasts, tugging on my nipples before finding its way down between my legs. They widen of their own accord as he drags my wetness up to my clit with his fingertips and gently applies pressure.

Within ten seconds, I'm moaning, needing more, but I'm not sure what. My hand grips the blanket underneath me. He moves his hand farther down until his fingers are at my entrance. Slowly he pushes one finger inside as he takes my nipple in his mouth. At first, it feels as though my body doesn't want to allow him entry.

"Relax, dolcezza," he whispers against my breast and I do on an exhale.

His thumb finds my clit, his tongue swirls around my nipple, and my body falls into the mattress. He pulls his finger out and slowly slides it back in. Tingles spread out from between my legs, traveling throughout the rest of my body.

My eyes drift closed as he works me until I'm close again, that tug of an orgasm dragging me closer to the edge. He carefully adds another finger, stretching me, and there's a bite of pain until it morphs into pleasure when he concentrates his efforts on my clit again.

He swallows my cries with a kiss as I come, then he drags his body on top of mine. My breasts press against his muscled chest, my sensitive nipples hardening further at the heat of his body on mine.

"Are you sure?" he asks in a soft voice.

I bring my hand up to his face and push it into some of the curls at the top of his head, falling over his forehead. "I told you, yes."

He nods, then looks down the length of our bodies and uses his hand to line himself up with my entrance. Antonio notches the head at my entrance. Immediately his gaze connects with mine as though he's checking in to make sure I'm okay.

When he pushes forward, it burns and I suck in a breath.

"Do you need a minute?"

I shake my head. I know it's going to hurt, and I want to get through it and on to the good part. Mira assures me there's a good part. An amazing part.

He keeps pushing and I squeeze my eyes shut, the pain becoming worse. When he comes up against a barrier, he sucks in a breath before he surges forward, eyes on me as if judging whether he should stop.

I yelp, I can't help it, and tears leak out. Antonio's breathing grows heavy and his mouth skims my cheek. He catches my tears with his tongue on one cheek and then the other before kissing my forehead.

I open my eyes and he's gazing at me with more patience and caring than I would have thought possible. He holds still and brings his face down to kiss me.

My arms and legs wrap around him, and I let myself get lost in his kiss. At some point, the pain between my legs becomes a low thrum of pleasure and I move my hips a bit as a test. The movement increases my pleasure and I move some more.

Antonio pulls away from my lips. "You're okay?"

I nod.

He pulls his hips back slowly, drawing his length from me before pushing back inside. It's slightly uncomfortable, but the next time he does it, the pleasure returns, then increases, then increases some more with every thrust.

My nails dig into his back muscles as they move under my fingers as he enters and leaves my body. Antonio lines my jaw with kisses before nipping on my earlobe.

"Fuck, Sofia. You feel so good," he murmurs against my heated skin.

His words ratchet my need and desperation higher. He pulls up so that he can see down the line of our bodies and watch as he enters me. I follow his line of sight and my breathing picks up.

Antonio's hand moves to where our bodies are joined and expertly manipulates my clit. The sensation of bliss radiates out from my core until I'm strung so tight I might snap. And then I do.

My climax rolls over me like a wave, dragging me under. Antonio's lips are on mine, swallowing my cries. My body contracts around him and he stills inside me, groaning into my neck, coming inside me.

Neither of us moves. We lie there together, unmoving, unspeaking. And when he pulls himself from my body and looks down at me, I worry that maybe this was a mistake.

Because the way Antonio is gazing at me makes me think that maybe he thinks it was, and though I will force myself to live without him, I'm not sure I can live knowing he considers me a regret.

CHAPTER TWENTY

ANTONIO

I look down at Sofia lying underneath me with all her innocence, all her trust, and know right away that things will never be the same. I'll never be able to look at her the same way. Never be able to pretend that our tryst or whatever the hell this is didn't happen. I am a changed man.

This is not something I bargained for.

And it's not because I took her virginity. She's not the first virgin I've slept with. It's because it's *her*. Plain and simple.

Fuck.

"Antonio?" Her voice sounds so small and vulnerable.

The last thing I want is for her to regret giving me this gift, this gift she can't take back.

"Are you okay?" I ask.

She senses the shift in my demeanor, and she lets out a long breath and nods.

"Let me get something to clean you up." I kiss her forehead before pushing up off the bed and walking to her bathroom.

Once I'm inside, I flick on the light and grab a washcloth, wet it with warm water, and wring it out. When I return to the room, she's in the same position I left her in. I kneel on the bed and my dick twitches when I see my seed leaking out of her. I stifle a groan.

My movement garners her attention and when her eyes flare

from just a touch, I look down and see that her blood marks the base of my cock. Fuck. I don't think I've ever seen anything more erotic in my life. She's the first woman whose blood has stained my cock and I don't ever want there to be another.

Fucking her without a condom was like heaven and I don't know if it's just because it was her or whether it's always like that when you're bare inside a woman. Trying to focus on her pleasure and not my own was difficult because I wanted so badly to lose myself in her body. But I needed to make sure that her first time was something she'd look back on with pleasure, not regret.

I press the cloth gently between her legs and she flinches—not much, but enough that I notice. I'm as gentle as I'm able while I clean her up, then I throw the washcloth in the nearby laundry hamper.

Though I should probably go and wash myself off in her bathroom, I don't. I want the evidence of what we did on my body for longer than a few minutes.

Sofia's watching me intently as I walk back toward the bed, and she looks surprised when I motion for her to crawl under the covers. When she does, I join her and pull her into my chest. I've never been a cuddler after sex, but I don't want to leave. There's a conversation to be had. I just don't know exactly how to start it.

We lie there in silence for a while, her cheek on my chest and her small fingers grazing over my abdomen. My dick is hard again under the comforter, but I ignore it. I have no idea if she would even want to have sex with me again or whether this was a one-and-done situation for us. The idea of that is tormenting.

Finally, I break the silence. "I don't know what happens from here."

Her hand stills for a breath before she starts again, drawing random patterns on my skin with her fingertips. "I know your future is set, Antonio. You don't have to make false promises to me."

I sigh. I wish her words weren't true, but they are, and there's nothing to be done about it.

"I like spending time with you." The words are hard to push off my tongue. They make me feel vulnerable—not something I'm accustomed to. I'm only able to voice them because of her admission to me earlier—that she's had feelings for me for years.

How did I not see it? Was I blind to her? If I had noticed, would I have pursued her, and if I had, would I be stuck in an arranged engagement with a woman I can barely stand?

"I like being with you too." Her voice draws me from my thoughts.

"Where does that leave us?"

She moves so that she's propped up on one elbow, looking down at me. "I guess that depends. Do you want more of . . . this?" She gestures between us with her free hand.

"Fuck yeah." The words are out of my mouth before I even consider them, but they're the truth. There's no sense holding them back.

She looks hesitant, but then she speaks. "So do I."

I bring my hand around the back of her neck and pull her down to my lips. After I've tongue-fucked her, I pull her back because there's only one problem with this.

"I don't want you to feel like a goomah. You're too good for that."

Her gaze sweeps over my face. "I want to share this with you, Antonio. I want to experience more of . . . this with you. But I can only do it for the rest of this school year. After you're married . . ." She cringes. "I can't be with you like this once you're married."

"You know I don't have any feelings for Aurora."

She nods. "I know, I do. That's the only reason I'll be with you now. But once you're married, it's different. I don't know why. It just is. I know it's not uncommon for the men in our world to mess around, but for me . . . you'll have made a commitment in front of God and everyone . . . you'll be sleeping with her to produce an heir . . ."

Sofia cringes at the idea. If I'm honest, my stomach turns at the thought too. I've tried not to focus on the fact that I'll have to take Aurora to my bed on our wedding night.

I want to ask Sofia what she plans to do about Giovanni, but it's not my place. Not when I'm engaged to another woman—arranged or not. Still, his blood will be on my hands if I find out she's fooling around with him at the same time as she is with me. The idea of watching him put his hands or lips anywhere on her body makes me want to rage.

"I get it." I bring her hand to my mouth and kiss her knuckles. "We have to be careful though. No one can know."

I'm saying it more for her sake than mine. I'm the heir to the La Rosa crime family. No one will bat an eye if they find out I'm sleeping with someone other than my fiancée. That's just the way it is in our world. Sure, I'd get a lecture from my dad about being more discreet, but no real judgment would be bestowed upon me.

Sofia, on the other hand, would be viewed as a tarnished woman and I don't want that for her. Only the two of us can possibly understand the pull we have to each other. I couldn't stomach being the reason she was looked at as less than.

"I won't tell anyone. Not even Mira."

I raise an eyebrow.

"I'm serious," she says.

I fucking hate that we have to be a secret, but that's the only way to protect Sofia's reputation and ensure her future within the family.

I wrap my hand around the back of her neck and tug her to me for a kiss, then sigh. "I should go."

It's the middle of the night and I don't want anyone to know I was in here. If I stick around, I might fall asleep and then I'd have to sneak out when everyone is up.

"I know." Her voice is almost a whisper.

She rolls away from me, almost as if she's afraid if she stays close to me, then she won't be able to let me leave. Or maybe that's just my own wishful thinking.

Jesus. One time inside this woman and I'm a total fucking sap. What the hell?

We both get dressed and she walks with me to the door.

"When do you want to get together to work on next Friday?"

I chuckle. Back to being Miss Responsibility. I just took her virginity, and these are her parting words. "How about tomorrow night?"

She cringes. "I'm supposed to do something with Giovanni."

I step forward and cage her against the wall. "After tonight, you're still going to see him?" She opens her mouth to speak, but I cut her off. "Don't bother answering. You probably think I'm an ass-hole for even asking, given my situation. Here's a little something to leave you with before you run off to your stronzo."

I remove any space between us, our bodies pressed together from chest to thigh, and I devour her mouth like a starved man. By the time I pull away, her chest heaves and her eyelids are heavy.

Let her think about that when she's sitting across from that ass-hole tomorrow night.

Then I turn, crack open the door to check that no one is in the hallway, and slip outside, forcing myself not to turn back and look at her.

If I did, I'd never leave.

In the stairway, I stop before walking to my floor because my body is begging me to go back to her.

I am so thoroughly fucked.

CHAPTER TWENTY-ONE
ANTONIO

I end up sleeping until a half hour before my phone call with my father, so I shower quickly and head downstairs. I'm anxious when I pick up the phone and dial my father's number. I just want to know if he knows anything more about Tommaso's dad since we last spoke.

He answers before the first ring has even finished. "Antonio." His voice is grave and a prickle runs up my spine.

"What is it?"

I hear his long sigh. The same one he always does before delivering the worst kind of news. "They found Leo's body."

The receiver slips from my hand, but I catch it before it falls. I slump back against the chair. It's not that I didn't know it was a possibility that Tommaso's dad would show up dead. I just thought it was more likely he'd turn up alive or badly beaten.

I school my reaction. "When?"

"He washed up on the beach last night. Our guy on the inside says it looks like he was badly beaten before he was shot in the head. Based on how decomposed the body was, they figure he was in there for a week."

"Fuck."

"There's something else."

I squeeze the phone in my hand. "What?"

"His eyes were cut out."

"Fucking Russians. Always so dramatic." I push my hand through my hair.

The Russians always leave that as their calling card when they waste someone. Just in case you'd hoped to have an open casket.

"I want you to go see Tommaso after this and tell him. I told Corinna we'd take care of relaying the news."

I dread being the one to have to tell him, but I know it's not the last time I'll have to deliver news like this. It's just the first and he's my fucking best friend.

"Okay. Any idea what happened?"

"No more than last week. I had our other capos bring their guys in, and no one thought he was into anything shady. But the Russians don't make it a practice to try to beat information out of someone for nothing. The question is, what were they trying to find out?"

If it was even the Russians. I think it but don't say it. It's just a gut feeling at this point, but it's something we need to consider.

"Could be anything," I say.

"Either way, we won't let them get away with it. First the guns, now this? It's a declaration of war."

Fire erupts in my belly. The kind you have when there's retribution to be doled out. The only problem is that I'm handcuffed here. And I'm sure Tommaso won't sit around here and wait to avenge his father's death. I have to find a way to keep him calm.

"We can't trust anyone." I throw the words out there to see how my dad will react. Will he catch my meaning? Is he considering what I am?

"Agreed." He doesn't say the words—probably out of respect for the fact that one of his longest-serving capos was just found mutilated and murdered—but I can tell from his tone that he's not above thinking it could be an inside job.

"When's the service?"

"Sometime this week. We'll send a vehicle to get you kids on Tuesday."

"All right."

"Tell Tommaso to call his mother after you speak with him."

"Will do."

"See you Tuesday, son."

We don't say anything else. I know we're both grieving the loss of a good man—at least as far as we know—but we've never been ones to discuss our feelings. I'm not going to pour my heart out to my dad. Never.

So I hang up and slide the chair back, pushing both hands through my hair, knowing it'll make the curls on top look as if I just rolled out of bed. I blow out a long breath and set aside my feelings. I have to deliver a blow to my best friend that's going to bring him to his knees. I can't imagine how I'd feel if it were my own father.

Actually, I can—like burning down the entire world.

I stand and make my way to the elevator. Thankfully, no one is inside, and I press the button for the third floor. I make my way to Tommaso's room, just down the hall from my own.

After three raps on the door, it swings open. Tommaso stills when he sees me. Obviously I'm not as good at putting my emotions aside as I'd hoped because something in my body language has tipped him off that this isn't a friendly visit.

Without a word, I step past him. He closes the door and his eyes follow me.

"We need to talk," I say.

"Did you just talk to your dad?" he asks.

"Why don't you sit down?" I gesture toward his couch.

"Just tell me, Antonio."

"Sit." My voice brooks no argument.

He does what I say, seeing clearly that he's not going to get what *he* wants until I get what *I* want. I don't bother to sit next to him because between the elevator and walking to his room, I've figured out what his reaction will be. I know what mine would.

"I have some news about your father."

"Just fucking tell me." He leans forward, eyes wide and anxious.

"They found his body on the beach last night. He was beaten badly and shot in the head." I give it to him straight, the way I would want it.

The air whooshes out of him and he slumps back against the couch, looking at me but not really seeing me. "They're sure it's him?"

I nod and his chin drops to his chest.

"There's more." His head snaps up and our gazes connect. "His eyes were gone."

As I expect, his reaction is immediate.

"Fucking Russians!" He bolts up off the couch and rushes toward the door. "They're going to pay!"

I intercept him, pushing against him so he can't reach the door.

"Let me go! They think they can take out my father and not pay? I'll show them what happens when they fuck with us!"

He keeps pushing to get past me and it takes all my strength to hold him back. I push him hard in the chest and he stumbles back a few feet. "There will be plenty of time for revenge."

"You think I'm gonna wait? Fuck that. I'm going to Moskva House. An eye for an eye. I don't care who the fuck it is, as long as Russian blood runs through their veins."

He makes a go of reaching the door again, but I don't let him. We wrestle for another minute until we're both breathing hard.

"Right now, your mother needs you. You need to call her."

That gets him to back off. He slides his back against the wall and hangs his head between his legs. "She's gonna be devastated."

Tommaso is right. Corinna loved Leo. Theirs was a love match and there was never any question that she was devoted to him.

"You need to put your thirst for revenge aside and focus on supporting your mother. We will figure out who did this and they will pay. You have my word."

His gaze meets mine and he studies me for a beat, then gives me a curt nod.

"I mean it. Whoever did this won't be breathing for long."

"I want to be the one to make them suffer. No one else."

If the same thing were to happen to me, I wouldn't feel any different, so I nod. "I'll speak with my father."

Jaw set, he nods again and pushes past me toward the door.

"Keep it together for another day and a half."

He stops, hand on the door.

"We're headed home on Tuesday for the rest of the week. We'll figure out more then."

Without acknowledging my words, he leaves the room.

What a fucking roller coaster the past twenty-four hours have been. I've gone from the highest high and then full force into this low.

My mind wanders to Sofia for the briefest moment now that I'm alone, but I give my head a shake. Duty is my number one priority. I need to make sure Tommaso keeps his shit together for the next couple of days until we go home and formulate a plan to exact revenge.

Something tells me that's going to be a full-time job.

CHAPTER TWENTY-TWO

SOFIA

"I still can't believe it." I shake my head and stare at the trees budding with new leaves.

Giovanni and I are sitting on a bench on one of the pathways as dusk approaches, and he snags my hand. It feels all wrong to me, but I'm too deep in my thoughts to pull away.

"Did you know him well?"

I look at him. "Of course. He was a capo, along with my father. I've known Tommaso since I was a child."

I still can't believe Leo Carlotto is dead.

Mira burst into my room without knocking early this afternoon and told me the news. I was in the middle of getting dressed and I about had a heart attack, but given what she had to tell me, I wasn't upset that she didn't knock.

Although she rarely comes by anymore, when she does, she acts as though it's still her room, which I secretly kind of love.

But I wasn't prepared for what she had to say. I don't think anyone in the La Rosa crime family was. Apparently Leo had been missing for some time, which explains Tommaso's strange behavior the past few weeks.

I feel terrible for him. His father is dead. I can't imagine how that feels, though being a child of a capo, I'm not naive enough to think I couldn't find myself in the same position one day. I've been to enough funerals with crying children and anguished young wives.

And Antonio . . . I can only imagine what he's going through too.

"I'm sorry. That's rough." He squeezes my hand, which is the jolt I need to remember what I'd planned to talk to him about tonight.

After last night with Antonio, I have to end this. I can't continue to date Giovanni while I'm sleeping with Antonio. It has nothing to do with Antonio's reaction when he was leaving my room and found out I had plans with Giovanni tonight, though I'd be lying if I said his obvious jealousy didn't send a thrill through me.

I pull my hand away from Giovanni's. "I wanted to talk to you tonight."

His forehead creases in concern. "Okay . . ."

"First, I wanted to thank you again for the surprise party. No one has ever done that for me before. And for the gift. It's too much, but I appreciate how thoughtful you are."

"I sense there's a but coming."

I frown. This is so awkward. Especially because I can't tell him the truth of why I can't be with him. "I can't see you anymore."

I let the words hang there between us and wait for him to respond.

"I know you don't want anything serious, Sofia, and that's okay."

I give him a small smile. "It's not just that. I think we're better as friends. I really like you, but I don't know that there's a romantic connection between us."

He cringes. "Ouch. You're friend-zoning me."

"I'm sorry. I feel terrible, especially after everything you did for my birthday. I just don't want to lead you on." My hands fidget in my lap. I've never had to do this before, and I can see why people hate it so much.

"Listen, I really like you, Sofia, but if you're not feeling it, I don't want you to pretend otherwise. Even if I did throw you an amazing party and give you a lavish gift." When my face falls, he squeezes my shoulder. "I'm only kidding."

"Giovanni, I'm so sorry."

"Listen, I'm disappointed, yeah. But I appreciate the honesty. It stings, but I'd rather know now than months from now."

"I'm sorry." It's like those words can't stop coming out of my mouth.

"Stop apologizing. I'll be fine."

And I know he will. Giovanni has no problem getting women.

"Do you want the watch back? I brought it with me in case you did." I reach into my spring coat and pull it out.

"I noticed you weren't wearing it."

Now it's my turn to cringe. "If I'm honest, I don't enjoy wearing stuff on my wrists. It always bugs me."

He laughs. "Blew that one, did I?"

"It's a really lovely watch."

He smiles. "You keep it. It was meant for you, so you should have it. Do what you want with it. Fence it if you want."

My mouth drops open. "I would never."

He chuckles. "I know you wouldn't. That's why I'm saying you should keep it. A lot of girls would."

"Okay. Well, thank you again."

He nods then stands. "C'mon. I'll walk you back to your room."

I stand, and we start along the path, headed in the direction of the Roma House.

"Will you guys be leaving school for Tommaso's father's funeral?"

I nod. "Yeah. We're leaving on Tuesday. I'm not sure exactly when the service and everything is, but I think we'll be back before next week's classes."

"I hope they catch whatever motherfucker did it."

His voice is more threatening than I've ever heard it. He's been so sweet to me, but I've heard rumors of how mean Giovanni can be. He's second to Marcelo for a reason and that was hard to see when he was so endearing to me.

"Me too." I don't like to spend much time thinking about all the things the men in the family have probably seen and had to do, but I hope whoever did this has to pay.

Giovanni walks me to my door, and before I go inside, he looks at me with regret. "If you change your mind and decide that I'm the man of your dreams, be sure to let me know."

I give him a look that must showcase how bad I feel.

"I'm just messing with you, Sofia. Jesus, I'm a hot-blooded male. I'll recover." Then he kisses my cheek before he leaves.

I go inside and close the door behind me, then flop onto my bed. What an insane weekend. First the surprise party, then I lose my virginity to Antonio before we find out that Tommaso's dad has been murdered.

My mind should probably snag on the part where my friend's father was murdered, but all I've been able to do since last night is obsess over my time with Antonio.

I don't regret losing my virginity to him. Not at all, even though I probably should.

The experience was everything I ever wanted it to be and I lost it to someone I have deep feelings for, even if we can never be together long term. I still can't get the expression on his face out of my head when he first entered my body.

The pain was distracting, but I'd never seen him look so vulnerable and overwhelmed. The way he gazed down at me made me think that maybe if things were different, he could have feelings for me too.

I groan out loud. I need to stop doing that—imagining what a future with him could be like. There is no future with him.

He'll be married to Aurora in the summer, and someday I'll go on to marry someone else connected to the family. I have to enjoy this time for what it is—two people who have a physical connection. I want to experience everything physical there is to experience with

Antonio. I want him to be the one to give me all my firsts. I want him to teach me how to be a good lover—how to give as good as I get. I'm determined for that to happen before the semester's over because, after that, I'll have to live with just the memories of our time together.

That will have to be enough, even if I know that nothing short of everything would ever be enough.

* * *

THE KNOCK ON my dorm room door that I'm expecting comes around nine o'clock.

I get up off my couch where I'm working on homework and unenthusiastically make my way over to answer.

"You broke up with Giovanni?" Mirabella pushes past me.

I close the door. She doesn't bother to sit. She's standing in the middle of the room between the bed and the couch with her arms crossed, looking like a concerned parent.

"Is it referred to as breaking up if you've only been on a handful of dates and made it clear you didn't want anything serious?"

"I thought you liked him. What happened?" She drops her hands to her sides and takes a step toward me.

"I do like him. Just not like that. I couldn't get past just seeing him as a friend."

She frowns and her shoulders sag. "Are you sure?"

I nod. "Trust me, I wish I liked him more."

That is one hundred percent the truth. My life would be so much easier if I'd fallen for Giovanni and not her brother. As it is, I feel like a deceitful liar because Mira doesn't know anything about what's going on between her brother and me.

"I'm so bummed." She walks to the couch and flops down onto it.

"I knew you would be." I join her.

"Is that why you didn't tell me before you broke up with him?" She arches an eyebrow.

"I didn't want you trying to talk me out of it. It's for the best."

She brings her hand to her chest. "I would never!" When I give her a look, she says, "Okay, I would. But really, all I want is for you to be happy. That's most important to me. I just hoped . . ."

"That Giovanni could make me happy. I get it. I would have liked that too, but it's not meant to be."

She frowns. "Is there someone else you're interested in?"

I school my features as best I can. The fact is that I've known Mira my entire life and she knows me better than anyone and the answer I have to give her is an outright lie. "There's no one else."

"You'd tell me if there was?"

Is she looking at me suspiciously?

"Of course I would." Needing to get her bloodhound nose off the scent of my lie, I change the subject. "Have you seen Tommaso? How's he doing?"

Her demeanor instantly changes. "I haven't seen him, but I texted my brother. Antonio's with him. I think he's just trying to keep him calm enough not to go and burn down the Moskva House. He called Marcelo over the other night."

I ignore the way my tummy feels fuzzy when Mira says her brother's name.

I'm glad we'll be gone most of next week. Things are always a little tense on campus between the different factions, but they're bound to be worse with all of this going on.

"I feel so terrible for him. I can't imagine."

"Me either." She does a full-body shake as though she's trying to rid herself of the image of being in the same position as Tommaso. "Let's hope neither of us is in the position of ever having to know what it's like to lose someone so close to us like that."

We sit in silence for a few moments, both deep in our thoughts, before she leaves to return to her room with Marcelo.

As soon as she's gone, I feel her absence, and I wonder if there will ever come a time here when I'm not always feeling the absence of a La Rosa.

CHAPTER TWENTY-THREE
ANTONIO

We return to campus on Sunday afternoon after a complete hell week back in Miami. Shit is as tense as I've ever seen it, and my dad and I agree that neither of us is one hundred percent convinced the Russians murdered Leo. Not because we don't think they're capable of it but because we can't see what they'd have to gain from doing so.

Starting a war with us will only result in losses on both sides—both people and money. If they're pinching our weapons from the port, that's one thing. They can either use them themselves or sell them on the black market and pocket the money.

But kidnapping, interrogating, and murdering one of our own? What information could Leo have had that they'd be willing to risk a war with us to get? Especially now that we're aligned with the Costa crime family through Mirabella's engagement to Marcelo.

The only thing that makes sense is that Leo was into something no one knew about and the Russians were somehow involved.

My dad ordered me to stick close to Tommaso. He wants me to try to figure out if he knows something about what might have been going on with his dad. I'll do it because it's part of my role in the family, but I can't say that it feels good to be distrustful of your lifelong best friend who's grieving.

Besides the funeral and wake, my week was full of meetings with my dad and Aurora's dad and the capos, discussing our plans for the Russians. I think that none of the capos understand my dad's order that we stand down for the moment. He sold it as wanting to be strategic in our attacks and that they'll be prepared for us, but I know he wants to make sure it actually was the Russians before we go start an all-out war with them.

I saw Sofia in passing at all the events for Leo, but I didn't get any time with her. Not just because duty called but because Aurora was glued to my side, wanting to make a big show out of how solid we were and how supportive she was of her fiancé. While we were in public, she put on a good show about being upset over Leo's passing, but in private, she pored over wedding details with her mother and mine, insisting that it was a good distraction for everyone from the sad events that had brought us home.

Seeing Sofia and not being able to touch her was torture. My hands felt as though they were on fire when she was within arm's length, but I couldn't reach out and feel her curves against my palms. I was hyperaware of her every move, and every night when I went to bed, Sofia was all I thought about, all I craved as I wrapped my hand around my cock and spilled my seed.

Now that we're back at school and she's only two floors above me, I feel as though a homing beacon is luring me toward her room. It's all I can do not to pace around until I know everyone is asleep.

I need to shed the weight of responsibility on my shoulders for a few hours. Forget all the chaos around me and the life laid out in front of me, including my engagement to a woman I have no feelings for. No positive feelings anyway. I want to lose myself in Sofia's body and the pleasure it provides until she's all I can think of, all I can feel, smell, and taste.

I watch the time on my phone like a man counting down the last minutes of his life, and as soon as it hits midnight, I bolt out of my room and head to the stairway. After making my way two floors up,

I'm standing in front of Sofia's door, feeling exactly like the desperate man I am.

I knock, not loud enough to wake her neighbors, but hopefully loud enough to wake Sofia. She must not have been sleeping because she opens the door seconds later with a hopeful expression that morphs into relief when she sees me.

Barely a second passes and I've stepped forward, hands in her hair, my mouth on hers. I am desperate for this woman after having to spend the last week in her company, unable to have my hands on her.

"I need you," I murmur against her lips as I close the door with my foot.

Truer words have never been spoken. I'm beyond desperate to lose myself in her. There's a violent, reckless urge inside me that demands I have her. It will be satisfied with nothing less.

Sofia wastes no time lifting my T-shirt up over my head. Our mouths separate only so the cotton can pass between us before she tosses the fabric aside.

She's wearing an oversized T-shirt that ends midthigh, and it has the effect of making her look absolutely fucking edible. I lift her, and her legs wrap around my waist. The warmth of her pussy is pressed against the hard ridge of my cock that's trying to strain out of my athletic pants.

I walk forward until her back is pressed against the wall and use my hips to anchor her there so that I can have free use of my hands. They dive under the T-shirt and move straight to her tits. Sofia moans when I hold their weight in my hands, then she strips her lips from mine, arching her neck when I pinch her nipples.

"This past week has been hell not being able to have you." I pull the T-shirt over her head in one swoop and her gaze meets mine. "Not being able to talk to you." I bend and pull a nipple into my mouth, sucking hard and playing with the tip between my teeth. "Not being able to taste you." I move to her other nipple and her hand pushes into my hair, snagging on my curls.

"I hated it." Her voice is breathy and as needy as I feel. "I hated watching Aurora pour herself all over you."

I drag my tongue across her collarbone and up her neck. "I couldn't stand anytime she touched me. I just wanted it to be you."

When I jerk my hips up, pressing my erection firmer into her heat, she moans. "Antonio, don't make me wait any longer."

With one hand, I push down my athletic pants until they pool at my ankles, thankful I'm not wearing any boxer briefs. Then I pull her underwear to the side and notch the head of my cock at her entrance. She's soaked already and my cock twitches.

I'm sure to lock eyes with her before I push inside. Her eyelids grow heavier and heavier with each inch I move deeper inside her. We moan in unison once I'm fully seated inside her.

God, she's so fucking tight. Like a goddamn fist. Tight and hot and wet and I can't hold still any longer. I pump into her, forcing myself to hold back the fervor with which I want to move. Sofia's only ever had sex one other time and I don't want to hurt her.

But after a minute or so, her legs are clamped hard around my waist and she cries out, "Harder."

I slam into her hard then slowly drag my cock out. Then I do it again. It's a savage pounding and a slow release.

The back of her head hits the wall, eyes closed. I watch her tits bounce with each thrust inside her wet heat. Her fingers dig into the muscles in my shoulders, squeezing a little every time I fill her.

A quick glance to our right gives me an idea, and I bring my hands to her waist and pull her up so I slide out of her. Sofia's eyes snap open, questioning.

I set her on her feet, careful not to let go until I know she's steady.

I push off my pants and shoes, kicking them to the side. "I wanna watch us fuck."

Her eyebrows press together into a frown, but when I take her hand and lead her over in front of the mirror, she looks from it to me and her cheeks color even more than they already are.

"Don't you want to watch me fuck you from behind?" I turn her to stand in front of me, facing the mirror.

Her gaze darts away from the reflection. I'm not sure if she's shy or embarrassed or something else, but I can't have this beautiful woman doubting herself. I force her legs a little wider with my foot. Then I push her chin up with my hand so she's forced to face the mirror. She meets my eyes in the reflection where I stand behind her.

"How could I not want to watch?" I whisper before sucking on the spot where her neck meets her collarbone. "You're perfect." I allow my hands to trail around either side of her waist and up. "These tits." My fingers seek out her nipples and a long breath leaves her lips when I squeeze the tips. "This face." I drag my tongue along her jaw while my right hand moves down between her legs. "This pussy." I cup it before rubbing small circles over her clit.

She moans and lets her head drop back against my shoulder. My cock is still slick with her arousal as I bend my knees a bit and drag it between her ass cheeks before finding her entrance, where I push inside.

Sofia's entire body shudders. I pull out and slam back into her, watching the two of us in the mirror. She grows more desperate as I pound into her and continue massaging her clit. My other hand moves to her hair, forcefully dragging her head to the side and holding it there. I suck on her neck while my movements become more frantic, as though I'm chasing a finish line that keeps moving farther away.

We look perfect together with our bodies joined, wringing the pleasure out of one another, and I vow to commit the image in the mirror to memory to be pulled out whenever I want to relive this moment—which will be often.

I increase the pressure on Sofia's clit. She attempts to fold into herself, but my hand is still in her hair, preventing her from bending forward.

"Oh god. Antonio . . . I'm gonna come. I'm gonna come." She keeps chanting the words and they spur me on. I want nothing more than to deliver pleasure to this woman.

I'm slamming into her without mercy, and when I pull my hand back and deliver a swift slap to her clit, she detonates, crying out and convulsing in my arms. Her pussy clamps around me and I spill into her on a long groan, holding myself there until she's milked me entirely.

We're left spent and panting, staring at each other in the mirror. Something passes between us—an understanding of how good this thing between us is maybe—and I can't help it, I need my lips on hers. I force her head back more, my hand still in her hair, and plunge my tongue into her mouth. Her tongue meets mine stroke for stroke, and when I pull away, I place a chaste kiss on her forehead.

Something about this woman makes me want to both defile her and covet her.

When I release her hair, she straightens and I pull myself from her body. My seed spills down the insides of her thighs and I groan. That's so fucking hot.

"Hang on."

I go to the bathroom, wet a washcloth with warm water, and get on my knees behind her. I drag the washcloth up the inside of one thigh, then the other, before I toss it in her laundry hamper. She expects me to stand, but instead, I spread her ass cheeks and drag my tongue through her center. She tastes like a mix of the two of us, and after a few more swipes of my tongue, I stand.

She's looking at me as though she wants more, but I don't want to overdo it. I was rougher than I should have been with her, given that she has no sexual experience, but I can't help myself when it comes to her.

"C'mon." I take her hand and lead her to the bed, climbing in under the covers and pulling her into me.

Sofia's leg rests over mine and her cheek lies on my chest while my hand trails up and down her side. I'm surprised to find that I enjoy this almost as much as I enjoy sex with her. In a different way, but it's no less enjoyable.

"Was that too rough?" I ask.

She lifts her head and looks at me, lips pressed together, and shakes her head, looking almost embarrassed. "No, I liked it. I like anything with you."

I pull her in for a kiss.

"I want to experience everything with you, Antonio . . . while I still can."

I cup her face in my hands. "I want that too." This woman makes me feel things I didn't think were possible for a man like me to feel.

She smiles and rests her head back on my chest. "Do you re-member the summer you were going into your junior year in high school and Mira and I always tagged along with you and Tommaso every time you'd go to the beach?"

I chuckle. "You two wouldn't take no for an answer."

"You know your sister." We both laugh.

"I hated when you guys came along because I had to look out for you and make sure no douchebags were trying to hit on you. Remember that one guy I beat the shit out of because I caught him ogling Mira's ass?" I shake my head.

"I remember," she says.

"What makes you bring that up?" My hand stills on her waist.

"That was the first time I remember seeing you as something other than Mira's older brother. I wasn't sure what to do with those feelings . . . especially as they grew over the years."

I roll her over until I'm on top of her. "The first time I saw you as something other than my little sister's friend was the night I knocked on your door and you answered wearing that little silk pajama set you have."

She grins. "Really?"

I nod. "I don't know why I didn't see you sooner." I run my knuckles down her face.

Her forehead wrinkles. "See what?"

"How incredible you are." I kiss her. "I think it was just that you were off-limits. You were Mira's friend, and I knew she'd kill me if I messed around with you."

She swallows hard. "I don't feel good about lying to her."

I sigh. "It's necessary."

"I know." Her voice is resigned as she pushes her hand into the hair at the back of my head.

"I wish things could be different."

She places her finger over my lips. "Shh. I don't want to talk about what can't be. Let's just enjoy this while we have it."

I give her a resigned sort of smile and trail my mouth down her body to the apex of her thighs. "How about I enjoy you while I can?"

She lets me. Twice.

CHAPTER TWENTY-FOUR
SOFIA

I've been walking around as if I'm in a dream for the past week since we returned to campus from Miami. Antonio has snuck into my room every night, and the time I share with him while everyone else is sleeping is my favorite part of the day.

I try not to dwell too much on the fact that our situation is temporary, but every meal when Aurora sits across from me, fawning over Antonio and talking about their wedding, it makes me want to flip the table. I'm not normally an angry person. I school my reaction as best I can, cut my meals short, or go sit with Mira at the Costa table. Anything so that I don't have to watch the Aurora show.

It's after dinner and I'm headed back to my dorm room to wait for Antonio. He's coming by earlier tonight under the guise of prepping for next Friday's event at the café—which we will. We'll just be doing part of that prep naked.

I was going to walk back with Mira, Marcelo, and Giovanni, but I made the excuse that I wanted to stop at the café for a drink. Things are still a little awkward around Giovanni, and for some reason, I feel as if I have a sense of duty to Antonio to stay away from him.

I'm taking the longer route through the school because it's raining outside. Not a ton of people are around since it's Sunday evening, but I spot a group of Irish roughhousing up ahead in the hall. I move as far as I can to the side of the hallway to avoid them.

Regardless, the guys jostle me as I pass, making a few disparaging comments about the Italian Mafia, which I ignore.

When I don't give them the attention they so obviously want from me, they walk alongside me.

"You think yer too good for the likes of us?" one of them says.

"We've got a real princess here, lads."

I finally stop and face the two guys closest to me. "Why are you bothering me? Are you looking for trouble?" I keep my voice strong, though I'm pretty sure everyone here knows I'm no threat to these three.

"We're just tryin' to have a conversation." The guy with dark hair raises his hands and looks at the guy with strawberry-red hair.

"Now why would you want to do that?" I raise an eyebrow and cock out a hip.

"We're just wondering what's the craic is all." He smiles at me as if we're friends or something.

I roll my eyes. "Speak English and maybe I'd know what you're talking about."

The guy with the red hair points his thumb at me and looks at his third friend. "This one's a dryshite."

All three of them laugh in unison. I turn to go, but a familiar voice from behind me causes me to turn around.

"Is there a problem?"

Antonio stands down the hall, Aurora by his side. He walks toward us and Aurora follows.

"No problem," the guy with the dark hair says.

"I suggest you keep away from anyone in the La Rosa family if you know what's good for you."

Aurora remains back as Antonio steps forward and stands chest to chest with the ringleader.

"What're you gonna do about it?"

"You don't want to find out." Antonio pushes him in the chest and he stumbles back a couple of steps.

The dark-haired one looks as if he wants to charge Antonio, but he apparently thinks better of it. "You all need to learn how to have fun. C'mon, lads."

They all follow him as he turns and heads back the way we came.

I turn to Antonio, avoiding Aurora's gaze. "Thanks, but I could have handled it myself."

"You're part of the family. You don't have to." He eyes me intently. So intently, I look away.

"Good thing he was here to step in, Sofia. Looked like you were getting a little cozy with them."

I turn toward Aurora, who has a saccharine smile.

"They were harassing me. I'd hardly call it getting cozy." Then I turn back to look at Antonio. "Anyway, thanks for your help."

I don't say anything else as I rush down the hall toward the Roma House. I know Antonio and Aurora are likely headed to the same place, but there's no chance I'm going to torture myself by walking with them.

I'll wait patiently for my turn with him, something I should be used to by now.

* * *

THE KNOCK ON my door comes a little earlier than normal. When I swing the door open, Antonio pushes past me, foregoing the kiss hello he usually gives me.

"You need to be more careful," he says by way of greeting.

I spin around to face him. "What are you talking about?"

"The Irish." He throws his arms out as though it should be obvious.

"They were just being assholes, nothing more."

He steps closer to me. "You don't know that."

I study his face and see genuine concern there, so I place my hand on his cheek. "Antonio, I was fine. They were being jerks, trying to get a rise out of me. Nothing more."

"Were they flirting with you?"

My head rears back and I laugh. "No!"

A crease forms between his eyebrows. "It looked like maybe they were flirting with you."

I let my hand drop from his face and wrap my arms around his waist. "I kind of like you jealous."

He glares at me. "I don't."

I grin at him. "Why don't you work off some of this angst you're feeling on me?"

The corners of his lips tip up. "What happened to the sweet, innocent woman who used to live in this dorm room?"

My hands slide down until I grab his ass. "Seems you've corrupted me."

"Maybe a bit. But not fully." He lifts me by the waist and tosses me on the bed and I yelp. "Let's see whether I can finish the job, shall we?"

* * *

AN HOUR LATER, we're still in my bed, with dried sweat on our skin, limbs tangled. I feel thoroughly worked over, and though I could fall asleep just like this in Antonio's arms, I don't want to. I don't want to miss a minute of the time I have left with him.

It's then that I remember something I fantasized about doing with him. I open my mouth to say it but shut it again. Maybe it's a stupid thing to want, but I wasn't kidding when I said I wanted to experience everything with him before school ends.

And because our time together becomes shorter with every second that passes, I force the words past my lips. "Do you want to have a shower together?" I lift my head to gauge his reaction.

"Hell yes." He rolls out of bed, perfection personified in his naked form, then bends and lifts me from the bed over his shoulder before walking into my bathroom.

I'm laughing as he bends over again and sets me on the counter before walking to the shower and turning it on. Our dorm rooms don't have bathtubs, just walk-in showers that are big enough to easily fit more than two people.

I don't have to look in the mirror to know there's an ear-to-ear smile on my face over his enthusiasm at my suggestion.

He stands beside the open glass shower door, eyes devouring me while he waits for the water to warm. When he sticks his hand into the shower to test the temperature of the water, he doesn't remove his gaze from mine.

I've never felt so much just from someone's gaze.

He nods to indicate that the water is warm enough and steps in under the spray. God, he looks good, eyes closed, head tilted back, cock erect as the water sluices down his body. I hop off the counter and join him, sliding the door closed behind me. The warm water hits my overworked muscles—overworked from nothing but sex with Antonio every night this week—and a soft moan leaves my lips.

He steps back so that I can get fully under the spray and wet my hair. Once it's soaked, he's apparently content to be a voyeur, so I reach for my shampoo and massage it into my hair. The berry scent fills the shower until I tip my head back and rinse it under the water. I repeat the process with my conditioner. When I lift my hands to work it out of the strands, Antonio's hands land on my breasts and massage them.

My breathing picks up and I grow slick between my legs despite the constant stream of water running down my body. Once the conditioner is washed out of my hair, I straighten my head and open my eyes. Antonio's erect cock bobs like an invitation between us.

There's something else I've wanted to do since discovering my sexuality with Antonio, but I've just been too nervous to try. What if I'm no good at it? But the look on his face—as though I'm a goddess brought to life—gives me the guts to push ahead.

Without a word, I drop to my knees in front of him.

His eyes widen and he cups my chin while the spray from the showerhead hits my back. "What are you doing?" There's avid interest in his eyes.

"I've never done this," I confess and grip the base of him.

He groans low in his throat as I pump him the way I've seen him do before we have sex sometimes.

"If I do something wrong, will you correct me?" I look at him and I feel the vulnerability radiating off me.

"Trust me when I say there's no way you're going to do anything wrong and there's not a chance in hell I'm going to stop you."

His words make me a little less nervous, so I lean forward and let instinct guide me. I drag my tongue from the bottom of his cock, just above where my fist is, up to the tip. Antonio's hand pushes into the wet hair at the side of my head as he groans. He seems to like that, so I do it again, a little more forcefully and with more confidence this time. His hold on my hair tightens and I take that as a sign that I'm on the right path forward.

Then I open my mouth and draw the tip of him inside, swirling my tongue around and around, and his grip on my hair tightens. Gaining even more confidence, I slide my lips over the tip again and take him farther into my mouth until I'm halfway down his length. I do this again and again and hear his breathing pick up over the spray of the shower, feel how he grows even harder between my lips.

I glance up to see his head tipped back so his chin is facing the ceiling, eyes closed. He looks like a man in rapture, and it spurs me on even more. At my attempt to take even more of him in my mouth, he reaches the back of my throat and I choke back a cough.

The hand in my hair moves to run over my cheek. "Breath through your nose. Relax your throat," he softly says.

I meet his gaze and do as he says. He rocks his hips gently at first, and when I don't choke again, he increases his tempo. The end of his cock reaches the back of my throat and moves past it. It feels strange at first. The urge to panic and pull away is there, but I force myself to remain in place, deciding instead to concentrate on the look of pure pleasure on his face as he gazes down at me.

He picks up speed until he's fucking my face in earnest. My eyes water, tears running down my cheeks. The water continues to spray on my back as he pumps into me, hands on my head.

"You make me want to throw it all away, Sofia." He holds himself deep in my mouth before pulling out and I suck in a deep breath. "You make me want to give it all up."

His need rises higher and higher as he uses my mouth for his pleasure and he's close to coming. Just when I think he's going to come down the back of my throat, he pulls out and jerks himself twice before ribbons of cum lash my face.

"I love being the only one to dirty you up." He gazes at me with awe.

He holds out a hand to help me up, then turns me around by the shoulders to rinse me off.

Once my face is clean, I turn back around to face him. "So, it was good?"

Antonio throws his head back and laughs. The sight of it nearly undoes me. "Just a smidge better than good." He shakes his head at me in exasperation and gives me a chaste kiss. "We should probably get out of here before we become prunes."

"Don't forget we have to talk about next Friday."

"The night is still young," he says.

After rinsing off with soap, we turn off the shower and get out. Once I'm dry, I grab my silk robe from the back of the door and slide it on while Antonio wraps a towel around his waist. We move into the main area of my dorm room to retrieve our clothes, but before I have time to gather them all, the door to my room whips open.

Antonio and I still. Staring at each other before our gazes move toward the door and Mirabella's voice.

"Sorry to barge in, but you're not going to believe what a—" She stops short and looks between Antonio and me, eyes wide, fists tight. "What the actual fuck?"

CHAPTER TWENTY-FIVE

SOFIA

"Mira!" I clutch my robe closed at the top of my neck as though that might somehow lead her to believe that the scene she's barged into isn't what it looks like.

"Don't you know how to fucking knock?" Antonio growls, obviously choosing to take the more aggressive approach.

"What are you two doing?" She steps up to Antonio and shoves his bare chest. "You're fucking my best friend?" When she goes to shove him again, he grips her wrists to stop her.

"Tread lightly, sis."

"I can explain." My heart hammers so hard that I can barely hear the words coming out of my mouth.

Mira whips her head in my direction. "It's pretty self-explanatory, I'd say. My brother is using you to get his rocks off. Probably because his fiancée is a royal bitch."

A growl rips out of Antonio's throat. "That's not what's going on."

"Oh yeah? What is then?" She crosses her arms and gives him her best "don't fucking lie to me" face.

"I don't have to explain shit to you." He bends at the waist to pick up his discarded clothes by his feet and stomps off into the bathroom, slamming the door behind him.

"I can't believe this." Mira throws her arms in the air and paces. All the La Rosas pace when they're upset.

I'm worried that my best friend will never forgive me for keeping this from her, but the truth is that I'm more worried this might mean that Antonio will want to end our arrangement early, something I'm not prepared for.

"Mira, let me explain."

She ignores me and continues to pace until Antonio comes out from the bathroom, fully dressed.

"Are you still going to marry Aurora?" A clear accusation is evident in her tone.

I turn to Antonio. "Do you mind letting Mira and me talk on our own?"

He looks between us a few times before finally giving me a terse nod. Then he places a chaste kiss on my lips, causing my cheeks to heat to volcanic proportions because Mira is in the room with us.

"Then I'll talk to my sister after." He faces her and she's looking at us as if we're little green men who just landed in our spacecraft on Earth. "Come see me in my room when you two are done. Don't make any detours in between." He doesn't wait for her to answer, sliding past her to head to the door.

"Don't make any detours in between," Mira says in a high-pitched mocking voice.

The sound of the door closing behind Antonio reverberates throughout the room and Mira and I stare at each other for a beat.

"How did you get in here?" I ask.

"I used my key." She shrugs as though it's no big deal, but at least she looks a little guilty.

I hold out my hand. When she doesn't immediately hand it over, I tilt my head and raise an eyebrow.

"Fine," she grumbles and drops it into my waiting palm.

I set it on my desk. "I'm sorry you walked in on that."

Her irritation morphs into concern and she takes my hands. "Explain to me what's going on."

So I do. I tell her how it all started. How at first, Antonio acted weird around me and I couldn't figure out why. How I've been pining for him since our freshmen year of high school. How I really tried to give it a go with Giovanni, but I couldn't get her brother out of my head. I confess it all and I wait for her to pass judgment.

"Why didn't you tell me?" she asks.

I sigh. "I promised your brother I wouldn't. If we were the only two who knew, there'd be less of a chance of anyone finding out. Besides, I didn't want you to have to keep it from Marcelo if I told you."

She nods, seeming to understand my position but still looking a little hurt. "So you two have . . ." I nod and her hands fly up to her face. "I can't believe my best friend lost her virginity and I knew nothing about it. And now I can't even ask you how it was because the last thing I want to hear about, or picture, is my brother having sex."

I laugh, unable to stop myself. Maybe because a ton of guilt and stress has been lifted off my shoulders now that Mirabella knows about her brother and me. It means I don't have to lie to her anymore. Regardless, talking to her about this feels good, even if I have to spare her all the bedroom details. Mira joins me in laughter, and it takes us a minute to gather ourselves.

She takes my hands again. "Is he going to call off the engagement to Aurora?" Her eyes look watery, which unnerves me. Mira doesn't often show her softer side.

"No."

The word hangs between us as if it's going to detonate.

"I'm worried about you. I know how you are, Sofia. You wouldn't have slept with him unless you're in love with him."

I don't bother denying it. It's true. I may not have confessed how deep my feelings go to Antonio, but I admit that I love him. "I've decided to take what I can get. Once the semester is up, so are we."

She squeezes my hands and frowns. "And that's going to be enough for you?"

I sigh, unable to hide my disappointment. "It has to be."

She chews on her bottom lip before drawing me into a hug. "Maybe there's something we can do to stop his wedding."

I squeeze her back, then pull away, shaking my head. "There's nothing to be done. Antonio has a duty to fulfill. I knew that going in. So did he." I'm proud of the way my voice doesn't wobble. "Trying to sabotage his engagement would only bring shame to the family, and that's the last thing either of us wants."

Mira's hands fist at her sides and she's gone from upset and concerned to angry. "See? This is exactly the kind of shit that shouldn't be a part of our culture anymore. Why shouldn't you two be able to be together if that's what you both want?"

I flop onto the couch, pulling my robe closed when it slides open. "That's not the world we live in, and you know it."

She walks over and joins me. "It should be though. I mean, what do you want for your future?"

"You know what I want." Mira doesn't understand it, but all I really want is to find love and fulfill my role as a traditional Mafia wife. That's enough for me, even if it's not for her. If I'm with a man I love, it's enough.

She blows out a breath and sinks into the back of the couch.

"I know you don't agree. It's not what you want. You want to be a part of the family business, but that's not for me. I'm not opposed to everything you believe in, Mira, but I think it's not *what* we choose that's important, just the fact that we *have* a choice."

She turns her head and studies me before taking my hand. "You're right. But that's exactly what I'm saying. If you and my brother—God, that sounds so weird—want that life with each other, you should be able to have it."

I squeeze her hand. "That we can agree on. But some things just aren't destined to happen."

She's quiet before she says, "This sucks."

A small laugh falls out of me. "In a lot of ways, yeah. But I'm grateful for the time with Antonio. It will always be special to me."

Understatement of the decade.

CHAPTER TWENTY-SIX
ANTONIO

The knock on my door comes about a half hour after I leave Sofia's room, and when I swing open the door, as expected, my sister barges in.

"Please, come on in," I say with false politeness after she's already inside.

"Cut the shit, Antonio. What's going on with you and Sofia?"

I arch an eyebrow and walk past her to go sit on my couch. If she thinks she's going to come in here and tell me how it's going to be, she has another think coming. She might lead her fiancé around by the balls, but I have rank over her and I'm not going to allow her to act otherwise.

"Pretty sure you figured that out for yourself when you barged into her room uninvited. What happened to all those manners Mom ingrained in you?"

"Oh yeah, Sofia told me all about how you two have been carrying on. What I want to know is, what does it mean for you? Are you just using her?"

My eyes narrow. I stand because she's standing in front of me, looking down at me. Now her eyes have to follow me up since I have damn near a foot of height on her.

"If I was, what do you think you'd do about it?"

Her lips press together in a thin line. "Tell you what an asshole you are for messing with my best friend and potentially our friendship, then go tell your fiancée."

I throw my head back and laugh. "No, you wouldn't because then you'd ruin your best friend's reputation in our family and she'd never get it back."

Mira voices a sound of frustration and stomps her foot like a child because she knows I'm right. "Explain to me why you'd mess around with her then. Why, after all these years, would you hook up with her?"

She stares at me, waiting for an answer, but I find I don't have one to give. Not one that will satisfy her question anyway.

Then her face drops. "Oh my god." Her hand flies to her mouth. "You actually have feelings for her. I know what a romantic and optimist Sofia is and I assumed that how she felt was mostly one-sided . . . I figured it was more about the sex for you, but you actually like her."

I cross my arms, unsure what gave me away. "Don't make it something more than it is. We're just having fun before school ends."

Mira shakes her head. "Bullshit. You like her. Oh my god, this is amazing!" She claps her hands together.

"How is this amazing?" I roll my eyes.

"Because you can do something so that the two of you can be together. She doesn't have any power in this situation, but you do."

I hold up my hand. "Slow down. I don't plan on doing anything. Sofia and I will have our fun this semester, then I'm getting married this summer . . . to Aurora. That's what's happening."

She frowns. "Why the fuck would you marry that viper when you care about Sofia?"

"You know why."

Mira scoffs. "Because of duty? Because you want to be Dad's perfect little son like always?" She opens her mouth and sticks her pointer finger inside as if the idea of what she just said makes her want to throw up.

"Because I made an oath to always put the family first, and blowing up my engagement with Aurora and insulting the underboss isn't putting the family first."

She steps toward me. "Antonio, you can't marry Aurora if you're in love with Sofia."

Now I'm the one who scoffs. "Who said anything about love? She's just a good lay and I want to keep it going while I can." The insult to Sofia tastes like acid on my tongue, but love? Where's my sister getting that?

She sticks her finger in my face. "Don't you dare do that. Not about Sofia."

I roll my eyes. "What you need to understand is that Sofia and I are not going to be together, Mira. Get that through your head and stop hoping otherwise. We're both in agreement about when things will end."

She shakes her head as if I've disappointed her. "I think you're both going to find that's easier said than done."

"I'm done with this interrogation. Why don't you go back to your room with Marcelo and do whatever it is that you two do? And keep your mouth shut about all this—that means Marcelo too." She opens her mouth to protest, but I don't bother letting her. "You're still a La Rosa at this point, Mira. Until you sign that marriage license and it makes you a Costa, you need to do what's best for the family, and that means the fewer people who know about this, the better."

After clenching her jaw for a second, she nods in agreement.

"Great. Now go. I'm sick of this conversation."

She leaves without another word, and I return to the couch, lying down and staring at the ceiling.

Just talking about things ending with Sofia makes my chest tight. What's it going to be like when it's a reality?

* * *

THE NEXT MORNING, I'm awoken by a knock on my door. I swear to God if this is my sister here to wake me up with another warning—

I grab a pair of pants and when the door swings open to reveal Aurora standing there, my thought ends abruptly.

Why is she here?

If this were a regular engagement, I suppose it wouldn't be weird, but Aurora has never been in my room before.

"Hey, what's up?" I yawn, covering my mouth with my forearm.

"Is that how you greet your fiancée?" She smiles and walks into my room.

I somehow hold back the sigh that wants to escape. It's way too early to deal with this woman.

"Did you need something, Aurora?" I walk to my closet to grab a T-shirt when I notice the way her eyes roam my chest.

"I thought we could walk to breakfast together this morning."

I arch an eyebrow. "Since when do we do that?"

"We don't, but . . . I've been thinking." She closes the distance between us and lays a hand on my chest, bringing the other one up to my face. "The wedding is getting closer and closer. It's time we start being a real engaged couple. Stop living such separate lives."

Her hand trails down my chest, then my abs, and I grab her wrist before she can reach my cock. "Now why would we want to do that?"

She gives me a coy smile. "Now, now. Don't pretend you don't like me, fiancé. The evidence suggests otherwise." Aurora looks between us to where my hard-on is pushing against my lounge pants.

"It's called morning wood. It's nothing personal—believe me." I toss her wrist to her side.

"We're going to spend a lifetime in bed together, Antonio. Why not have fun a little early?"

I bark out a laugh. "Any time I spend in bed with you will be out of duty, Aurora. Nothing more. Now, I have plans to meet up with Tommaso, so you'll have to excuse me."

She narrows her eyes, the sultry persona gone. "What would our fathers say if they knew you were talking to me like this?"

"Is that a threat?" My jaw is clenched so hard it hurts. Our fathers have probably talked to our moms worse than I just did.

She shrugs. "Just a question."

I swear she adds a little extra hip action to her walk as she struts to the door. I follow her. Not because I have actual plans to meet Tommaso before we head to the dining hall for breakfast but because it's the easiest way to get her out of here.

Aurora opens the door and turns to face me. "I'll save you a seat beside me at breakfast."

"Perfect," I say with false politeness, adjusting myself in my pants so my dick is held down by the waistband, and follow her out into the hall.

She heads one way to the elevator while I go in the opposite direction toward Tommaso's room. I knock on his door, and Aurora watches me from the far end of the hall while she waits for the elevator.

It's all I can do not to dance in place. I have to take a piss so bad.

When he doesn't answer right away, I knock again. Tommaso isn't an early riser, so I can't imagine he's gone to work out or already left for the dining hall.

The elevator door dings, and I watch as Aurora gets in. As soon as the doors close, I race back to my room and into the bathroom to relieve myself.

Once I'm showered and dressed in my uniform, I head back to

Tommaso's room around our usual meeting time to head to the dining hall for breakfast. This time, he answers right away.

"Hey," he says as he answers the door. "Come in. I'm almost ready."

He appears tired. There are bags under his eyes and the smile that used to be ever present has given way to a crease between his eyebrows. We haven't talked much about his dad since we returned—a bit here and there. I've had to stop him from rushing the Russians' table in the dining hall a few times, but he doesn't seem to want to discuss it.

I wouldn't know how to anyway. It's not like we're raised to explore our feelings. We're raised to act, not feel.

Something has been bugging me though. For all the tension on our end when we're looking at the Russian section in the dining hall, why aren't the Russians tense?

They're carrying on as normal. Nothing has changed in their habits or their demeanor and certainly not toward us. They still show the same mutual disdain we've always had for each other. The only explanation is that they don't know there's a reason to be tense. They don't know that we think they killed one of our capos—or they're pretending not to know. Which is it?

I follow Tommaso inside his room while he slips his tie with the colors of the Italian flag on and does it up in front of the mirror.

I pick up his blazer that's hung over the back of his desk chair and toss it to him. "I came by earlier and you weren't here."

He stills for a beat while he's pulling on his blazer. It's only a half second, but I clock it.

"Went for a walk early. Couldn't sleep. Was thinking about my dad."

Tommaso isn't a "leisurely walk to work out his feelings" kind of guy. He's a "beat the shit out of a punching bag" kind of guy. I want to call bullshit but now isn't the time. The guy's father was just murdered, had his eyes gouged out, and washed up bloated on the beach a week later. That'll fuck up anyone.

So instead of grilling him, I say, "If you want company next time, let me know."

He nods and makes his way over to the door. "Ready?" He seems eager to end the conversation.

"Yup." I pretend to believe him.

We head out of the Roma House, but I can't shake the feeling of unease that plagues me the entire walk to the dining hall.

My best friend is lying. The question is, what's he lying about?

CHAPTER TWENTY-SEVEN
SOFIA

The next day in embezzlement class, the professor announces that we're going to work on a project in groups of three. I stifle a groan. I've always hated partner work in school. Probably because I'm a perfectionist and always have the urge to take over. Unless it's with Antonio. I've really enjoyed partnering with him on the Friday events.

Unfortunately, Mira isn't in this class with me. In fact, there are very few Italians in this class. Aurora's the only member from the La Rosa family here, and there's no way I want to partner with her. But after the professor tells us to get into groups of three, I see that the Italians from the Accardi and the Vitale families have already paired up. As have most of the people from the Moskva and Dublin Houses. There are a couple stragglers—politicians' kids—but there's no way I'm working with them.

When I turn back around to look at the other side of the classroom, Aurora is there, grinning at me.

"Looks like we're going to be partners." She's pretending to be happy about this, but we both know she likes me about as much as I like her.

"Great," I deadpan. "Who's going to be our third?"

"Don't worry, lass, I'll join this group." I turn at the sound of the Irish accent behind me and see the same guy with dark hair who was pestering me in the hallway the other day.

He sticks out his hand. "Conor Murphy, pleased to meet you both."

I glance at his outstretched hand for a beat before I feel rude and end up accepting it. "Hey."

Before any of us say anything else, the professor claps at the front of the room to get our attention. "All right, now that the groups are set, why don't you all have a seat and I'll explain what the assignment is."

I spend the rest of the class taking notes about what's required and pouting internally that I'm going to have to spend extra time with Aurora and this jackass of an Irishman.

When class ends, Aurora sprints up out of her seat and pulls aside Conor and me. "Let's head to the dining hall together. We can talk about our ideas and when we're going to get together after class to work on it."

The entire way, Conor tries to talk me up, much like he did when he was annoying me in the hallway that night. I can't tell if he's actually trying to hit on me or just annoy me. It's the latter that's working.

"So, you seeing anyone, Sofia?" he asks.

After a quick glance from the side of my eye at Aurora, I shake my head. "Nope."

"How's a looker like you not have a boyfriend?"

I narrow my eyes. "Maybe I don't want one."

He laughs and pulls open the door to the dining hall and we step inside. "I can assure you, lass, if you were with me, you wouldn't stop wanting me." He winks.

What is this guy's deal?

"All right, remember, we're going to meet at the library at eight tonight. Don't be late," Aurora says before rushing off toward the La Rosa table.

"It was great getting to officially meet you." Conor grabs my hand before I can stop him and pulls it up to his lips.

As soon as I realize his intentions, I rip my hand away. A quick look around tells me that more than a few people noticed, as they should. I mean, I'm Italian and he's Irish. I glance at the La Rosa table and Antonio's watching—jaw set, fire in his eyes. Then Aurora reaches the table and slides onto his lap, taking him by surprise.

I look back at Conor. "Don't touch me again."

I stomp away from him until I reach our table, then slide in beside Mira and across from Antonio and his lapdog Aurora.

"What was that about?" Mira asks me, eyes wide.

I'm sure she's sitting at our table today because of everything she found out last night. Most days lately, she eats at the Costa table with Marcelo.

Before I respond, Aurora butts in. "We were paired with him for embezzlement class. Seems he's quite taken with Sofia," she singsongs.

"It's not like that." I glare at her.

"That's not what it looked like the other day when Antonio and I came upon you guys in the hallway." She brushes her hand over his chest.

I move my hand under the table onto my lap and squeeze it into a fist. A fist I'd love to place right between her shit-disturber eyes.

"What's she talking about?" Mira looks at me with concern.

"Nothing. He and his friends were harassing me, trying to get a rise out of me." I look at Aurora, steadily avoiding Antonio's gaze. "Not flirting with me."

"If you say so." She waves off my argument.

"Stay the fuck away from him."

Everyone at the table turns to look at Antonio. How could they not? His voice is filled with venom you don't often hear from him.

"He's my group partner in class, that's all." I keep my gaze steady on Antonio's.

"That better be all."

Mira shifts uncomfortably next to me.

"He's Irish. He's the enemy."

Antonio's add-on statement appeases everyone else at the table. After all, we're all a little high-strung after what happened with Tommaso's dad.

Speaking of whom, Tommaso arrives at the table and stands at the end, looking between everyone for a beat. "What'd I miss?"

I don't bother waiting for anyone to answer, pushing up off the bench. "I'm going to get my food."

"Me too." Mira's up and beside me as we walk away from the table.

"You okay?" she asks under her breath.

"Never better," I lie.

* * *

WHEN ANTONIO KNOCKS on my door that night, I'm still annoyed about lunch. I managed to avoid his and Aurora's PDA at dinner by sitting with the Costas. But I knew I'd have to face him eventually since we'd made plans to meet up this evening to get some work done for Friday's event since last night's planning session was a bust.

"Hey." I swing open the door and don't bother waiting for him to say anything, turning and making my way back to where I was sitting on the couch, getting a head start on everything that has to be arranged for our karaoke night this Friday.

"Why are you acting like you're pissed off?" He stands in front of where I'm sitting, glaring at me with his hands on his hips.

I wish he didn't look so gorgeous when he's clueless.

"Maybe because I am." I look back at my notebook, where I'm listing all the tasks to be done.

"What do *you* have to be pissed about?" His tone implies that he thinks he's the one who should be mad. When I keep writing in my book and don't answer him, he rips it from my hands and tosses it across the room.

"What the hell, Antonio!"

"Don't make me repeat myself." He crosses his arms.

"What the hell was that in the dining hall at lunch?" My voice is loud and shrill.

"That's a great question." He leans in and cages me against the back of the couch. "Why did that Irish asshole feel like he had the right to touch you? Try to put his lips to your skin?"

My anger reaches new levels. He's questioning me when Aurora was practically dry-humping him through lunch and dinner today? "Why do you even care? Seems to me that you and your fiancée were a little preoccupied."

His jaw flexes. "Don't change the topic, Sofia. Why'd he touch you?"

"I have no idea. You'd have to ask him. Probably to piss me off."

His hand moves in a flash to the back of my neck. "There's only one man who's permitted to have his lips on you and that's me. If I see him touch you again, I'm going to cut his fingers off one by one."

"Oh? And how would you explain that to your fiancée?" I say *fiancée* with as much attitude as I can muster. Being this close to him, when he's this intense, makes it hard to think straight and remember why I'm pissed off at him in the first place because my body is screaming at me to bridge the distance and kiss him.

"I don't have to explain anything to my fiancée. That's the great thing about being next in line to lead the family."

Our gazes lock and hold.

"And how would you explain it to me?" I ask in a near whisper.

He doesn't answer, but his lips crash onto mine in a searing kiss.

He'd do it because it's his duty. He'd do it because seeing another man's hands on me makes him insane with jealousy. He'd do it because I'm the woman he cares about, not her.

We're both breathing heavily by the time he pulls away and straightens up, pushing a hand through his hair.

"We should probably get to work. Otherwise, we're going to spend the whole time with me inside you."

"You won't find me complaining."

But he's right. Time is running out for us to get everything together for this Friday's event.

We're saved from our voracious appetite for each other when there's a knock at the door. I frown, wondering who that might be, and get up off the couch.

When I open the door, there's a young woman, probably in her late twenties, and she holds a small envelope out to me. "Here's your new key."

"Oh! Thank you so much. I didn't think it would be that fast. Appreciate it."

She nods and turns to leave.

"What's that about?" Antonio asks.

I open the envelope and drop the key into my palm. "I lost my key, so I had to go to administration to get another one made."

He steps toward me. "How'd you do that?"

I shrug. "No idea. But it was a good thing I made Mira give me hers back last night so I could use that today." I hesitate. "Do you want this one?" When he looks at me quizzically, I rush to explain. "Then you can come and go as you please. That way, if we're planning to meet up and I'm not here yet, you can just go inside so no one sees you in the hallway."

He plucks the key out of my palm. "I'd be honored." He shoves it into his back pocket before stepping into me and wrapping his arms around my waist and resting his hands on my ass.

"I thought we needed to get to work?" I moan when he gently sucks on my neck.

"There will be plenty of time for that later," he murmurs against my skin.

Turns out, he's right.

CHAPTER TWENTY-EIGHT

ANTONIO

"I swear to God, if I have to listen to another ABBA song, I'm going to shoot myself in the head." I stare at the stage where yet another group of girls is singing a terrible rendition of an ABBA song.

"At least it's not 'Bohemian Rhapsody,'" Marcelo murmurs.

Tommaso's not here tonight. He said he's not into it, which is fair, but he's still acting cagey. I tried to get him to commit to going to the gym with me a few times like we usually do and he put me off. Said he didn't feel up to it.

Mira claps her hands in front of her. "I think I'm up next."

"I can't believe you're even doing this," Marcelo says.

She whips her head in his direction. "Why? You've never heard me sing. Maybe I'm amazing."

"She's not," I deadpan.

Aurora laughs beside me. She's been like a second skin to me all week and it's wearing on me.

Mira rolls her eyes and turns around to continue watching the performance. When their song ends, Sofia takes the microphone from them and looks at the sign-up sheet in her hand.

"Next up is Mirabella La Rosa." She grins at my sister but doesn't look my way at all.

It hasn't escaped my notice that Sofia's been avoiding looking at me. Probably because Aurora's all over me. At least she hasn't been looking at Giovanni, who's sitting to Marcelo's left, either.

Mira bounds out of her seat and rushes up to the small stage, grabbing the mic out of her friend's hand. "I have to insist that you sing this one with me, Sofia. As my bestie, it's your obligation."

Sofia shakes her head and tries to walk offstage, but my sister snags her arm and drags her back.

"Who wants Sofia to join me?" Mira says loudly into the microphone.

Most of the crowd cheers and claps, and eventually Sofia relents, cheeks pink. She takes the second microphone off the stand, ready for whatever song Mira picked. My sister looks at our table with a Cheshire grin.

"The Boy Is Mine" by Brandy and Monica plays, and my sister sings Brandy's part and Sofia does Monica's. While Mira will do nothing but look at us, Sofia steadily avoids looking in the direction of our table.

I'm not worried about anyone reading into it. Everyone here will just think that Mira's staking her claim over her fiancé, but I'm still fucking pissed that she's pulling this shit. Especially because she knows I can't say anything to her about it here.

Well played, sis.

When the song wraps up, Sofia returns to hosting and Mira returns to our table, glancing at me with an expression that dares me to call her out.

"Well, if there's anyone who didn't know that Marcelo is yours, they know now," Giovanni says and laughs.

"That's the idea," Mira says, glancing at me.

I return my attention to the stage until the night is over. Aurora's hands roam my leg the entire night, and as soon as the last person has finished, I shoot up out of my chair and head to the stage.

"You did a good job hosting," I tell Sofia.

She glances at me while placing the mics back into their cases. "Thanks!"

"Honey . . ."

I cringe at the sound of Aurora's voice behind me.

"Let's head back to Roma House now." She comes to stand beside me and wraps an arm around my waist.

"I need to stick around to help Sofia clean up." I gesture to where Sofia's taking down some of the decor we set up before anyone got here.

Aurora sticks out her bottom lip. "Don't make me walk back alone, honey."

"It's fine," Sofia says. "There's not much to do. And I'm sure Mira doesn't mind staying to give me a hand."

I give Sofia a look that says, "Why'd you have to say that?" and "I'll use my key to meet you in your room" at the same time. "If you're sure . . ."

"I'm sure," she says with false brightness.

"Perfect!" Aurora interlinks our fingers. "See you later, Sofia."

Though it feels all wrong to be leaving here with Aurora, I do it to keep our secret.

Aurora tries to make small talk the entire way back, but I'm not much into talking, so I respond in mostly one-syllable grunts. If it bothers her, she doesn't indicate as much. She has more patience for my disinterest these days for some reason.

We reach her door on the fourth floor, and I drop her hand, taking a few steps back. "I'll see you tomorrow, I guess."

"Wait!"

The urgency in her voice startles me.

"Why are you rushing off?" Aurora wraps her arms around my neck. "Do you want to come in?" She presses her front to mine and goes up on her tiptoes, leaning in for a kiss.

I rear my head back and attempt to disentangle myself from her. My skin feels as if it's crawling with fire ants when her hands are on me.

"What are you doing?" I look at her with a mix of disdain and confusion.

"I told you, I want to act like a couple."

I manage to unwrap her hands from around my neck and place them at her sides. "That's not happening. Now I've gotta go. See you tomorrow."

She doesn't protest any further as I head to the stairwell as though I'm going to the third floor and my room. Instead, I head one level up, fish the key to Sofia's room out of my pocket, and slip inside while no one is in the hallway.

The scent of her perfume and shampoo fills the room and mixed together, they remind me wholly of her. I breathe it in and wander around the room, anxious for her to join me.

Since this is my first time alone in her room, I use the time to study everything on her walls. There are a few retro-looking posters in shades of peach, tan, and light green. A romance novel rests on her nightstand, along with some hand cream, a candle, and her phone charger.

Above her desk is a collage of pictures, so I walk over there to take a closer look. Are we in any of them together?

The bulk of them consist of her and Mira, but there are some newer ones that also include Marcelo, Giovanni, Andrea, and Lorenzo. I clench my jaw, seeing the way Sofia's standing beside Giovanni in one.

But there are some older ones from high school, in particular, a few from our summers spent on the beach. We're in them together, as are Mira, Tommaso, and some other friends from home. I study them with the newfound knowledge that Sofia was into me at the time and I was completely clueless. I still don't see anything that would indicate to me that I missed anything.

Then my gaze snags on one from Christmas a couple years ago. Mira, Sofia, and I are standing in front of the giant Christmas tree my mother erects every year in the great room. It's a candid shot as my sister and Sofia are looking at me while I'm saying something.

It's there that I see it. The way Sofia stands between my sister and me and looks up at me. There's an unguarded light in her eyes, something I only see nowadays when she looks at me in private. Her interest is clear in this picture.

To think that this magnificent woman was in front of me the entire time and I was too dumb, too immature, and too blind to see it. Things could have been so different if I hadn't had my head up my ass.

I turn away from the desk when something catches my eye—the colors orange and green. There's a sliver of fabric poking out of the bottom drawer of her desk. It looks like whatever it is got caught when she tried to close the desk drawer.

Though I shouldn't, I reach for the handle and pull the drawer open.

My stomach squeezes painfully when I realize what it is.

I grab the corner and pull out one of the school-issued ties for the Irish. The white, orange, and green pattern in my hand makes it feel as if I'm holding photographic evidence of Sofia in bed with some other guy.

How did she get this?

Is it a little token left behind by a lover?

No, I took her virginity, of that I'm certain.

That doesn't mean she couldn't have been doing other stuff with someone else before you came along.

No. She wouldn't. Even if she was, it wouldn't have been any of my business.

The sound of voices in the hall causes me to quickly close the drawer and roll up the tie, shoving it in my pocket. I rush to the couch and take a seat seconds before Sofia appears in the room.

"Hey, you used your key." She grins across the room.

"Sure did." I try to keep my voice even.

A part of me wants to ask her about the tie, but a bigger part of me doesn't want to ruin the short amount of time we have left with each other. Is it my business if she was messing around with an Irishman before I came along?

It is if he's Irish.

I push the thought out of my mind for now. I'll examine all the possibilities of how that tie ended up with her another time.

What is she doing to me? I'm knowingly lying to myself.

CHAPTER TWENTY-NINE
ANTONIO

When Sunday morning rolls around, I'm still thinking about the tie I found in Sofia's room. But I still haven't mentioned it to her. Why? What am I so afraid of?

You're afraid of ruining what little time you have left with her.

It's true. As weak and pussy-whipped as that makes me, it's true. I'd spend a lifetime with her if I could and we only have weeks left. Still, I can't stop the niggling feeling that there's something more to the tie, but I guess that's what you get for being in this life. You're always distrustful of everyone.

But Sofia is the most trustworthy and loyal person I've ever known. If there was something I needed to know, she would have told me.

On my phone call with my dad, I run an idea by him, and when he agrees, I go in search of Marcelo. He's in the lounge at the Roma House with my sister on his lap, Giovanni on his one side, Sofia on the other, and Andrea on the opposite couch.

"Hey." I lift my chin and address the group as a whole when I approach. I don't want to pay too much attention to Sofia and I can't look at Giovanni without wanting to glare at him, knowing he's had his lips on the woman I wish I could claim.

"You just get off the phone with Dad?" Mira asks.

I nod.

"I spoke with Mom earlier and all she wanted to talk about was your wedding. It's like I'm not even engaged." She arches an eyebrow.

It's a challenge. I know it. She knows it. And Sofia knows it.

I ignore it and turn my attention to Marcelo. "You got a second?"

Our eyes meet and it's clear he knows this is business related. He gently taps Mira's side to get her off him.

"Be back in a few," he says to her once he stands from the couch.

Mira looks perturbed that she's not in on the conversation. Marcelo's free to include her as much as he wants in his family business, but in the La Rosa crime family dealings, she's not involved—even if she hates that fact.

We head outside into the spring sunshine. It's a nice day, and feeling the sun on my skin again, like I'm used to at home, eases some of the uncertainty that's been plaguing me the past couple of weeks.

"What's up?" Marcelo asks.

"I need your help. Spoke to my father this morning and we'd like to lay a trap as bait. We'll buy a shipment of guns from you. Keep it a little less quiet than normal. Not enough to arouse any suspicion, but enough that if someone were digging, they could find out when and where it's coming in. In the shipment, we need you to plant a GPS tracker so we can see where it ends up."

He stops on the path and turns to face me. "You're not worried about the shipment being intercepted by authorities and them tracing it back to you?"

"My dad agrees that it's worth the risk. We need to know if it's someone on the inside. The Russians haven't made any other moves since Leo's murder if it was even them. We need to know whether we need to prepare for war or flush out a rat."

"There's a chance whoever's taking the shipment will locate the tracker and ditch it."

I nod. "True. But it's worth trying. We've got a tech guy on our crew, and he makes them himself. They're small . . . can fit inside the barrel of a gun."

Marcelo nods. "All right. We'll help you out."

"Think you can arrange for all this to happen on your phone call this afternoon? The sooner, the better."

He shrugs. "I got ten minutes. I'll make 'em count. I'll call my nonno first, then your dad. Consequences be damned."

"Great, thanks, man." I stick out my hand and he shakes it. "It's gonna be good having you as a part of the family."

He chuckles. "You remember you said that when our interests don't align."

I grin. He's right. At the moment, it's easy because we're on the same side, but inevitably one day, we'll be on opposing sides of an issue and we'll each have to put our own family first. Hard when his family includes my sister.

We turn and head back toward the Roma House. When we get inside, I make a beeline for the elevator.

"You not gonna hang with us?" Marcelo asks.

I shake my head. "Nah, I'm gonna go back up to my room."

I can't sit around and watch Giovanni still try to flirt with Sofia.

I'm pretty much going to spend the rest of the day counting down the minutes until I can head to Sofia's room tonight under the guise of getting organized for our volunteer activities.

As I wait for the elevator to arrive, I force myself not to glance back at Sofia. It's like my body is finely attuned to her and can approximate the exact distance we're apart, even with my back to her. I swear, the moment her gaze flicks my way, I sense it.

The elevator arrives, the doors sliding open to reveal Dante Accardi. He's next in line in the Southwest sector of the country. He's always been a bit of a dick, but I tolerate him.

"Hey, man." I raise my chin at him when we pass each other, him exiting and me entering the claustrophobic box.

"What's good?" he says. "Where's that fox of a fiancée of yours?"

I narrow my eyes at him. Not because I feel proprietary over Aurora, but because this stronzo knows as well as I do that he's completely offside and asking for a fight. "Wouldn't know."

I let the elevator doors slide closed between us, annoyed by Dante's shit-eating grin. That guy likes nothing more than instigating shit.

When I get in my room, I turn on some music and relax in bed, hoping to drift off because it will save a few hours of me counting down the minutes until I can go see Sofia.

I do end up drifting off, and I don't know how much later it is when there's a knock on my door. The music is still going and She Wants Revenge's song "Out of Control" is playing. I yawn as I approach the door and swing it open, my mood souring when Aurora's there.

She has on a long coat, so I assume she must've just come from outside. It was nice when I was out there earlier though, so I think she's a little overdressed.

"What's up?" I ask.

She pushes past me, and I close the door.

"What were you doing?" she asks, turning to face me with a smile.

What's up with this new, more pleasant version of her? Did she get a lobotomy at some point over the past few weeks?

"Nothing, I was just lying down." I push a hand through my hair and wait for her to say something. "What's up?" My arms go up at my sides.

"I wanted to talk more about what I was saying before."

A long, drawn-out sigh leaves my lips and I step to the couch, lying on my back. "There's nothing to talk about. I've made it pretty clear that I'm not interested. We'll do what we have to for the sake of producing an heir once we're married, but beyond that . . . I wouldn't expect much."

Honestly, when the time comes, I'll be happy if I can even get hard for her. I might have to use a little blue pill in order to make it happen.

"Oh, come on, Antonio. You can't tell me you're not attracted to me at all."

In general, I like a woman with a certain amount of confidence. But as she struts toward me, swaying her hips, it's all I can do not to laugh at what I think she means to be a sexy walk. She reaches the side of the couch and undoes the tie on her coat, letting it drop to the floor, and I choke on my tongue because she's practically nude. She's wearing a pair of black see-through underwear and a matching bra that her nipples poke out of.

"What the fuck?" I sit up, but she pushes me back down by the shoulders and straddles me.

"I want to be with my fiancé. Is that really so bad?" she purrs, moving her hips so they coast over my dick.

It doesn't even stir at the contact. If this were Sofia above me, half-naked and grinding on me, I'd be as hard as a baseball bat.

"I already told you I'm not interested." I give her my best "don't fuck with me" glare, but she's unaffected.

She bends to place her lips on mine and rubs her tits on my chest, but I grab her shoulders and stop her before she can kiss me.

"Cut the shit, Aurora. What's really going on?"

She gives me the pouty look she's perfected. "I told you. I don't want to wait for the wedding night. Don't act like you're some angel, Antonio. I know you've slept with women before."

"I'm not going to sleep with you. I already told you that."

She laughs off my comment and snakes her arm between us, grabbing my dick through my jeans. I wrap my arms around her and, in one fell swoop, roll us off the couch so we're lying beside it, her under me.

She blinks up at me in shock, mouth open.

I remove my arms from underneath her and roll off her, then glare at her. "If you're so desperate to get laid, go find someone else to do it."

I almost miss it. Almost, but I don't.

The flash of her face falling that's gone in an instant tells me there's way more to this.

"What's going on? Why are you here pretending to want to sleep with me?"

She sits up and raises her chin as if she has any dignity left, sitting there in lingerie after being discarded. "I'm not going to explain myself again."

"You're lying." The corner of her mouth twitching tells me I'm right. "Might as well tell me what's up now. It's gotta be big if you're trying to seduce me."

In a huff, she gets up and yanks her coat off the floor before putting it on and tying it around her waist. When she looks back at me, there are tears in her eyes.

I pin her with a stare and wait for her to decide whether she's going to be stupid or smart about this. Whether she tells me or not, I'll get to the bottom of it. It will be my mission.

"Sorry for giving a shit about this upcoming marriage." She moves to pass me, but I snag her arm and pull her to a stop, meeting her gaze in a game of chicken that she loses.

She blinks and a tear runs down her cheek, unsettling me. I've never seen Aurora cry. Not even in elementary school when she fell off the swings and broke her arm. There's nothing soft about this woman.

"Fine. I'm only telling you because you'll figure it out eventually." She yanks her arm out of my hold and turns to face me fully. "I'm pregnant."

All the blood rushes from my brain because it takes me a moment to put the two words together and make sense of them in this context.

"By who?" There's anger in my voice, but not because I'm jealous. Yeah, it's a double standard, but Aurora is promised to me. And whoever touched her and took her virginity, got her pregnant, will have to answer to me.

"It doesn't matter."

I figure it must be someone from one of the other Italian families, some loser she's embarrassed to admit to fucking. Or maybe she actually cares for him and doesn't want me to rip off his nuts for touching what's mine—whether I want it or not isn't the point.

Then her plan dawns on me and I stop worrying about who the father might be because this bitch . . . "So what? You thought you'd get me to sleep with you so you could say I was the father?" I resist the urge to pin her against the wall and instead fist my hands at my sides. I'm so worked up my heartbeat pulses in my neck. I take a step toward her. "I can't fucking believe you."

I don't have to ask whether she's going to have an abortion or not. She was raised the same way I was. That's not an option.

"Oh, so what? We're going to be married anyway and it's not like you want to touch me. We can just say that this child is ours. We never have to even consummate the marriage now. You'll have your heir."

The distraught woman from minutes ago is gone and she's back to being the woman I know.

I chuckle at her assumption. "Do you actually think I'm going to marry you now? You've given me one of the few outs I have. I should thank you and say congratulations." I look at her with a smug smile.

Her eyes narrow and a grin I don't like crosses her face. "You're still going to marry me."

I can't help but laugh again and shake my head at her. "You're delusional."

"If you don't, I'll tell everyone you've been sleeping with Sofia for months."

My stomach drops to the floor and oozes out of my pant leg.

"That's right. I know all about you two. You think you're being so stealthy, sneaking around." She rolls her eyes. "Please. You two practically eye-fuck each other every time you're around one another. I can't believe Mirabella is so stupid she didn't figure it out herself. It's so obvious you've been sneaking off to her room at night."

Is it possible she's seen me? How does she know? I have no idea. But one thing is clear, she definitely knows.

"Leave Sofia out of this," I warn her with barely restrained fury. My chest is so tight I can barely push the words out.

"She has everything to do with this! If it weren't for her, you probably would have slept with me by now."

"And that would have solved all your problems, wouldn't it? I wouldn't have been the wiser and I'd have raised a child that wasn't mine."

"Oh please, don't act like you're so innocent. You're anything but. And if you don't cooperate, I'll tell everyone how she's been your little whore for months. She'll be ruined. She'll never find a respectable marriage within the family. No one will want her. She'll end up some gangster's goomah and produce bastards for him. Is that what you want for your little angel?" Her voice is filled with vitriol, and she'll make good on her promise. Aurora is totally the kind of woman who will take others down with her no matter the cost.

I hate that everything she's saying is true. Sofia will be ruined. Everything she hoped for in her future will be out of reach, at least out of reach in the way that she wants it.

The urge to scream presses against my vocal cords, but I somehow refrain.

What's my better option? To go along with Aurora's plan and say the child is mine and never have to touch her or tell the truth and be free of her? The problem with the latter is that even though I'd be free of Aurora, I still couldn't have Sofia. She'd be looked at as unpure. People would question whether she's slept with anyone else . . .

An image of the tie with the Irish colors flashes across my mind.

She still might not be accepted by my family as worthy of being the don's wife and she'd be ruined anyway.

Fuck!

I need to do what I have to in order to protect Sofia's future, as hard as it is. And I want to enjoy the small amount of time I still have with Sofia.

"Fine. We'll pretend the child is mine and you won't breathe a word about me and Sofia to anyone else. But I don't want your pregnancy coming out until after the wedding. Agreed?"

Though I'd never hit a woman, the urge is so strong when I see the self-satisfied grin slowly form on Aurora's face because she's gotten what she wanted.

"Agreed," she says with a nod. "Glad you came to the correct conclusion."

"Get out of my room. I can't stand to look at you anymore."

"That's fine, I'll go. But make sure you keep things more discreet with Sofia from here on out. I don't want gossip flying around that my fiancé is sticking his dick in Little Miss Goody Two-Shoes."

I don't even respond to the insult to Sofia. If I open my mouth and address Aurora, I'm liable to rage and then everyone will know our business.

But the minute she's out of the room, I take my phone from my pocket and throw it against the door, where it shatters to the floor in pieces.

I stand, breathing heavily, trying to gather my thoughts. I need to talk to someone, and I don't have a lot of options. It can't be my sister. She'd no doubt use this pregnancy to ruin Aurora and, in the process, ruin her best friend. Mira can be shortsighted at times. I can't talk to Sofia about it for obvious reasons. That leaves one person.

I go knock on Tommaso's door, but he's not there. Again.

Where the fuck is he spending his time these days?

As if I don't have enough to deal with. With a frustrated growl, I step away from the door and stomp to the stairwell, taking the steps two at a time until I reach the fifth floor. I don't bother knocking when I get to Sofia's door. I just take the ever-present key from my pocket and let myself in.

She's not there, must still be downstairs.

That's okay. I feel a little calmer just being surrounded by her things, her scent.

I'll wait. I have no choice. She's what I need.

CHAPTER THIRTY
SOFIA

After saying goodbye to everyone in the lounge, I make my way up to my room. I have some homework I need to finish before Antonio arrives tonight.

I enter my dorm room, and I'm surprised he's already here, standing in the center, staring at me with an intense, raw need. He says nothing as he stalks over to me, cups my face, and brings his lips to mine. He devours me—there's no other word for it. This kiss is filled with a desperation I don't understand, and when he pulls away, studying my face and tracing his fingertips down my cheek, that same desperation is reflected in his eyes.

"I need you." His voice is hoarse and filled with vulnerability.

One of my hands goes to his cheek, the other into the hair at the back of his head. "I'm here. I'm here."

It seems to be what he needs to hear because a look of relief passes over his features and he kisses me again.

We're naked within minutes, barely able to stop kissing while we undress the other as though having our lips on each other's is providing us with oxygen to breathe.

Antonio picks me up and walks me to the bed, never once diverting his eyes from my gaze. Somehow, he makes it there without stumbling, as if he's memorized the path. He sets me down before he climbs on top of me, and I part my legs. Antonio holds himself up with his elbows and studies my face, his fingertips lightly brushing over all my features as though he's trying to memorize them. Then he gently rocks into me with a sigh.

His pace is slow and steady but somehow still intense. I not only feel my orgasm building in my core, but my chest expands. As if it's being so shoved full of feelings, they have nowhere to go.

"Sei la mia vita," he whispers, bringing his lips to my forehead. "La mia anima." His mouth trails a path up the side of my neck to my ear. "Cuore mio."

My eyes sting with unshed tears, listening to this man pour his heart out to me. Before I can return the sentiment, his lips are on mine. I pour everything I'm feeling, everything I've ever felt for this man into our kiss, and when he pulls away, I cup his face.

"Antonio . . ."

He shakes his head. "Don't say it. Don't. It will make it too hard."

I suck back the words—that I love him—and nod in understanding. If I hear him tell me he loves me, will I be able to let him go? This feels like a shift in our relationship to another level and a goodbye all in one.

As he pushes and pulls himself in and out of my body, my climax draws nearer and nearer. When it hits me, rather than feeling as though I'm being shot out of a cannon, it feels like a slow rolling wave overtaking me and I'm lost under an ocean of bliss until I breach the surface and come up for air.

Antonio holds himself inside me, groaning with an expression of pure rapture as he empties himself inside me, then he collapses on top of me. It's only seconds before he rolls us over so that I'm lying on him. We're still connected.

Neither of us speaks. We lie there holding one another, basking in our lovemaking. It feels almost as though we'll break the spell if one of us utters a word.

I drift off in the afternoon sun that streaks across my dorm room, lying in the arms of the man I love, wishing we could stay like this forever.

* * *

MONDAY NIGHT AT the dining hall, Aurora is all over Antonio again. It's enough to kill my appetite, but I force down some food, trying to act as normal as always.

Mira sits with us and gives me a few looks through dinner as though she feels sorry for me. It doesn't make the situation any better. Antonio is in no way encouraging Aurora. He never does, but the fact that she's the one who holds the *right* to touch him in public stings like the lash of a whip.

It's just the four of us at the table. Mira and I came early in the hopes of avoiding Antonio and Aurora. He must have had the same idea.

Aurora barely touches her dinner. In fact, she's mostly just moving it around her plate, from what I see.

After the four of us sit in strained silence for over a minute, Mira pipes up beside me. "What's up, Aurora? Trying to lose a few extra pounds before the big day?"

"I don't have a few extra pounds to lose. You, on the other hand, might want to get started on your diet. Our wedding isn't far off now, is it, sweetie?" She pulls Antonio's hand to her.

He looks as though he wants to rip it away, which is some consolation, but just seeing her touch him makes me want to vomit.

"As if." Mira glares.

"I'm feeling a little nauseous, if you must know."

Antonio stiffens, and I look between them with some sort of sixth sense drawing my attention.

"How come?" I ask her.

Aurora directs her cunning smile at me. "Can you keep a secret?"

"Aurora—" Antonio says, eyes wide.

She leans in. "I'm pregnant," she whispers.

The floor drops out from under me. That's the only explanation for why I'm falling with no end in sight.

Mira jolts out of her seat and leans in over the table. "What did you say?"

My gaze snaps to Antonio, waiting for him to say it's not true, but he looks away from me. Bile races up my throat and I swallow it back.

"You heard me." Aurora takes Antonio's hand on the table and intertwines their fingers. "We weren't expecting for it to happen quite so fast, but we should be okay to keep it under wraps until after the wedding. It's still early days." She smiles at him as though they couldn't ask for a happier surprise, while Antonio's face is a blank slate.

"Excuse me." I stand. "I just remembered that I have something I have to do."

"Don't run off, Sofia. Don't you want to congratulate us?" Her thrilled laugh echoes after me as I race out of the dining hall.

"Sofia! Wait!"

Mira's voice sounds behind me, but I don't stop running. I can't. I need to be anywhere but here, in this reality where the man I love lied to me and betrayed me for months. I keep running until my legs burn and each breath pulls fire into my lungs. Then I stop and bend at the waist, the tears unwilling to stay at bay.

A hand rubs my back and Mira bends beside me. I straighten and so does she. Her arms wrap around me in a tight embrace. Tears leak out, free-falling down my cheeks.

"I'm sorry, Sofia. I'm so sorry." She squeezes me harder the more tears that come.

I pull away and wipe my face. "You have nothing to be sorry for. This isn't your fault. This is me and my stupid heart that got me into this position."

A pair of Russian girls scoot past us on the path, eyeing us curiously.

Mira wraps an arm around my shoulders. "Come on. Let's go back to your room, where we'll have some more privacy."

I move but shake my head. "Not my room. He'll come looking for me there . . . if he comes looking at all."

"My room then."

I nod morosely. Less than five minutes later, Mira unlocks the door to her and Marcelo's room. Thankfully, he's not there.

"He's probably gone to dinner with the guys," she says.

I nod and head straight for the couch, where I flop down and bury my face in the cushions, letting the tears loose again. Mira sits on the edge and rubs my back while I sob.

"He told me she didn't mean anything to him . . . that they weren't sleeping together."

She sighs and gives me a pitying look. "Did you see how much she enjoyed telling us? God, she's so evil."

"She knew it would piss you off." Poor Aurora doesn't even know that she scored bonus points with me and my reaction, though she's probably wondering where the fire is with how I raced out of there.

"I'm so sorry."

I take her hand. "Stop apologizing. This isn't on you. It's on him. And on me because I was stupid enough to believe the lies he told me." That makes a certain type of dread settle in my stomach. "Maybe it was all a lie."

How he pretended to care for me, to make love to me . . . maybe I was just another body to get his rocks off. Maybe he has a thing for virgins.

I can't even say the thought out loud. It's too painful.

"I'm going to kill him," she seethes.

I sit up and shake my head. "No, this has nothing to do with the two of you. This is between him and me."

"The hell it is—"

A knock sounds at the door and we freeze and look at each other. Neither of us moves. Then another knock comes, followed shortly after by Antonio's voice.

"I know you're in there, Mira. Open the damn door before I bust it down."

Mira eyes me as though waiting for me to tell her what to do. I nod sharply.

Might as well get the inevitable over with. I knew there would be an ending to this thing between us eventually. I just didn't think it would be this soon or this painful. But maybe it was always going to be this painful, regardless of the circumstances.

Begrudgingly, Mira gets up off the couch and opens the door. Antonio pushes past her as soon as the door is cracked open and stops when he sees me on the couch, staring at me with something in his eyes—what, I can't quite tell.

Maybe I never could. I once thought love lived there, true deep feelings, and obviously, I was way off the mark.

"You're a piece of shit." Mira whirls, slamming the door. "You can tell *your fiancée* that she can forget me being a bridesmaid at your wedding. I don't care what people think."

"Get the fuck out of here, Mira." He doesn't break eye contact with me.

I glance at Mira and she's infuriated. Her face is red. "This is my fucking room!"

"Mira." Her head snaps in my direction. "Can we talk alone, please?" I ask.

She draws in a deep breath through her nose and looks between the two of us, turning silently before leaving.

Antonio and I continue our standoff, staring at each other, neither of us saying a word.

Finally, I break the silence. "When did you find out?"

He hesitates before speaking. "Yesterday." Only now does he drop his gaze from mine to look at the floor.

That's why he came to me so desperately yesterday afternoon. He knew it would be our last time together.

I press a hand to my stomach and try to suck in some air. Antonio steps toward me and I bolt up from the couch, arm outstretched. "Don't come any closer."

My words seem as though they hit him like a dagger if his expression is anything to go by. I've never denied him.

"She wasn't supposed to tell anyone until after the wedding."

My eyes narrow. "Is that supposed to make me feel better somehow? You told me there was nothing between you two. You said you weren't sleeping with her."

His hand fists at his side. Open. Closed. Open. Closed. "I'm sorry."

My hands fly out to my sides and now I'm bridging the distance between us, pushing him in the chest. "You're sorry? That's all you have to say is that you're sorry?"

He catches my wrists and holds me in place. We're inches apart, both breathing heavily, staring at the other. But unlike a day earlier, I have no desire to kiss this man—I'd rather spit in his face.

I rip my wrists from his hold and step back. "Was any of it real, or was it all a big lie?"

A pained look crosses his face, and he pushes his hand through his hair, but he says nothing.

Some sort of sound echoes through the room. I think it's coming from me.

"You don't even have the balls to admit that this meant nothing to you." A caustic laugh leaves my lips. "Just leave, Antonio. I don't know why you bothered chasing after me in the first place."

He opens his mouth as if he wants to say something, eyes full of despair, but he snaps his jaw shut, a look of resolve twisting his features. "Take care, Sofia."

Those are his parting words before the shattered pieces of my heart crush underneath his feet as he walks out of the room.

"Go fuck yourself, Antonio!" I yell as the door shuts behind him.

CHAPTER THIRTY-ONE
ANTONIO

I never should have trusted Aurora to keep her mouth shut. She's cruel to the core.

Most people would say I'm not a good person because of the things I have to do as a member of the Mafia, but there's a difference between Aurora and me. I do what I have to in order to survive and for the good of the family. Aurora gets some sick sort of pleasure from causing people pain, riling them up.

Which was exactly her goal when she announced the pregnancy at dinner tonight.

God, the look on Sofia's face when the words left Aurora's mouth. I felt as if someone had poured bleach down my throat.

It was even worse being alone in that room with Sofia standing in the crater that was the aftermath of the bomb Aurora had detonated.

I wanted to tell Sofia I love her. That I know beyond a doubt that I will never feel for anyone the way I feel for her. That leaving her hurting in that room and knowing I was the cause felt like ripping off a limb.

But I couldn't. It's better for her if she hates me. It will make it easier for her to move on. And with her reputation intact, she'll be able to find someone worthy of her.

"Fuck!" I punch the wall in the room and my fist flies through the drywall from the force, leaving a jagged hole of damage behind.

The pain in my fist doesn't even register because of the pain in my chest.

Before I can think much about it, I'm out of my room and barging into Tommaso's. He looks up from where he's typing something into his phone on his bed. His eyes flare, and he tosses the phone aside.

"Hey, man. What's up?"

Something about his reaction to seeing me makes the hair on the back of my neck stand on edge.

"What are you doing?" I ask, nodding toward the phone.

He shrugs. "Nothing." Then his forehead creases. "What happened to your fist?"

I glance down and see that my knuckles are red and scraped up. I hadn't even noticed.

I came in here with one purpose—to ease my burdened soul—but now I have another. I've let this weird shit with him linger too long anyway.

"What's going on with you?"

He straightens where he sits. "What do you mean? My dad was just tortured and murdered, isn't it obvious?" His expression challenges me to suggest otherwise.

I will. "Cut the shit. What's really going on? You've been acting weird, you're barely in your room, and you looked like a kid caught with his hand in the headmaster's daughter's panties when I walked in."

"You're losing it, man. Nothing's going on."

I am not in the mood for this. With two long strides, I eat up the space between us and grab him by his shirt, hauling him up off the bed.

"What the fuck?" he shouts.

"Tell me what the hell is going on. Otherwise, my mind is going to go to some places you'd probably prefer it didn't."

Does he know something about his dad and his death that he's not telling me? Were Tommaso and his dad involved in something he doesn't want me to know about?

"Nothing—"

I punch him in the face before he can even finish speaking and let him drop. "I'm not in the fucking mood. Tell me what you're hiding."

Eyes narrowed, he looks up at me from the floor and wipes his lip with the back of his hand. "Fine. I'm fucking that hot Russian chick."

I study him for a beat before I realize he's telling the truth. When I hold out my hand to help him up, he takes it.

"You're fucking a Russian after they killed your father? You in love with her or something?"

"I'm fucking her *because* I thought they killed my father, but now I'm not so sure."

"Explain." I cross my arms.

He sighs and flops down to sit on the edge of the mattress. "I could tell she was attracted to me, so I made it happen. Figured after a good fuck or two, a little pillow talk wouldn't be far behind."

I arch an eyebrow. "And?"

"Nothing. Either she doesn't know anything, or they had nothing to do with it. I'm not sure which."

So we're no closer to knowing what the fuck is going on and whether the missing weapons are somehow tied to Leo's murder.

"You're lucky no one else found out. Dimitri and his crew would've cut your dick off if they knew you've been banging one of their girls."

He shrugs. "I'd like to see them try."

"End it." When his mouth drops open, I add, "Immediately."

His jaw flexes, mouth tight, but he nods.

Then I punch him in the face again and he falls back onto the mattress.

"What the fuck was that for?" he shouts, holding his jaw.

"For fucking someone from one of the other houses and for not bringing me in on the plan. You're lucky I didn't find out and think you're disloyal. Don't keep shit from me again."

"Fine. I deserve that." He gets up off the bed and heads into his bathroom and grabs a hand towel, then he goes to the small fridge and pulls some ice out of the freezer portion and sets it in the middle of the towel before holding it against his face where I hit him. "What'd you come in here for anyway?" His voice is muffled behind the towel.

I say the first thing that comes to mind. "Wanted to see if you were paired with anyone for orientation day."

This Friday and Saturday, students who will attend the school for the first time next year are welcomed to campus and paired up with someone to show them around. Saturday night, there's a dance as the capstone to the whole two-day event.

"Yeah, I ended up with Riccardo Rizzo. Remember that guy? We used to screw around with him when he was a freshman in high school and we were seniors."

I chuckle, remembering some of the shit we used to pull. "I got Paolo Caruso. Guess I got luckier than you."

"Seems that way."

We settle into silence for a beat before I say his name. When he looks me in the eye, I make him a promise I intend to keep. "We'll figure out what happened with your dad and we'll make them pay."

"Hai promesso?"

With a nod, I respond, "Prometto."

I can't do anything to ease Sofia's pain, but at least I can help my best friend.

CHAPTER THIRTY-TWO

SOFIA

After my world explodes on Monday, I miss three days of school, pretending to be sick and not leaving my room. Mira takes care of me and brings me all my meals and hangs out with me to keep me company and keep my mind from wandering too much.

It's nice to spend more time with her, but it dawns on me that sometimes you get what you wish for but not in the way you want it. I've been missing my best friend all semester and wanting to spend more time with her, but not because I was heartbroken and she felt sorry for me.

On Friday, I have no choice but to rally. Today the new students for next year are on campus and I've been paired with someone from the La Rosa crime family. I'll act as her mentor for the next two days. I don't know much about Anna Bernardi except that her father is a soldier in my father's crew.

We all meet up in the auditorium to find our pair, and I'm proud of the way I don't even glance in Antonio's direction once I know where he's standing. Mira sits beside me, and when she sees me noticing him and looking away, she takes my hand and squeezes. As far as I know, she hasn't spoken to her brother since Monday, but I haven't asked. It's like an unspoken rule between us that we'll avoid the topic of her brother.

It's just the Italians here. The Irish have already been in and paired up, and the Russians will come after us, then the cartel and the politicians' kids.

We're waiting for things to start when Marcelo and Giovanni join us. Giovanni says a quick hello and chooses to sit on the opposite side of Marcelo, who's beside Mira. That's pretty much how it's been since I broke things off with him.

Anger pours into my chest like someone's pouring hot tea when I realize that it's possible that I ruined what could have been a good thing with Giovanni because I was so obsessed with Antonio.

"Feeling better, Sofia?" Marcelo asks and looks between Mira and me.

I'm sure he knows something more is up than me not feeling well with how much time Mira's been spending with me.

"Much, thank you. Is your sister going to be here?" I ask.

Marcelo's younger sister, Aria, is due to start at the academy next year.

He lets out a long-suffering sigh. "Yep, there she is." He raises his hand.

I turn in the direction he's looking and see Aria making her way over. She has the same dark hair and eyes as he does and she smiles when she spots us, rushing over.

"Hey, guys." She takes a seat beside me.

I like Aria. She's always been sweet the few times I've met her since Mira and Marcelo were engaged.

"Excited for this weekend?" I ask.

She nods enthusiastically. "A weekend of freedom, are you kidding me? I'm counting the days until I get to move into the dorm next year." Aria grins wide.

"Don't get too excited," Marcelo says with clear warning in his voice.

Mira swats him. "Leave her alone. It's okay for Aria to be excited. I was."

"That's what I'm afraid of," Marcelo grumbles and turns to talk to Giovanni.

I return my attention to Aria. "Do you know who you're paired with?"

She nods, pressing her lips together as though she's trying to keep herself from smiling, then she leans in and says in a quiet voice, "Gabriele Vitale."

My eyes widen and I glance at Marcelo to see if he overheard, but he's still talking to Giovanni.

Mira, however, is looking at me questioningly. "What?" she mouths.

I whisper in her ear, "Aria's matched with Gabe."

Mira leans back with wide eyes and stares at me for a beat.

Gabriele is next in line to run the Vitale crime family in the Northwest portion of the country. He's some kind of computer hacker genius—which is saying a lot because Mira is pretty good herself—but no one knows much about him. He keeps a low profile on campus and rumors are always swirling about him.

One thing I know for sure is that Marcelo won't be happy that his sister has been matched with Gabe.

Aria leans over me and whispers to us both, "Don't tell him." She nods at her brother. "He'll try to ruin it for me."

"He's going to find out," Mira says.

"Find out what?" Marcelo asks.

"What I have planned for Mira's bachelorette party," I say with as much enthusiasm as I can muster—given the state of my heart, it isn't much. But it seems to appease him.

Still, Marcelo gives me a weird look and goes back to talking with Giovanni.

Shortly after that, Chancellor Thompson begins, thanking everyone for coming and talking about what a meaningful thing it is to have current students showing new students around and giving them an idea of what campus life is like.

I zone out about halfway through his speech, my mind running over and over what it felt like the last time Antonio touched me. The look in his eyes as he hovered over me and made love to me. How can all of that have been fake?

When I can't stop myself and I glance toward where he's sitting about twenty feet from me with Aurora and Tommaso, it feels as if my newly mended glass heart shatters all over again because he's staring at me with eyes full of regret.

Regret that he hurt me or regret that he started something with me in the first place?

Aurora leans in and says something to him, and his attention snaps back to the chancellor finishing up his speech.

"To our new students, if you have any problems while you're on campus for the next couple of days, don't hesitate to come see me. I know it can be overwhelming and an adjustment, but my team and I are here to help. You've all been partnered, and I suspect some of you will know the person you've been partnered with. If that's the case, when I'm done speaking, you can make your way to them if you see them. If not, just head to the front of the room and we'll get you paired off. Thanks, everyone. We'll see you all at tomorrow night's dance."

There are murmurs through the crowd as people move, pairing off where they can. I know what Anna looks like, but I don't see her, so I suppose I'll head to the front and look for her.

Before I do that though, I spot Gabe strolling toward us, hands in his pockets and looking pretty relaxed for a man who's about to piss off the don of the Costa crime family. I decide to stick around for a minute in case Aria needs backup.

Gabe's let his facial hair grow. His cognac-colored eyes divert to Aria when he reaches us.

"You lost or something, Vitale?" Marcelo says, standing.

Gabriele gives Marcelo the once-over. "Not at all." Then he turns his attention back to Aria, who's practically beaming under his gaze. "Ready?"

Marcelo shoulders his way between them. "What do you mean ready?"

Gabriele sighs as though he expected this reaction. "Aria and I are partnered together. And don't get on my ass. I had nothing to do with it. I asked administration about it, and apparently, there were more girls than guys this year and the numbers didn't match up." He shrugs.

Mirabella steps forward and sets her hand on Marcelo's chest, giving him a look that says he should let it go.

"You keep your hands to yourself, or else I'll cut them off," Marcelo says through a clenched jaw.

Gabriele guffaws. "I told you I'm not into kids, Costa."

Aria's demeanor deflates and I wish I could say something to make her feel better, but I know better than anyone how much a man can hurt you. The best I could do for her is to warn her not to get her expectations up.

I wish someone had warned me.

CHAPTER THIRTY-THREE
ANTONIO

My Friday and Saturday are spent showing Paolo around campus. He has a million fucking questions that I don't feel like answering, but I decide to use his presence for what it is—a distraction from thinking about Sofia and an excuse not to have to be around Aurora.

But the moment we step into the dance on Saturday night, I've had enough. Tommaso's had enough of Riccardo too, so we tell them both to take a hike and go mingle. Somewhere, anywhere but where we are.

"I'm glad we only have one more year of showing freshmen around," Tommaso says to me, pulling a flask from the inside of his suit pocket. "Want some?"

"Where'd you get that?" I glance around to make sure none of the administration is watching.

"I have my ways." He unscrews the cap and takes a swig before passing it over.

I take a quick nip and pass it back. "Vodka?" I arch an eyebrow.

"Relax, I got it from the Russian before I ended things." He puts the cap back on and slides it into his jacket.

We're still standing near the door, so it's impossible to miss when Sofia walks in with my sister and Marcelo and his crew. She looks phenomenal. Of course she does. She always does.

Sofia's makeup is a little heavier than normal but not overdone, and she's wearing a black body-con dress that accentuates her curves. I notice more than a few guys watching as she makes her entrance.

"Hey, guys," Tommaso says when he sees them and Marcelo. Being none the wiser, he leads them all in our direction. "How'd it go with your freshmen?"

Marcelo doesn't bother answering his question. "You guys see my sister and Vitale yet?"

"Can't say that we have." I dart my gaze toward Sofia, but she refuses to look at me.

Marcelo looks back at Giovanni, Andrea, and Lorenzo. "I wanna know where the hell they are. Spread out and find them. Text me when you do."

No one argues with him, and they all take off in different directions.

"I'll catch up with you in a bit," he says to Mira and places a chaste kiss on her temple before taking off.

Tommaso laughs beside me. "Now I know the best way to get under his skin."

Mira rolls her eyes. "Don't even start. It's all I've had to listen to since yesterday. I told him she's a big girl and can make decisions for herself."

Tommaso opens his suit jacket pocket and pulls up the flask so the girls can see it. "Either of you want some?"

Mira shakes her head. "I need my wits about me in case Marcelo gets into it with Gabriele tonight."

Sofia surprises me by grabbing the flask. "Thanks." She removes the lid and gulps back a healthy portion before pulling it from her lips and cringing.

"Never knew you were such a big drinker, Sofia." Tommaso smiles and takes the flask from her.

"People just drive you to drink, you know? Excuse me, I'm going to mingle." She takes off.

My sister gives me a scathing look before following her.

Tommaso turns toward me. "What's up with that?"

"What do you mean?" I shift in place.

"She was kinda cold, no? Sofia's normally so nice and bubbly. Your sister was off too, but Mira's always temperamental."

I shrug. "How am I supposed to know what the hell is going on with her?"

He raises his hands. "Sorry, man, my bad."

My night gets worse when Aurora sidles up beside me, hooking her arm around mine. She leans into me as if we're a happy couple. "Hey, honey."

"Hey." I don't even spare her a glance but continue looking through the crowd to see if I can spot Sofia and whoever she's talking to.

A quick glance at Tommaso and I see that he's looking between Aurora and me, sensing the tension radiating off us.

"I'll see you two later." He takes off before I force him to stay so that I'm not alone with Aurora.

"I haven't seen you since yesterday. How was your time with your freshman?" she asks.

I give her a derisive glance. "Let's not pretend to be cordial when no one's around, okay? I don't have the energy for it."

She presses her lips together in a thin line. "You can't act like this forever, you know."

I arch an eyebrow. "Like what?"

"Like I took your favorite toy away. At some point, you're going to have to accept that we're going to be together."

I lean and speak directly into her ear. Her perfume is cloying. "I have accepted it, and that's the only reason I'm going along with your little plan. Don't think that's ever going to mean I'll be happy about it or happy about being stuck with you."

Before she can respond, I head off through the crowd. I'd rather talk to anyone other than her, even my freshman.

I catch a glimpse of Sofia. She's standing with Tommaso, taking a pull from his flask again. I don't know why that irks me so much. Maybe it's the idea that she'll get drunk and lose control and consider messing around with someone. Maybe it's just her being in proximity to another man, even if it is my best friend.

By the time I've made it over there, Sofia is gone and Tommaso is chatting up some other girl. Disappointment flares in my chest.

The next hour goes by with me trying to catch glimpses of Sofia through the crowd without anyone noticing. A few times, I feel my sister's narrowed gaze on me, but when I look at her, she looks away as though she can't stand the sight of me.

The first slow song of the night comes on, and of course, Aurora approaches me immediately.

"Let's dance." She takes my hand and drags me out onto the dance floor.

No piece of me wants to, but it's part of the role I play for my family. All the other factions are here, and they need to see a united La Rosa family. We can't show any sign of weakness. So even though I feel sick inside, I wrap my arms around my fiancée and dance.

On our fifth rotation, I spot Sofia standing at the edge of the dance floor. She's with Tommaso again and he's handing her the flask. She glances our way while she takes a swig and I look away. I feel so ashamed standing here holding Aurora in front of her.

"Would you stop looking at her like a sad little puppy dog?" Aurora snipes as we slow dance.

"Fuck off. I'm already going along with your lie. It doesn't mean I have to like it."

"No, but it does mean you have to sell it."

I shake my head and look away from her, back at Sofia.

"Kiss me."

I stop dancing and stare at Aurora. "Are you kidding me?"

She shakes her head. "Kiss me. People need to think we're in love. Especially those two over there who know about the baby. And who knows whether your sister's told Marcelo." She nods toward where my sister now stands next to Sofia with Marcelo.

"He doesn't know." I dance again.

"How can you be sure?"

"I can tell. You wouldn't have to worry about it at this point anyway if you'd stuck to our deal." I'm seething, remembering the devastation on Sofia's face in the dining hall when Aurora dropped the news.

"I had to make sure you didn't get any crazy ideas like ditching me for Sofia. You can blame yourself and the way you moon over her." She rolls her eyes.

"I don't want to hear her name out of your mouth anymore. Do you understand me?"

Aurora meets my gaze. "Kiss me, or I blow up your lover's life. And you'd better sell it."

There's no question she's serious. She might go down if her secret comes out and I couldn't care less about that, but she'll inflict as much damage as she can on her way down.

So I dip my head to hers, my stomach turning over, and bring my lips to hers. Her hand comes into my hair and it's all wrong. These fingers have long, fake nails and I miss the feel of Sofia's short, natural nails. The mouth is all wrong. Instead of Sofia's pillowy lips, these feel hard and thin under mine. And the taste of her tongue makes repulsion flow through my veins like thick tar.

When I pull away from Aurora, I instinctively glance at Sofia and it's like a bullet to the chest. She's staring at us, eyes glistening with so much devastation on her face I want to strangle the woman in my arms for forcing me to hurt the woman I love in order to protect her.

I've done a lot of terrible things in my life, but somehow this feels like the worst.

CHAPTER THIRTY-FOUR

SOFIA

I know I've drunk a lot, but I blink a few times to be sure I'm seeing what I think I am—Antonio and Aurora on the dance floor, kissing.

Not just kissing, making out.

It's not like I didn't know they'd been physical with each other—she's pregnant, for God's sake—but this is the first time Antonio has really returned her affection in front of me.

My hand goes to my stomach. I'm going to be sick, but I can't stop myself from staring at them.

"Are you okay?" Mira leans in and asks me.

The bass from the song pounds in my chest, or maybe that's my heart trying to leap out of my rib cage and commit suicide by diving onto the floor.

Antonio pulls away from Aurora and his eyes find mine.

Why?

To make sure he's inflicted even more pain? To make sure I've received the message that I never really meant anything to him and he's where he wants to be? I have no idea, but I can't be here and bear witness to the man I'm woefully still in love with, twisting the dagger through the scar tissue on my heart.

"I have to use the bathroom," I say to no one and everyone around me.

"I'll come with you." Mira grabs my hand, but I pull away.

"No, I'm fine. I'll be right back."

She gives me a look like she's not sure if she should let me leave, but she has no choice as I pull away and Marcelo moves to ask her something over the music.

I'm more unsteady on my feet than I realize, and I have to work to walk in a straight line toward the entrance. The only thing that could make this night even worse would be someone from administration realizing I'm drunk.

When I make it into the hall, I don't go into the bathroom. I continue walking to the end and push through the double doors into the night. It's not overly warm, but the air isn't cold and being out of the same room as Antonio helps me feel as though I can breathe a little better.

I wander for a bit, doing my best to navigate the pathway in my inebriation until I make it to the semicircle courtyard on the other end of the school. There's an inlaid brick patio in the center and it's surrounded by hedges. On the other side of the hedges are a series of benches that line the greenery, and that's where I head.

My legs are tired from walking this much in heels and I just want to sit down. When I reach the benches, I lie down on one, staring at the night sky. Stars twinkle against the black backdrop, and I wonder what it would feel like to be all the way up there. Would the pain still feel as raw and real if I were millions of light-years away?

Of course it would. No amount of distance from the source of my pain will make it go away. A part of me thinks that I'll be carrying this agony around with me for eternity.

Tears silently stream down the sides of my face into my ears. Eventually my lids grow heavy and my breathing evens out and I pass out.

* * *

SOMETHING STARTLES ME awake and it takes me a moment to realize what it is. The sound of people arguing. I'm still lying on the bench. It sounds as if they're on the other side of the hedge and have no idea I'm here. Should I try to creep away without them noticing or make my presence known and excuse myself?

"I don't know what you're getting so bent out of shape about."

Wait . . . was that . . . is that Aurora's voice?

"Bullshite." The distinct Irish accent makes me stop breathing. What is she doing out here talking to one of the Irish?

"You're making out with him now?" he says, a clear accusation in his voice.

"We are engaged."

"And what about us?"

I press my lips together to stop myself from making a sound. There's an *us* between her and him? One of the Irish? Does Antonio know?

"I told you it was over with us last week. What didn't you understand?" Aurora's voice holds all the anger and disgust I'm used to hearing from her.

"So that's it then? You've had yer fill and we're done."

It's only now that I realize it's Conor's voice. Conor, who's part of our threesome for our group project. But they acted as though they didn't know each other. I'm so confused, the vodka from earlier still swirling through my veins and making it difficult for my brain to make the connections it needs to.

"We'll talk when we have to, but beyond that, yeah, we're done," she says.

What the hell is going on?

He chuckles, but it doesn't sound as though he finds what she said funny. "I suppose we will. I guess there's not much left to say then, but thanks fer the fun. I'll see you around."

I hear his heavy footsteps head off into the night, then a grunt of frustration from Aurora before the sound of her heels clicking on the brick patio grows more and more distant.

I wait at least ten minutes before I sit up on the bench and look around. I'm alone again.

What the hell just happened?

I don't even know how long I've been out here. I didn't want to carry a purse tonight, so I didn't bring my phone with me.

One thing is for certain, Aurora is up to no good. I mean, it's not as if I didn't already know that, but this is on a level that surprises even me. There's a decision to be made . . . do I keep my mouth shut and stay out of it? Do I tell my best friend and let her do what she thinks is best with the information, or do I do what I know I should and tell Antonio?

He's the highest ranking of the La Rosa family here on campus and therefore is the one I should bring the information to. If something goes down and my father finds out I had information and didn't pass it along, he'll be more than disappointed in me. He'd probably disown me.

"Oh my god!" My hand flies up to my mouth.

What if Antonio isn't the father of Aurora's baby? The conversation I overheard definitely made it sound as though she and Conor had something going on. What if Conor is the father? Would that even change anything? I mean, it could if he wanted it to. But Antonio obviously has feelings for Aurora since he was sleeping with her and lying to me about it.

I push up off the bench and start on the path in the direction of the Roma House. What I should do is clear to me, but it means being alone with the man I yearn for and can no longer have. But what if this changes everything?

One thing is for certain—sneaking around and lying brought me nothing but heartbreak. Maybe the truth will piece my heart back together.

* * *

I KNOCK ON Antonio's door early the next morning. A restless sleep caused me to wake early and I figure most people will be sleeping late today. I don't really want anyone spotting me going into his room.

It takes a second knock before his door swings open. He's bleary-eyed and midyawn, wearing a pair of pajama pants. The curls on top of his head are chaotic and unruly and he blinks a few times as if he thinks I'm a mirage.

My gaze roams his muscled chest and I remember how it felt to have it pressed to my bare breasts while he thrust inside me.

"What are you doing here?" He doesn't seem happy to see me outside his door, but I don't really care.

I don't wait for him to invite me in before I push past him. "We need to talk."

He releases an exasperated sigh, then the door clicks closed. "We've already done that. There's nothing left to say."

He crosses his arms, mouth in a thin line, and widens his stance as though he's ready for a fight. He's fully turned on his intimidating mafioso persona, but it's not going to stop me from saying what I came here to.

"It's not about us. I have to tell you something I heard last night."

With a sigh, he walks back to the bed and flops down on it, leaning forward with his elbows on his knees. "Make it quick."

I push back the hurt and start in on why I came here. "Last night when I left the dance . . ." Our eyes catch and hold because we both know it was due to his public make-out session with Aurora. "After I left, I wandered around outside and ended up in one of the courtyards. You know the one that has the semicircle with all the hedges around it?"

"Are you quizzing me on the geography of the campus grounds?"

My lips press together in annoyance before I continue. "Anyway, I laid down on one of the benches and I must've fallen asleep."

"You mean passed out?"

I ignore him. "I woke up to two people arguing on the other side of the hedge. They had no idea I was there. It was . . . it was Aurora and that Conor guy we're doing the project with in embezzlement class. The one from Dublin House."

He doesn't say anything, but I can tell he's now zeroed in on what I'm saying.

"It sounded like Conor was jealous because she'd been . . . kissing you." I can barely get my mouth to shape the word *kissing*, let alone push the words past my lips. "They sort of argued for a bit. I don't know, it was weird."

He stands from the bed and walks toward me. "Jesus, you're pathetic."

My head rocks back and my eyes sting as if he struck me. "What?" The word is barely a whisper.

"You come here making shit up about my fiancée? Are you hoping that I'll believe you and call the wedding off and marry you?"

The derision on his face, coupled with his words, makes my knees almost give out.

He steps closer to me. "Listen, the two of us were good together in the sack, no doubt, but I was never going to be with you, let alone marry you. You need to let this little girl fantasy you have about the two of us go and move on. Stop trying to cause trouble in my relationship with Aurora. We're having a child together. We're going to get married."

"But what if the baby isn't yours?" I'm hopeful my words sink in.

Antonio rocks his head back in laughter. "Are you really that desperate? I'm telling you, Sofia, if you repeat this bullshit to anyone else, there will be consequences and you won't like them. Do you understand me?"

The way he looks at me . . . it's like he's not the same man I allowed into my body. I don't know this man. This version of him is 100 percent the leader of a crime family and not my Antonio.

"Do you understand me?" he asks again through his teeth.

I nod weakly, but my own anger takes hold and turns from a small flicker of a flame into a forest fire. He can pretend all he wants that what we shared was small and insignificant, but he forgets one thing—I was there too. And I know that what we had was real, for however short of a time we had it.

"You know what, Antonio? You can lie to yourself all you want, but I know that what we shared was real. Even if it's over now, even if you have something with Aurora, we were real. You can't ever take that away from me. So go fuck yourself if you want to say otherwise."

I push past him with tears in my eyes, but I refuse to let him see them fall. There's a chance I will never really get over what I thought Antonio and I could have had if things had been different, but I'll be damned if I let him bring me to my knees any longer.

CHAPTER THIRTY-FIVE

ANTONIO

Sofia leaves my room in a fit of fury, leaving me with so many emotions swirling in my chest I feel as if I'm being whipped around in a tornado. A part of me is proud of her for finding her inner strength and telling me to go to hell. Another part of me just wanted to grab her by the shoulders and kiss her. And the biggest part of me wanted to confess to her that I'm not the baby's father, but now I have an idea of who is. Not that it matters all that much—except for the part where my fiancée was fucking an Irishman and not a fellow Italian like I assumed. How did she think we'd fake an Irish baby for being mine?

Where exactly do Aurora's loyalties lie?

I'm not sure, but I will find out.

Having to be cruel to Sofia to get her to believe my commitment to Aurora felt like ripping open a wound that hasn't scabbed over fully, but I have to protect her. Especially now that I know Aurora is somehow in cahoots with our enemy. Who knows what she's capable of?

But before I deal with this new piece of information, I have to get ready for my phone call with my dad. I want an update on the gun shipment. I need to know if whoever is ripping us off took the bait.

After I've showered and eaten, I head down to the lowest level of the Roma House and am told to go to room number nine. Once I'm inside and seated with the door closed, I dial my father's number.

"Antonio," he answers.

"Any word on the shipment? Did everything get in place?"

"It did, and whoever it is hijacked our shipment. It's still on the move."

I smile. Step one is complete. Soon we'll know exactly who dares to fuck with us.

"Any idea where it's headed?" I ask.

"Looks like they've moved it into a vehicle. It's traveling all around, one direction, then the next. Not sure if they're trying to take an inconspicuous route or if they think we might be tailing them and are trying to lose us. Once they're settled somewhere for more than an hour or two, our guys will move in."

"Who knows about this?"

"No one. Me, you, and a few people in the Costa family who helped make it happen. I won't be informing anyone on our payroll where they're going or what they're doing until they're leaving."

"Good."

"You still think there's a rat?"

I sigh. "Not sure. But what I do know is that the Russians here sure don't seem like a group of people afraid and readying themselves for retribution."

"That could be an act."

"Could be. But my gut tells me it's not."

He contemplates my words. "You've always had good instincts."

I don't say anything, but his comment fills me with pride. My father isn't a terrible man. Sure, he's done some terrible things and taught me to do the same, but I've always seen him as fair, level-headed.

"If anything comes up before our call next Sunday that you need to know, I'll call you."

"How are you gonna do that? They won't put the call through."

My father laughs. "If I say it's an emergency, they will. We're one of the four founding families of that place. Who do you think helps hire and fire around there?"

"All right, well . . . hopefully I'll hear from you before next Sunday. I'd like to know who's behind this so we can figure out whether it has something to do with Leo's death."

"How's Tommaso?" my father asks in a grave voice.

"Not great."

"Hmm. Although I'm sure he wants retribution and it may help slightly, it will take time. I'll talk to him the next visit home. Have a good week. I'll talk to you soon. Ciao."

He hangs up, then I set the old-school phone on the receiver.

"One problem dealt with. Now for the next one." I push up off the chair and leave the room.

When I get into the elevator, I press the button for Aurora's floor. Time to get to the bottom of her and that Irish prick.

My anger grows with each level the elevator ascends, and by the time I step off and stand in front of her door, her betrayal feels like a slick oil over my body I need to wash off. I bang on the door, not bothering to temper my anger. It swings open and my darling fiancée stands there, wrapped tightly in a fuzzy robe.

"Is your roommate here? We need to talk."

She sniffs and it's then that I realize she's been crying. Her skin is sallow and there're bags under her eyes.

I sigh and pinch the bridge of my nose. Nothing ever comes easy with this one. "What's wrong?"

She waves me in with another sniffle and closes the door. I step into her room and see that her roommate's bed is made and she's not here.

"What's going on?" Irritation is still coloring my words, but this rare display of vulnerability from Aurora has thrown me for a loop.

"I had a miscarriage. There's blood all over the floor in the bathroom. I felt some cramping when I was lying in bed, and by the time I got up, it was too late."

She bursts into tears, and I do the only thing I can think of—I step forward and draw her into my arms. She shakes, clearly still in shock from the experience. The first real emotions I've ever felt from her.

"Do you need to go see the doctor?" I ask.

She pulls away from me, head shaking. "No way. He'll know if he examines me."

I look her up and down. "Are you still bleeding?"

"Not as bad. I put a sanitary pad on." Her voice wobbles. "But the bathroom is a mess and if I don't clean it before my roommate gets back, she's going to know and—"

I raise my hand for her to stop speaking. "Go lie down and relax. I'll clean up the mess."

I might be an asshole, but I'm not completely heartless. I'm not going to accuse her of treason in the midst of her loss. It can wait a day or two.

"But . . . Antonio—"

"It's not the first time I've cleaned up blood." I arch an eyebrow.

She nods and slowly walks to her bed and lies down. Meanwhile, I go into the bathroom to assess the mess. She's right. There is a lot of blood on the floor and some more on the toilet and the side of the cabinet where she's touched it. I get to work cleaning up the mess with the supplies she has in her bathroom, and when I'm done, I toss all the bloody towels in one of the garbage bags. A quick wipe down with a cleaner under the bathroom sink takes care of the metallic smell of blood in the air, and I turn on the bathroom fan for any lasting effects.

I step out of the bathroom, garbage bag in hand. "How are you feeling?"

Aurora rolls to face me. She's crying again. "Still a little crampy."

"I'm going to go dispose of these bloody towels. Do you want me to bring you back something?"

Her eyes well with more tears. "Can you bring me some soup from the café?"

I nod. "Sure. I'll be back in a bit. If your roommate comes back, just tell her you aren't feeling well."

She nods and I head for the staircase so that no one will see me carrying a bag of bloody towels. It's not that I don't want answers to what the fuck was or is going on between her and Conor, but I remember when I was nine years old and my mom had a miscarriage. She and my father had tried for a while after Mira to have another baby—I remember my mom talking about it a lot with Sofia's mom when she came over.

When my mom got pregnant, she was far enough along that they told my sister and me about it, but a month or so after that, my dad had to explain to us that we would no longer be having a baby brother or sister. My mom stayed in bed for weeks, and it was a good couple months before she was back to being a constant presence in our lives.

It's only human for me to give Aurora a bit of time to come to terms with her loss before I grill her. But one way or another, I'm going to get to the bottom of what's going on.

* * *

A couple of days pass, and by Tuesday night, Aurora is still in bed. Physically she's feeling better, but I think she's still having trouble dealing with the emotions of her loss. Regardless, I can't pussyfoot around what Sofia told me any longer. I need to confront her.

So, that night I stop by to bring Aurora dinner because she, once again, doesn't want to go to the dining hall and face everyone. I decide now is the time to ask her about Conor. Her roommate is in the dining hall and Aurora's finally out of bed, sitting on the couch and eating the bowl of penne I got her.

"Are you going to tell the father you lost the baby? You never even said whether he knew you were pregnant." I keep my voice nonchalant, as though her answer doesn't matter to me one way or the other.

She looks up from the bowl, fork pausing halfway to her mouth. "He didn't know I was pregnant. I thought it was best that way."

I nod. Sure, she did. That way, he couldn't cause any problems for her if he wanted any claim to the baby. "You never did say who it was."

She shrugs and goes back to eating. "It doesn't matter. It's over."

I stare at her until she feels my gaze and looks at me. "Is it? Over?"

"Yes. Is this the part where you chastise me for seeing someone else while you were out secretly fucking your little sister's best friend? Maybe I should ask you if you're still sleeping with Sofia."

For the first time in days, the Aurora I'm used to creeps in. She's definitely feeling better.

"Sofia and I were done the moment you announced your pregnancy, and you know it." I can't keep the derision from my voice.

She rolls her eyes and stabs some penne onto her fork.

"So who was the father?" I ask.

Aurora must hear something in my tone because, for the first time in this conversation, she looks at me with something akin to concern. "Why are you just now so interested?"

There's no point in keeping the information I have from her. She'll never back down unless she's cornered, that's just how she is. She needs to think I already know if there's any chance of getting her to admit what I suspect is true.

"Who's Conor to you?"

Surprise flashes in her eyes for a beat before she recovers. She leans forward and sets her bowl on the side table.

"Conor?" Her head tilts.

"Yeah, heard about a little argument the two of you had at the dance last Saturday. Sounded interesting."

Red colors her cheeks and she swallows hard. I can practically see the wheels turning in her head. Should she admit it and tell the truth? Should she lie? Is there any chance I'll believe her if she does?

"I did talk to him because he pulled me aside to talk about Sofia. He has a thing for her. I already told you I thought that."

I nod slowly, keeping eye contact. "Funny, that's not how I heard it."

"Who told you? Oh, let me guess. Little Miss Angel, right? You can't believe anything she says. She's practically obsessed with you. She'd probably do anything to try to get you back." She grabs the half-eaten bowl of pasta off the table and tosses it in the garbage.

"Not hungry anymore?" I arch an eyebrow.

She scowls at me. "Seem to have lost my appetite, what with my fiancé accusing me of being a traitor."

"I didn't call you that."

"You didn't have to."

I decide to employ a different tactic. "Listen, I can understand you falling for someone you shouldn't. That's no different than what happened between Sofia and me. But if you lie about it, that just makes it worse."

She steps up to me and jabs her pointer finger into my chest. "I have never betrayed this family and I never would. For you to insinuate otherwise is unbelievable. One day I will bear the child who will take over the empire you've built. I wouldn't do anything to put that in jeopardy."

Aurora holds my eye contact. She's good. I'll give her that. It's almost like she believes her own lies. It's not that I necessarily think she was giving away our family secrets to the Irish—she's not in a position to really know any of them anyway. But I do believe that she was sleeping with Conor. Whether just for kicks or because she had real feelings for him, I don't know.

But I will find out.

"You're right. I should know better. Sofia probably made it up, thinking I might break our engagement if I thought you were disloyal. Your dad is the underboss, for God's sake. Can you imagine?"

She looks mollified enough that she gives me a curt nod. "Good. Now, I'm tired and need to lie down. Make sure you close the door behind you."

I'll let her think I believe her lies today, but my dad told me a long time ago that patience always wins.

CHAPTER THIRTY-SIX

SOFIA

It's Thursday and I've done my best to avoid Antonio all week, which actually hasn't been that hard. We don't have an event to plan this Friday and he hasn't been around the dining hall during mealtime very much. When he was, I sat at the Costa table.

At first, I thought that maybe he believed what I told him and he was dealing with Aurora, or something had gone down with them because she hadn't been in the dining hall all week. But I overheard one of the other girls talking about how sweet it was that he's been bringing Aurora food to her room all week because she'd been sick. Morning sickness is all that comes to mind, and the idea of Antonio caring for his pregnant fiancée fills me with grief. Whether the baby is his or not, or whether he believes anything I overheard, he obviously plans to stick with her.

I push down my disappointment and remind myself that I don't care anymore. Antonio was so cruel to me. Why should I? I need to forget him, forget everything we ever had, and move on with my life.

"You want to study for our creative accounting class?" Mira asks me on the way back to the Roma House after dinner.

I shake my head. "Nah, I already went through all my notes last night. I'm ready for the test tomorrow."

She frowns and looks at me with concern, then behind us to see how far away Marcelo, Giovanni, and Andrea are. "Are you okay?"

I take her hand and give it a good squeeze. "I'm fine. I swear. Well, getting there anyway."

"If it's any consolation, I've barely spoken to my brother since Aurora's announcement."

"You don't have to do that for me, Mira. He's your brother. I understand that eventually, you two will be okay again."

She looks at me with what I think is pity and I hate it. More than I can say.

We arrive at the Roma House, and I hold the door open for her and the guys who aren't far behind us. Giovanni gives me an awkward smile and thanks me as he passes. We haven't spoken much since I broke things off with him, but I'd like to think that someday we'll be back to being friends like we were before we dated.

They all head to the lounge area and I say my good nights and tell them I'm heading to my room. There are a few protests, but they let me go easily enough.

The smile slips from my face the moment the elevator doors close between us. Pretending to be okay in front of others has felt like a full-time job lately. I like being able to take the mask off when I'm by myself.

I unlock my door and head inside, closing it behind me. I'm on my way to the couch when I notice a pink piece of stationery on my desk.

That's odd. I don't have any pink paper. I pick it up and see that it's a letter addressed to me.

Sofia,

We need to talk. I know about you and Antonio.
Meet me on the roof at midnight.

Aurora

I drop the letter onto the desk. What the hell? How does she know? Better question, how the hell did she get in my room to leave it here?

My stomach flips like a waffle maker, making one giant lunge so that I feel sick.

Antonio still has my spare key. Maybe he gave it to her. Or maybe she stole it from him. I wouldn't put it past her.

What does she want to talk about? Is she going to scream and yell at me? Is she going to cry and tell me how upset she is? Maybe she's going to warn me off him or beg me to leave him alone? I have no idea.

What I do know is that I have to meet her. She's not going to drop it and the fact is that I don't like her, but I made my choices. If she wants to talk to me for messing around with her fiancé, I deserve her wrath. I won't shy away from it.

Maybe this is exactly what I need to finally put Antonio La Rosa behind me.

* * *

SINCE THE ELEVATOR doesn't go all the way to the roof, my only option is the stairs. I've never been up here before and I'm not sure what to expect.

I ignore the sign that says that no unauthorized personnel are allowed on the rooftop and push open the heavy metal door. When I step out onto the roof, I see some equipment I assume are heaters or air conditioners for the building, but no Aurora.

It's kind of creepy up here. At least under these circumstances—in the dark, late at night, under a cloudy sky without moonlight. A handful of orange-colored lights are sporadically placed along the edge, but they don't emit a lot of light. Just enough to tell you you're getting close to the edge—which, as it turns out, is only a small lip, maybe a foot tall.

I spin around when I hear footfalls behind me. Aurora is hard to make out because she's wearing all black, but it's her.

"I got your note," I say to start the conversation. I want to get this over with.

"Thanks for coming." She paces to the far side of the roof, and I follow.

"About Antonio—"

She whips around to face me. "It was no big surprise to me, Sofia. I've seen the way you've panted over him for years. You reminded me of a puppy with her tongue hanging out of its mouth."

I narrow my eyes and decide to ignore her insult in the interest of getting this over with. She has every right to be pissed at me. "It should never have happened. He told me that your engagement was one of convenience. If I'd known about the—"

Her eyes widen and she cuts me off. "An apology hardly makes up for the fact that you were sleeping with the man I'm engaged to."

My chin hits my chest and I look down at the rooftop. "You're right."

"Or the fact that you ran off and tried to turn my fiancé against me the first chance you got."

My head whips up to face her. "What are you talking about?"

"Oh please. You think I don't know that you tried to convince him I'm a traitor?"

"Hello, Sofia."

The male voice from behind me startles me and I whip around. It takes me a second to figure out who it is in the dark. "Conor. What are you doing here?"

"Aurora informed me we had a little problem on our hands." He steps toward me.

Since I'm between the two of them, I instinctively step back. The only issue is that it takes me toward the edge of the roof, and eventually, I'll run out of space.

My heart rate picks up and my breathing grows shallow. "There's no problem. I told Antonio and that's all. I never planned to tell anyone else." My head ping-pongs one direction then the next, trying to keep an eye on both of them.

"How can we be so sure?" Conor steps forward again, as does Aurora.

"Because I don't care who the father of Aurora's baby is. Antonio and I are done! Nothing is ever going to happen between us again!"

Conor's forehead creases and he whips his head in Aurora's direction. "Yer with babe?"

Aurora looks furious at me for a second, then morphs her expression to one of innocence when she looks back at Conor. "I didn't want to tell you yet. It was still early."

"But you told that bastard?" His focus is on her now. He turns and steps right to her.

I slowly shift, trying not to draw their attention so that I can escape.

"I didn't plan on it. He found the test and cornered me. I never told him who the father was."

"I can't believe you didn't tell me. I thought you loved me."

I keep one eye on them and one in the direction I'm trying to go, sliding over a little more.

"I do love you." Aurora steps up to him and places her hands on his face. "So much. That's why I had to end things with you. Antonio was suspicious and trying to figure out who the father was. I was protecting you. I would've told you once I knew everything was okay with the baby."

"Was?" Conor's voice breaks on the word.

I shift forward toward the door to the roof, rolling my feet and trying to make as little noise as possible.

"I lost the baby last weekend. That's why I've been in my room all week. I've been so devastated," she says. "I didn't know how to tell you."

A pang of sympathy hits me, but I push it away. I can't allow myself to sympathize with this woman. I have no idea what her plan is tonight, but I know it's not in any way good for me.

Conor pulls her into his chest.

"And yet again, Sofia is ruining everything. Telling you before I could that we lost our child."

I still where I am and look back over my shoulder at them.

Aurora pulls away from Conor and looks to where I had been. Her head whips around and finds me. "She's getting away!"

Conor's eyes land on me in the dim light, and he gently sets Aurora to the side.

I spin around, running as fast as I can toward the door, knowing that if I don't make it there, I won't be leaving this roof alive.

I'm two feet from reaching it when I'm tackled from behind. My body slams against the ground, knocking all the wind from my lungs. As I lie there beneath Conor, panting and trying to find my stolen breath, all I can think about is how I'm glad that if I'm going to die tonight, I was able to experience real love with Antonio.

CHAPTER THIRTY-SEVEN
ANTONIO

A sharp bang on the door shortly after eleven has me rushing from the bathroom to put something on after my shower. The knock sounds again as I pull my pants up my legs.

"Hang on!" I yank a shirt over my head and go to the door and swing it open.

Tommaso stands there, eyes wide, with a drink from Café Ambrosia in his hand. "You gotta get to the chancellor's office."

My face screws up. "What?"

"Your dad needs you to call him. I was on my way back when the chancellor saw me. Told me to tell you."

"Shit." I rush back into my room to put some shoes on then push out into the hallway past Tommaso.

"I'm coming with you. It could be about my dad."

I could argue with him, but what's the point? He's right. And if it's not something for his ears, I just won't tell him whatever my dad has to say.

"All right. Hurry."

We rush across campus until we reach the administration building and head straight to the chancellor's office. He's clearly come from his place, and unlike usual, he's not dressed in his expensive suit but in a pair of plaid pajama pants and a T-shirt with a robe.

He stands at his open office door, and when he spots us, he motions us inside. "You can use the phone in my office. I'll give you some privacy."

Tommaso and I enter the chancellor's office and he closes the door behind us while he remains on the other side. I head straight for his desk, pick up the phone, and dial my father's number.

"Antonio."

"What's going on?" I flop down into the chancellor's chair while Tommaso paces in front of the desk.

"You were right. We had a rat."

"Who?" I practically growl.

"Oronato."

The word hangs between us.

Aurora's dad?

What the fuck?

"Are you sure?"

"We traced the shipment once it stopped ping-ponging all over the map. Found a few of our soldiers there. With a little incentive, they talked."

I know what kind of incentive he's talking about. I've been the one to deliver it from time to time. I also know those guys are already dead.

Tommaso must see the look on my face. "What is it? Do they know who murdered my father?"

I look away from him and push a hand through my hair, blowing out a long stream of air. "Why would he do that?"

"Apparently he's been using what he knows to steal the shipments and then sell them back to the Irish and pocketing the money. I guess Leo figured out something was going on since these guys worked under him, so Oronato took him out before he could tell anyone. I don't know yet how the hell he got an audience with the Irish, but I'll get my answers in due time. I promised Tommaso he could be the one to take out his father's killer, so he's in the regular spot, waiting to be interrogated. I'll send a plane for you two in the morning and you can join us."

My gaze flicks to Tommaso. "We'll be on it."

He widens his eyes in a "tell me what's going on now" gesture.

"Good. I know Marcelo helped put the plan into place, but don't divulge anything to him. It makes us look weak when one of our own betrays the family."

"Yeah, all right." Then something clicks into place. "Wait. You said he was working with the Irish, not the Russians."

"Apparently."

Like the rush of water through a tunnel, everything Sofia told me hits me full force.

Aurora's relationship with Conor.

Sofia's missing key.

The Irish tie in Sofia's room.

And then I went and basically told Aurora that Sofia was on to her.

"Shit!" I bolt up from the chair.

"What is it, son?"

"I think I know how Oronato got an in with the Irish. I gotta go. I'll fill you in when I see you tomorrow." I hang up before he can protest.

"What's going on?"

"We gotta get back to the Roma House. I'll fill you in on the way."

We rush out of the chancellor's office, and as we run back to our dorm, I fill Tommaso in on everything. He's shocked. First, that one of our own betrayed us and killed his father, then about Sofia and me, and finally, Aurora's pregnancy and relationship with Conor.

"I can't wait to put a bullet in that fucker's head. I'm going to make him pay, make it more painful than he made it for my dad."

We push through the doors of the Roma House. Because it's so late, the lounge is basically void of people.

"First, we have to make sure Sofia is okay. I don't know what Aurora is capable of, and now that she's feeling better, who knows what she'll try." I stab the button for the elevator and wait impatiently for it to arrive.

"You really think Aurora's capable of hurting Sofia?" he asks as we step inside.

I think about how manipulative she is and how easily lies roll off her tongue. Aurora is out for number one and anyone she sees as a threat to that is in her way.

"Absolutely."

When the elevator doors open again, we rush down the hall and I bang on Sofia's door. When she doesn't answer immediately, I bang some more. I don't have her key with me, but I don't need it to know that she's not in there.

"Fuck!" I turn to Tommaso. "I want you to go round up my sister and Marcelo and his crew. Start looking for Sofia. We need to find her." I rush off.

"Where are you going?"

"I'm going to see Gabe. That guy has his eyes on everything around here. Text me if you find her." I run to the stairwell without waiting for him to answer.

When I reach Gabriele's room, I bang on the door. I already know he knows it's me because he has cameras pointed at his door. "Open up, Vitale. This is important!"

The door opens and Gabe stands there looking unimpressed, though it's clear he wasn't sleeping. "What do you want, La Rosa?"

"I need you to look up where Sofia went when she left her room tonight."

He smirks. "Afraid your little sidepiece has a new man in her life?"

I narrow my eyes. "You know?"

He shrugs and steps back to open the door farther so I can walk in. "I have eyes and ears everywhere."

I step into his room, which looks more like a CIA surveillance van than a college dorm room. "Perfect, get me the info I need then."

He folds his arms over his chest. "What's in it for me?"

"Whatever you want! Just make it happen!" I usher him toward his bank of computer screens. I highly doubt school administration has any idea he has all this shit in here.

He stays where he is. "I want another favor. Remember, you owe me one from last semester. I'll call it in at a time of my choosing and you can't say no."

My teeth grind together. The last thing I want is to owe this fucker anything, but what choice do I have? I know for certain that Sofia's not out on a leisurely walk at damn near midnight.

"Fine."

Gabe nods and folds himself into his chair, then types away on his keyboard. I have no idea what he's doing, but he's flicking through different camera angles until I recognize the one that shows the hallway near her room.

"That's it!"

He looks back at me over his shoulder, annoyed. "I know." He flicks a few more keys on the keyboard and the video starts. "Let's see what—or who—Miss Moretti is doing this evening."

"Careful," I warn and he chuckles.

He speeds up the tape. There's no sign of Sofia after she arrives at her room after dinner. Other people on her floor come and go, but not Sofia. Then finally, the door to her room opens and she carefully closes it before heading to the stairwell.

"What time was that?" I ask.

"Eleven fifty-five."

I yank my phone from my pocket. "That was only ten minutes ago. Where did she go?"

"There're no cameras in the stairwell. Let me see what floor she came out of the stairs on." He checks all the other floors, one by one. "Nothing."

I straighten from where I'm crunched over looking at his screen and push a hand through my hair. "What the fuck? So she's either still in the stairwell . . ." A vision of Sofia's lifeless body lying at the bottom of a set of stairs flashes through my mind.

"The roof," Gabe says. "There're no cameras on the roof."

My blood instantly chills. There aren't a lot of ways to kill someone on campus—what with no weapons and without drawing suspicion to yourself—but falling from a rooftop would do it.

I race from his room to the stairwell and take the stairs up two at a time.

I've never felt so much terror in all my life. I swear to Christ, if anyone hurts my Sofia, I will not rest until I've sent them to hell. I reach the top of the stairs and the door that leads to the roof, and I burst through.

Conor is dragging Sofia toward the edge of the building. He's about five feet from the ledge and she's kicking and screaming.

Without considering the risk, I charge forward to tackle Conor. I'm going to save the woman I love or die trying.

CHAPTER THIRTY-EIGHT

SOFIA

I'm kicking and screaming, trying to do anything I can to dislodge myself from Conor's grip, but he's too strong. There's nothing I can do, but I won't stop trying until my last breath.

I jerk in his arms, and for a split second, I see Antonio charging at us. He tackles Conor, who drops me in the mayhem, and they both hit the ground and slide toward the edge.

"Antonio!" I watch in horror as he stops a foot from the edge.

But before I can get up to help, Aurora is on me. "You bitch! You ruined everything!" She jumps on top of me and punches me in the face.

It takes me a second to get my bearings, but when I do, I roll her off me. I punch her in the face, giving it everything I've got, which isn't much for someone who's never punched anyone in her life. I go try to help Antonio. He and Conor are rolling around, fighting each other and still dangerously close to the edge.

I make it one step before Aurora rolls over and latches on to my ankle with both hands. I hit the ground with an "oomph," kicking my leg and trying to get her off me. It works when I connect with her face, and her nose crunches under my shoe.

I scramble to stand again and rush toward the guys, but I'm not sure what to do. I don't have anything to hit Conor with, so I do the only thing I can think of. He's on top of Antonio and punching him, so I yank Conor's hair from behind as hard as I can.

He cries out and instinctively reaches for his head. That's all Antonio needs to gain the upper hand. He flips Conor off him and drills him in the face with his fist.

A flash of movement to my left causes me to turn. Aurora's running at me, looking unhinged as she screams. Two seconds later, she makes contact with me and sends me hurtling toward the edge of the roof. I scream and scramble to grab anything to prevent my fall. When my hand meets with something cold and metal, I latch on to it. My body hits the side of the building as I fall over the edge, and I gasp for air.

Aurora's scream echoes through the night until I hear a sickening thud on the pavement below, then silence.

"Sofia!" Antonio's voice is frantic, then there are more scuffling sounds of fighting.

"Antonio!" I call so he knows I'm still alive.

Lights around the top of the building jut out before reflecting down on the side of the building, and I'm holding on to the post of one of them. But I won't be able to hold on for long.

"Antonio, I'm slipping!" I call frantically.

These can't be my last moments. They just can't be.

Conor's face appears over the edge of the roof, and his eyes widen as he looks down below. I assume he's spotted Aurora's body. I haven't looked. I don't want to know how far down I'm going to fall if my hands give out.

Antonio's on top of Conor, pulling him up and bashing him down on the rooftop edge. Conor tries to fight back, but it's obvious he's losing steam. With a bellow of rage, Antonio flips him over the side. Conor reaches for me as he falls, but I sway as far as I can, escaping his grip.

"Sofia!" I look up to Antonio's hand outstretched. "Give me your hand and I'll pull you up!"

I look down—I don't know why—and I squeeze my eyes shut, shaking my head. "I'll fall."

"You'll fall if you don't let me help you. Give me your hand."

The urgency in his voice confirms what I know—he's right. But even as I have to readjust my grip because I'm slipping, I can't force myself to take one hand off the pole.

"Sofia!" I open my eyes, watching as Antonio positions his body against the edge with his hand out. "Do you trust me?"

After everything we've been through, it feels like a much bigger question than how he means it. But as I look into his eyes, the color of a summer sky, time seems to slow down and everything stills around me and within me. I do trust him, even after everything.

With a deep breath, I let go of the pole with one hand and reach for him. He takes my hand in both of his and tugs me up with a grunt until finally, he pulls me over the edge and I collapse on top of him. We pant, unable to speak, realizing how close we both came to losing our lives tonight.

Without warning, Antonio's hands are on my face and his lips are on mine. He kisses me deeply and I don't resist.

When he pulls away, he squeezes me tightly to his chest. "I thought I'd lost you. Oh God, Sofia, I thought I'd lost you." I cling to him—for how long, I don't know. But then he pushes me away and helps me to stand. "We need to get out of here."

"What?" I'm still in such shock from everything that's happened that I can't make sense of what he's saying.

"Before anyone finds us here." He grabs my wrist and drags me to the door.

"But what about . . ." I can't say either of their names.

He shakes his head. "Let someone else find them. They can think it was suicide. Some Romeo and Juliet shit."

"But . . ."

He grips my face in his hands. "Sofia, that's probably what they planned to say when someone found you on the ground in the morning. Why do you think you were up here?"

I nod numbly. He's right. I know he is. "Won't they know when Conor's face is messed up?"

He drags me into the stairwell. "Maybe he hit the building on the way down. I dunno. Regardless, if anyone asks, you know nothing, you understand?"

"Okay."

We burst out of the stairwell onto my floor. When I don't immediately reach for my key, Antonio reaches into my pocket and grabs it and unlocks my door, pulling me inside my room. Then he takes out his phone and sends a message to someone before shoving it back in his pocket.

He places his hands on my shoulders and dips his head to meet my eyes. "I need you to have a shower and go to bed. Tomorrow, you act like nothing happened. When you hear about Aurora and Conor, you act as shocked as anyone, understand?"

"Yeah."

"I have some things to take care of back home, so I won't be here. I'm leaving on a plane with Tommaso first thing in the morning. The less you know, the better. But when I return, we'll talk, all right?"

"You're leaving?" I grip his shirt.

"You can do this, tesoro. You're so much stronger than you think."

I draw in a deep breath. He's right. I can. "How long will you be gone?"

"I don't know." Antonio rests his forehead on mine. "But I'll get back here as soon as I can."

I nod, then he plants a chaste kiss on my lips and he leaves.

This time though, I'm confident he'll be back.

CHAPTER THIRTY-NINE
ANTONIO

When Tommaso and I return home to Miami, we explain everything that went down at Sicuro Academy to my father. Since he hasn't received a phone call, I have to assume administration doesn't think anyone else from the La Rosa family had anything to do with Aurora and Conor's deaths.

After a three-day interrogation and torture session with Oronato, my suspicions were confirmed that he used Aurora as an in with the Irish and all their deal-making was done through the secure lines and Sunday calls at the academy. They'd pass information and messages back and forth that way.

I think it came as a surprise to Oronato that his daughter was also fucking the Irishman and that he'd knocked her up, but the real surprise was when I told him she was dead because of the wheels *he* set in motion.

In the end though, we let Tommaso deliver the kill shot. He deserved to be the one to send that man to hell after what he did to his father. And as fucked as it might sound, it's like some burden has been lifted off Tommaso's shoulders ever since. He's back to being more like his old self. Not entirely—but close.

"Salute." My father raises his glass.

The rest of the room echoes his sentiment. We're all celebrating the fact that we've exterminated the rats within our ranks. It's just my father, me, Tommaso, and the other capos. We're minus one underboss since he's now rotting at the bottom of the Atlantic five miles off the coast.

I knock back some of my drink and set the glass back down, waiting for my dad's speech. I know what's coming. He asked for my opinion and I agreed wholeheartedly with his decision.

"As you all know, we have a very important position to fill now that Oronato has left us."

There are some grumbles around the table and cursing about what a traitor he was.

My father says, "I've given a lot of thought about who exactly I want by my side, and I'm appointing Stefano Moretti as my new underboss."

Sofia's dad stands from the table, all smiles, and walks to hug my father. Stefano is a good choice. He's loyal to the family and has been for decades, and he keeps a good head on his shoulders.

"Did you know?" Tommaso leans in to ask me.

I nod.

"That ought to help your chances with Sofia." He laughs, and I roll my eyes.

Though I've been preoccupied with everything going on here the past few days, now that it's all wrapped up, I'm desperate to return to the academy to see her. Only two people might stand in the way of me being with her and I intend to figure out tonight whether either of them will be a problem.

The night passes in a blur of drinks and dirty jokes between all the men. When some of the guys finally clear out, I approach my father and Stefano, where they're talking in the corner. I can tell it's business related, but I need to interrupt regardless. I'm on a private plane in the morning to head back to the Sicuro Academy.

"Can I speak with the two of you in private?"

They turn to look at me with matching looks of concern. I don't know if they can read the nerves coming off me or what, though I try to keep it in check. But the truth is, if they don't agree, I don't know what I'll do because I refuse to live without Sofia.

"Everything all right, son?" Dad arches a graying eyebrow.

"We'll see." I motion with a nod toward the adjoining room.

My dad frowns but leads the way into his office. Once we're inside and I've closed the door, Stefano pulls me into an embrace.

"I haven't had a moment to properly thank you for saving my Sofia. Your dad tells me she wouldn't be with us any longer if it weren't for you."

I clap his back before pulling away. "Of course. That's actually what I wanted to talk to both of you about. Sofia."

My dad sits behind his desk and pulls out a cigar, motioning to the two of us to ask if we'd like one. We both wave him off.

"I don't see any reason to not come out with it, so I'm just going to ask . . . I'd like both of your permission to marry Sofia."

My father stills with his cigar halfway to his mouth.

Stefano looks at my father, obviously going to take his lead on this.

"We've developed feelings for each other, and I'm not afraid to tell you that I love her. I'd like to make her my wife." I look between them and swallow hard, waiting for either of them to give me some indication of what they think of this idea.

They both laugh, then look at me.

My forehead creases. "What's so funny?"

"What do you think we were discussing before you pulled us in here?"

"You were talking about me marrying Sofia? How did you know we care about each other?"

"We didn't," Stefano says, smiling huge. "We just got to talking and thought it would be a good pairing, but after what happened with Aurora . . ."

"We wanted to figure out a way to make you think it was your idea," my father finishes for him. "Didn't think you'd be too receptive to me choosing your bride again after how it turned out the first time."

Tension eases in my shoulders. "So is that a yes?"

"That it is, absolutely," my father says and comes around his desk to give me a hug. "Congratulations."

"Don't congratulate me yet. She still has to say yes."

Stefano chuckles. "My daughter has always been smart. I have no reason to think she won't be when you ask her."

I wish I had their confidence. After everything we've been through, will Sofia be able to trust and forgive me?

CHAPTER FORTY

SOFIA

Mira tells me that Antonio is coming back to campus today and my nerves are shot. We haven't spoken since that terrible night on the roof, so I have no idea what, if anything, all this means for us. If there even is an us.

Everyone at school suspects that Antonio and Tommaso had something to do with Aurora's and Conor's deaths, given that they disappeared the next day. But the official word is that they had to return home to deal with something for the family and administration seems happy to accept that Aurora and Conor must have jumped off the roof together. Either that or they were struggling for some reason and fell accidentally.

Whether they're willingly looking the other way or were told to, I have no idea. Nor do I care. I feel awful about what happened, but it was us or them. And though I may not be as outwardly tough and strong as Mira, turns out I am strong and I refuse to go down without a fight.

Mira suspects I was somehow involved with what happened on the roof, but when she comes straight out and asks me, I deny it. I don't know if Antonio would want me to say anything, so I figure it is better to keep my mouth shut until he gives me some kind of directive.

The day passes without any sighting of Antonio, and by the time I return to my room after dinner, I'm in a funk. Maybe he wasn't able to return to school today? All this waiting and not knowing is driving me crazy.

I unlock my door and step inside my room.

I gasp.

It's filled with flowers, all kinds of flowers. I recognize roses, peonies, tulips, dahlias, hydrangeas, asters, and more. Standing in the center of the room is Antonio, looking as handsome as ever. His blue eyes glisten as he takes me in.

"What's all this?" I step farther into the room.

"I realized that we never had a proper date, so I was never able to buy you flowers. Then when I went to, I realized that I didn't know which is your favorite, so I covered my bases." He chuckles.

"This is . . ." I circle around to take them all in. "Wow."

"The guards at the gate hate me. They had to inspect each vase and flower."

We both laugh and when the laughter dies down, we stare at each other.

"How are you?" he asks.

"Okay. I keep hearing Aurora's scream and then the thud."

Antonio embraces me. I inhale his scent deep into my lungs and feel a calmness I haven't felt since he left campus settle over me.

"I'm sorry you had to go through all of that. Jesus, Sofia, I thought I'd lost you." His voice breaks a bit on the last few words and he squeezes me tighter.

"I was so scared."

He rubs my back. "I know. But it's all been dealt with now."

I nod into his chest and don't ask any questions. I don't want to know. I just want to know that we're both safe now. Or as safe as any of us connected to this life can be.

He pulls away and settles his hands on my upper arms, looking at me. "I did a lot of thinking while I was away."

I swallow hard, afraid of what he's going to say next. Will he tell me that he thinks it's better if we just stay friends?

"First, I need to explain myself and apologize for saying such terrible things to you. I didn't mean a word of them."

A relieved rush of air leaves my lungs.

"Aurora knew about us," he says. "She told me about the pregnancy and threatened to out us and paint you as a whore and ruin your chances of securing a good marriage. I know how much you want a stable marriage with someone you love and to raise a family. I couldn't let her steal that chance from you.

"I knew the baby was never mine because I'd never slept with Aurora, but I went along with her plan to protect you. You and I knew we'd have to end things sooner than later and I figured protecting you was worth the cost of ending things early. But God, Sofia . . . hurting you and seeing that look on your face when I said and did some of the things I did . . ." He shakes his head and his eyes glisten. "I don't ever want to be responsible for putting that look on your face again."

"So you didn't mean any of the things you said?" I'm afraid to hope, afraid to believe, only to have it all ripped away from me again.

"Not a word. I hated Aurora for forcing my hand. And when you came to me about the Conor thing, I believed you. I wanted to get to the bottom of things and see how I could use them to my advantage, but I couldn't put you at risk by telling you that. And then Aurora had a miscarriage and I wanted to wait a few days before pressing her for answers, but waiting almost cost you your life. Can you ever forgive me?"

I place my hand on his cheek. "There's nothing to forgive. You were trying to protect me."

He turns my hand and kisses my palm.

"But . . . what does all of this mean for us? Is there even an us?"

As soon as the words leave my lips, I hold my breath, waiting for his answer.

He smiles wide. "Of course there's an us. I love you, Sofia. More than I ever thought I could love anyone."

He kisses me and I sink into his embrace, full of joy and possibility.

I end the kiss and pull away because he needs to know how I feel. "I love you too, Antonio. It's only ever been you."

Antonio takes my hands and drops onto one knee. My heart skips a few beats and I gasp as he reaches into his pocket and pulls out a ring box.

"Sofia Maria Moretti, I may not have been as quick as you were to see what we could have together, but now that I know, I can't bear to ever let you go. You are my one true love, my anima gemella, and I want to spend the rest of my life with you. I want you to be the mother to our children, and I want to come home to the peace and safety of your arms after a long day, every day. Will you do me the honor of becoming my wife?"

I open my mouth to respond, but he speaks again before I can answer.

"You should know that I already asked permission to marry you from both my father and yours while I was home."

Tears well in my eyes. "You did?"

He nods.

"Yes, I'll marry you! Of course I will. I want nothing more."

He opens the ring box to reveal a five-carat oval-shaped diamond in the center of a ring flanked by more diamonds on the band.

"It's gorgeous." I lift my shaking hand so he can slide it on, and once it's settled there, I am never, ever taking it off.

Antonio stands and kisses me. It starts out as a celebratory kiss but quickly morphs into a lust-filled one before he pulls away, cringing.

"What's wrong?" I ask.

"I'd love nothing more than to continue this, but I told everyone to meet us down in the lounge. Figured we should announce our engagement and celebrate the news a bit."

I grin wide. "You want everyone to know right away?"

He scoffs. "Of course I do. We've had to sneak around for too long. I don't plan to do it for another second. I want everyone to know who you belong to."

Heat pools between my legs. "I like the sound of that."

He arches an eyebrow. "Oh yeah?"

I nod, and he leans in and kisses me again.

When my hands wander over his body, he pushes me back. "All right, we really have to go. Otherwise, we're not going to make it out of this room for a week."

I giggle and take his hand, leading him to the door.

We take the elevator down to the lounge, and when we step out, we find it filled with people. Tommaso, Mira, Marcelo, Giovanni, Andrea, and Lorenzo are near the front, along with some other members of the La Rosa family. I even spot Gabriele and Dante in the crowd.

Before anyone can ask what they've all been summoned here for, Antonio takes my left hand and holds it out in front of me. "I wanted you all to know that I've asked Sofia to be my wife and she's accepted."

Sounds of surprise fill the room and some congratulatory cheers, but it's Mira's yelp I hear most. Then she's racing forward and enveloping me in a hug.

"Oh my god. I'm so happy! We're going to be sisters now!"

I laugh and hug her back. It almost feels surreal. This all started with me having a secret crush on her brother and now I'm marrying him.

"Sisters for life," I say with tears in my eyes.

The guys all head up to Antonio to offer their congratulations before stepping toward me to do the same. Giovanni is grinning when he reaches me and I spot Antonio watching from the corner of his eye.

"I should've known." Giovanni chuckles and pulls me into a hug. "Congratulations, Sofia. I hope you guys are really happy together."

I look at Antonio and wink. "We will be. You'll find your happy ever after someday too."

He chuckles. "Maybe. Maybe not."

Giovanni moves on, and I accept congratulations from the next person. It goes for a while.

About an hour later, Antonio and I slip out of the party and up to his room. We've never spent time in his room before and he insists that he wants to christen every surface in there.

And we do, some even twice.

SOFIA

It's the start of a new school year, and Antonio and I spent the day getting settled into our new room. The new room that we share, because we're a married couple now.

Antonio wanted to get married right away, and after I checked with Mira to make sure she didn't mind—I know how miffed she was when Aurora had their wedding pushed ahead of her and Marcelo's—we decided to keep the date that was originally scheduled for Antonio's wedding.

Sure, it's kind of weird, but it made sense. The venue was already chosen and booked, but that's about the only detail we kept from the original affair. I chose all my colors and decor, and providing a huge monetary bonus to the wedding and bridesmaids' dresses designer made sure our dresses were ready on time.

It was a very special day—not only for Antonio and me but for the La Rosa family as a whole. It signaled a new beginning after all the terrible things that had resulted from Aurora and her father's betrayal.

After our wedding, we spent two weeks in Fiji having sex in the sun, in the shower, in the sand, and anywhere else we could steal a moment alone. It was magical.

This is Antonio's last year at the academy since he'll graduate at the end of second semester, but it's also my last year. I only ever came here for Mira, and I have no plans to stay if my husband isn't here.

I most look forward to next year when we'll be settled in our new home and hopefully working on a family. All I've ever wanted was to be a wife and mother and maybe that's not very progressive of me, but isn't the whole point that I'm able to make my own choice for my life?

And nothing will make me happier than filling our home with children and providing a loving place for my husband to land after he's done dealing with all the terrible things he'll see in a day.

"That the last of it?" Antonio comes up behind me and kisses my neck as I place a pile of shirts into a dresser drawer.

"That's it." I straighten up and turn in his arms, winding my arms around his neck.

"What do you think of being late to meet everyone so we can spend some time naked?"

I chuckle into his chest. "We were just naked on the plane before we arrived."

Since we were alone on the plane (besides the pilots and flight attendant), we joined the mile-high club on our way here.

"I can never get enough naked time with my wife, you know that." He nips on my earlobe.

I sigh and tilt my neck to give him better access. "I love when you say that."

"Naked?" He laughs, knowing what I mean.

"Wife." I pretend to scold him with a swat on the arm.

"Well, I would very much like to fuck my wife now. And if my wife is feeling generous, maybe my wife can suck my cock first. But only after I eat my wife's pussy and make my wife come on my face." He grins at me, knowing I can't deny him.

We end up being forty-five minutes late meeting everyone in the lounge. We all planned to meet up to welcome Marcelo's little sister to campus since it's her first year and also because we haven't seen much of anyone over the summer. Mira spent most of her time with Marcelo and his crew in New York. Tommaso was busy handling a lot of stuff for Antonio since he was busy with the wedding and honeymoon.

The elevator dings open and we see everyone hanging around one of the sections of couches and chairs, so we make our way over, hand in hand.

It's no longer awkward for me to be around Giovanni. In fact, he was at the wedding, so he knows better than anyone how happy I am. He brought a gorgeous date with him, but I have no idea whether it's serious or not.

"There's the happy couple. Married sex isn't boring yet, I see." Tommaso nods toward Antonio's jeans, which are unzipped.

He pulls the zipper up with a grin.

Mira gives me a big hug. It's good to see her.

"How are you?" I ask.

She rolls her eyes. "Well, now that your wedding is complete, my mom has shifted her focus to me. There are a million decisions to be made, most of which I don't even care about."

I laugh. Italian weddings are no joke. "Well, if you really don't care, let her do some of the choosing and put your foot down on the things that really matter to you. I'm happy to help too, if you want."

"That would be amazing."

Once we've all said our hellos, I take a seat beside Aria on the couch and Antonio sits on the other side of me, never too far from me since we became public.

"How are you feeling about starting school in a few days?" I ask Aria.

She grins excitedly. "I can't wait. I'm finally out from underneath my mom's thumb. A little bit of freedom will be good for me, I think."

I chuckle and look at Marcelo, who's sitting on the couch opposite us, then I lean in. "I think you might find your brother is just as bad," I whisper.

She rolls her eyes. "Tell me about it. Do you know he tried to get my room beside his so he could keep a better eye on me?"

My mouth drops open. "He did not."

Aria nods. "He did, but I found out about it and put a stop to it, which was not easy, believe me."

"How'd you manage that?" I ask.

A little smirk forms on her lips. "I have my ways."

Interesting. I wonder if perhaps Marcelo's angelic little sister isn't that angelic after all.

The elevator dings and Gabriele Vitale steps out. He was never a small man, but I think he must have spent more time at the gym over the summer because he's definitely more muscular than he was the last time I saw him.

"I'm going to go say hi to Gabe," Aria says, standing.

"The hell you are," Marcelo says to her.

She scowls at him. "What's the big deal?"

Marcelo stands to his full height, clearly trying to intimidate his sister. "First, he's a Vitale. Second, he's too old for you. Third—"

"Are you too old for Mirabella?" She crosses her arms and cocks out a hip.

I have to work to stop myself from laughing. Poor Marcelo has Mira *and* his sister to contend with on campus this year. I have a feeling they're going to keep him busy. Either that or make him crazy.

"That's not the point." The line between Marcelo's eyebrows deepens.

"I'm not a baby."

"Stay away from him. I mean it."

"Fine." Aria flops back down on the couch.

It doesn't escape my notice that when Gabriele passes by our little group, his eyes go straight to Aria and hers to him. She may be only eighteen and figuring out her life, but I have a feeling Aria knows exactly what kind of man she wants and it's the exact opposite of the one her overbearing brother would choose for her.

This should be interesting. Or deadly.

Can't get enough of Antonio and Sofia?
Turn the page for an exclusive new bonus
scene from *Corrupting the Innocent*.

ANTONIO

Six Weeks Before the Epilogue

The women loitering outside the room of my parents' home that's housing my fiancée gasp when I walk down the hallway.

"Is something wrong?"

"You can't be here."

"It's back luck."

I ignore all of them and knock on the door. A few seconds later, it opens, my mother's head poking out, her jaw dropping at the sight of me.

"Antonio, what are you doing here?"

"I want to see my fiancée." My tone brokers no argument.

"You can't see her right before the ceremony. It's bad luck!"

I roll my eyes. "That's just a stupid superstition."

We're getting married in a church, of course, but my parents requested that we all get ready in their home so that the photographer could get pictures of both the men and the women before the ceremony. Since their place is large enough, we didn't see a problem with it.

"Antonio, you need to leave now."

"I want to speak to my soon-to-be wife—alone." I meet my mother's perturbed gaze and don't back down.

She sees that I have no intention of leaving because after a long, drawn-out sigh, she steps back from the door and directs everyone out.

I wait in the hallway, earning scathing looks from each one until they're all out of the room.

My sister is the last and she stops in front of me. "If you mess up her hair or makeup, you're a dead man," she warns.

I chuckle before entering the room and closing the door behind me.

The air leaves my lungs in a whoosh.

Sofia stands in front of me, a little more done up than normal, but looking like a goddamn princess. Like the Mafia princess she is.

Her long hair is pulled back loosely off her face and diamonds drip from her ears. The white dress she wears is somehow modest and sexy as hell in a way that only she can pull off.

My cock twitches in my tux in response to the knowledge that in a very short time, this woman will be all mine.

"What are you doing here?"

She tries to sound stern, but she can't quite pull it off when the corners of her lips tip up. She's happy I'm here.

"I didn't want the first moment I see you to be in front of hundreds of people." I step up to her and run my hands down her sides, letting them settle on her hips.

"And what do you think?" Her big doe eyes look at me expectantly with a bit of anxiety in them.

"I think you're the most beautiful woman I've ever seen in my life and I'm one lucky bastard when you say 'I do.'"

The color in her cheeks deepens as she runs her hand down my chest. "You look very handsome." Her lids drop just a bit and I know she's turned on.

I know all Sofia's tells. I know when she wants it soft and slow. I know when she wants it hard and fast. And right now, her gaze tells me she wants me to show her she belongs to me.

"There was one other reason I wanted to see you before we left for the church." My voice is rough with lust.

"Oh?" She arches a perfectly shaped eyebrow.

"I want my fiancée's pussy one more time before it belongs to my wife."

Even I'm not depraved enough to fuck in a church. But I do want to fuck her in her wedding dress. There's nothing I like more than sullying up her innocence.

She giggles, but doesn't make any attempt to stop my line of thinking. Instead, she turns and presents her back to me, bends at the waist, and leans her forearms on the dresser set against the wall.

She is fucking perfect.

After some work I manage to pull the many layers of her dress up, revealing that gorgeous ass of hers, clad in a white lace thong.

It's only seconds before my pants are around my ankles and I'm sliding into her. We moan in unison the second I'm fully in.

It's a herculean effort not to let my hands dive into her hair and yank Sofia's head back, but my sister and probably my mother would kill me if I undid all the hard work the hair stylist had done.

We both come on a groan, and I hold myself inside, cherishing the feel of her before I reluctantly glide out.

"Hang on." I rush to the adjoining en suite and quickly get a washcloth to clean her up before anything gets on her dress.

Once I'm done, I straighten up, toss the washcloth in the laundry basket, and help her arrange her dress. She doesn't look quite as put together as she did when I came in here, but the glow on her cheeks makes me chub.

"Now that I've checked the first thing off my list, I need to fulfill the second reason I dropped by."

"There was more you wanted to do besides ravish your bride in her wedding dress?"

I step forward and cup her cheek. "There's not much I enjoy

more than putting my cock in you, but we'll only have one wedding day and what I want to say to you I won't be able to say during the ceremony."

Her forehead wrinkles.

"We'll say our vows in the church in front of God and everyone else, but I want to make my own vow to you, here and now." I brush my thumb back and forth over her cheek. "Sofia, I vow to love you for a lifetime and to never put anyone or anything above you and your happiness. I vow to keep you safe from harm, and I want you to know that I will exterminate any threat to our lives together. You are what is most precious to me in this world, and I vow to never lose sight of that. And when we're blessed with children, I will be the best father I know how to be, though I know I'll never come close to topping the mother you'll be to them."

I brush away a lone tear cascading down her cheek with my thumb.

"I have never and will never love anyone but you, this is my most sacred promise to you on our wedding day." I hold her gaze so that she sees how serious I am.

Her lips press together, and she nods once then sniffles, trying to hold back her tears.

I lean and press a chaste kiss against her forehead whispering the words I mean more than anything against her skin. "Ti amerò per sempre."

"Are you trying to ruin my makeup?" She laughs and then sniffles, wiping the tears from her eyes.

"You look gorgeous either way."

A knock at the door interrupts our moment.

"That's probably one of our moms or Mira," Sofia says with disappointment.

I feel the same that I'm going to have to wait until after the wedding tonight to spend time with her alone.

With one last quick kiss, I leave the room, ready to get on with today. I can't wait to call this woman my wife.

* * *

SOFIA

Antonio leans in and kisses the corner of my jaw, speaking low so only I can hear him. "What's wrong?"

"Is it that obvious? My feet are killing me."

Between the long Catholic wedding ceremony, hours of pictures, a receiving line, and walking around and greeting all the guests, I can't wait to slip these heels off my feet.

"I don't know how you women wear those things. I'd sooner wear a thong every day than four-inch heels."

I chuckle. "I'd like to see that."

"Not likely." He grins and leans in to place a chaste kiss on my lips. "Why don't we go sit. We can take a break before we finish saying hello to everyone."

My eyes widen. "We can't do that."

He shrugs. "It's our wedding. We can do what we want."

"No, it's *our* wedding, which means we have to give everyone face time and make sure they're enjoying themselves." I hook my arm around his. "C'mon. Let's just get this over with."

We move onto the next table and the next and eventually we come to a table that holds Gabriele Vitale, his father, the underboss of the Vitale family, and a few of the caps and their wives.

There's a table for the Accardi family where Dante sits as well, and of course the Costa family has a few tables given that their don is marrying Antonio's sister. I was happy to see Giovanni with a date he's enamored with.

We do the usual chitchat and while Antonio is charming everyone at the table, I pull Gabriele aside.

"You look gorgeous today, Sofia. Congratulations," he says, leaning in to kiss one cheek then the other.

"Thank you. Maybe I'll be attending your wedding this time next year?" I arch an eyebrow and he chuckles.

"I'm in no hurry to find a wife. I have pretty particular tastes." The way he says it makes me curious to know more, but I need to say what I have to before we're interrupted.

After everything went down at school with Aurora and Conor, I was forbidden from mentioning my involvement to anyone, but Antonio confessed to me that Gabriele helped him figure out where I was. I wasn't able to mention it at school for fear of someone overhearing or us being caught on camera, so I'm taking my opportunity now.

"Antonio told me what you did for him to find me that night and I want to thank you. There's a good chance I wouldn't be alive today if it weren't for you."

His lips press into a thin line. I'm not sure if it's because he's annoyed Antonio told me or if it's because I'm bringing it up. Regardless, I continue.

"I want you to know that the favor you're owed in return extends to me. After all, you saved my life. If there's ever anything I can do for you, you just have to ask."

One corner of his lip tugs up. "That's very kind of you, Sofia, but I suspect your husband will be able to offer much more of what I need than you will."

"Still. If that ends up not to be the case, you need only ask me."

He shoves his hands in his tuxedo pant pockets and nods.

"Everything okay over here?" Antonio asks, sliding up beside me and wrapping his arm around my waist.

"I was just telling Sofia how sorry I feel for her now that she's stuck with you for a lifetime," Gabriele says.

Antonio rolls his eyes but doesn't take the bait.

"Hey, guys."

We all turn to see Aria Costa join us. She looks lovely in a deep red silk dress that hugs curves I didn't even know she had.

A quick glance at Gabriele tells me he's noticed how much more mature she looks than normal this evening too. I watch as his nostrils flare just the smallest amount and his jaw sets.

"Hi, Aria. Are you enjoying yourself?" I ask.

"Absolutely. My mom and brother are so involved in making sure they talk with everyone that I'm almost able to do my own thing."

"I'm starting to understand why you and Mira get along so well," Antonio says.

The four of us all laugh.

"Your brother is going to have his hands full," I add.

Aria blushes and sneaks a look at Gabriele. It's clear to anyone who's watching that she's a goner for him. Something I don't think he's enthused about and something I know her brother would not condone.

"I'm going to get back to my date," Gabriele says, emphasizing the word *date*. "Congratulations again, you two." Then he turns and walks the short distance back to his table, slinging his arm around the back of the chair of the blond woman beside him.

When I turn back to look at Aria, it's clear she's put on a brave face, but she gives the impression of a flower that's wilted.

"I'm going to go see if I can sneak some wine off someone's table," she says, disappearing into the crowd before I can say anything to her.

"Marcelo's going to have his hands full with her next year," Antonio says.

"That's for sure."

"Can't wait to watch it all unfold." He laughs, then takes my hand before we venture off to the next table.

The night is long, but I have an amazing time despite my sore feet and when we finally climb into bed, Antonio rubs my feet before he makes love to me as my husband for the first time in what is our lifetime together.

ACKNOWLEDGMENTS

We hope you enjoyed your time on campus!

Corrupting the Innocent *was a lot different to write than the first book in the series,* Vow of Revenge. *First, we changed our writing process and then we had a new set of characters with their own motivations.*

Antonio took his duty to his family seriously and at first when he was told he was going to marry Aurora, he accepted it because that's what a good Mafia son, soon to be Don, does. He was pretty happy moving through his life the way it was. But as he began to fall for Sofia, he saw his arranged marriage for what it was—handcuffs on the future he really wanted. You can see that shift in his attitude toward Aurora throughout the book the closer he and Sofia became.

As for Sofia, we were nervous about how readers might respond to her. She's very different than Mira in Vow of Revenge *and readers really seemed to love Mira. But we had to stay true to Sofia's character . . . Sofia did want to be a Mafia wife. She wanted everything her best friend despised, and we think that's okay, as long as she's the one who gets to make the choice—something she tried to point out to Mira.*

The more we write in this world, the more spin-off possibilities we see for some of the characters attending the Sicuro Academy. If there's someone whose story you hope to see, please let us know!

A big thank-you to everyone who helped get this book into your hands . . .

Nina and the entire Valentine PR team.

Cassie from Joy Editing for original line edits.

My Brother's Editor for original proofreading.

All the bloggers who have read, reviewed, shared, and/or promoted us and this new pen name!

Every reader who got this far in the book! We hope you were entertained!

To May Chen, for loving this series enough to bring it in under the Avon publishing umbrella and helping to get this series into reader's hands. Such a pleasure to work with this team!

Of course, Kimberly Brower, our agent, for championing the Mafia Academy series to Avon.

Gabriele and Aria are up next. Who can't wait to see big brother Marcelo's reaction? We can't! Hope you're ready for The Mafia King's Sister!

Ciao,
Piper & Rayne

ABOUT THE AUTHOR

P. RAYNE is the pen name for *USA Today* bestselling author duo Piper Rayne. Under P. Rayne, they write dark, dangerous, and forbidden romance.

DELVE INTO P. RAYNE'S
MAFIA ACADEMY
SERIES

A dark romance series set at a boarding school for the sons and daughters of the most powerful Mafia lords, now with new bonus content exclusive to the print editions.